D1825941

Full Circle
d'Arrent Honor
Ann Jacobs

ELLORA'S CAVE
ROMANTICA PUBLISHING

$\mathcal{W}$hat the critics are saying...

ℰ

Vampire Justice

4 Rating and Heat Level S "This book is an engaging paranormal romance. There's a hint of darkness to drive the suspense that sets the scene not only for this entertaining story, but also for the future of this sexy vampire clan. [...] It was completely rewritten and expanded. Vampire Justice is an entertaining love story that hooked me on wanting more stories about the d'Argent family!" ~ *Just Erotic Reviews*

Eternal Victory

"Eternal Victory" is a fun, fast-paced book. It is only 69 pages, so it is great for a quick break. The erotic aspects of the story are incredibly well written. If you have vampire fantasies, Mara's character acts them out. Enjoy!" ~ *Reader Views Book Reviews*

Eternal Surrender

4 Rating and Heat Level H "Their love play was erotic and sensual, and had me turning my PDA pages as fast as they could go for more action. Even though it is part of a series, it stood by itself without any problems. Ann Jacobs did a fabulous job of pacing the story and Alina and Sam were fabulous characters that were well matched for each other; in and out of the bedroom." ~ *Just Erotic Reviews*

An Ellora's Cave Romantica Publication

www.ellorascave.com

Full Circle

ISBN 9781419956935
ALL RIGHTS RESERVED.
Vampire Justice Copyright © 2006 Ann Jacobs
Eternal Surrender Copyright © 2007 Ann Jacobs
Eternal Victory Copyright © 2007 Ann Jacobs
Edited by Sue-Ellen Gower.
Cover art by Syneca.

This book printed in the U.S.A. by Jasmine–Jade Enterprises, LLC.

Trade paperback Publication November 2007

With the exception of quotes used in reviews, this book may not be reproduced or used in whole or in part by any means existing without written permission from the publisher, Ellora's Cave Publishing, Inc.® 1056 Home Avenue, Akron OH 44310-3502.

This book is a work of fiction and any resemblance to persons, living or dead, or places, events or locales is purely coincidental. The characters are productions of the authors' imagination and used fictitiously.

Also by Ann Jacobs

෨

A Gift of Gold

Another Love

A Mutual Favor

Awakenings

Bittersweet Homecoming

Captured

Colors of Love

Colors of Magic

Dallas Heat

Dark Side of the Moon

Enchained (*anthology*)

Firestorm

Forever Enslaved

Gates of Hell

Gettin' It On

Gold, Frankincense & Myrrh (*anthology*)

Haunted

He Calls Her Jasmine

In His Own Defense

Love Magic

Love Slave

Mystic Visions (*anthology*)

Out of Bounds

Roped

Storm Warnings (*anthology*)

Tip of the Iceberg

Wrong Place, Wrong Time?

About the Author

စာ

Ann Jacobs is a sucker for lusty Alpha heroes and happy endings, which makes Ellora's Cave an ideal publisher for her work. Romantica®, to her, is the perfect combination of sex, sensuality, deep emotional involvement and lifelong commitment—the elusive fantasy women often dream about but seldom achieve.

First published in 1996, Jacobs has sold over forty books and novellas, some of which have earned awards including the Passionate Plume (best novella, 2006), the Desert Rose (best hot and spicy romance, 2004) and More Than Magic (best erotic romance, 2004). She has been a double finalist in separate categories of the EPPIES and From the Heart RWA Chapter's contest. Three of her books have been translated and sold in several European countries.

A CPA and former hospital financial manager, Jacobs now writes full-time, with the help of Mr. Blue, the family cat who sometimes likes to perch on the back of her desk chair and lend his sage advice. He sometimes even contributes a few random letters when he decides he wants to try out the keyboard. She loves to hear from readers, and to put faces with names at signings and conventions.

Ann welcomes comments from readers. You can find her website and email address on her author bio page at www.ellorascave.com.

Tell Us What You Think

We appreciate hearing reader opinions about our books. You can email us at Comments@EllorasCave.com.

FULL CIRCLE
By Ann Jacobs

ॐ

VAMPIRE JUSTICE

ഔ

Prologue
The Beginning
ℰ

A chill wind blew across the Channel that night in the year of Our Lord 935. The moon was nothing but a sliver of silver in the black void of a winter sky. Rolfe d'Argent, youngest brother of Rollo the Viking, paced in the great hall of the stone keep he'd completed the previous summer, shivering despite his fur robe in the draft that had flames dancing in the fire. There! Above the whimper of the wind and the crackling fire he heard a lusty cry. The babe was born. Please the gods of his ancestors, 'twas a son. First of a dynasty to rule this fiefdom he'd carved out above the rugged cliffs of Normandy's shores.

Rolfe bounded up the stairs, only to be met halfway by the terrified-looking girl who was his wife's maid. "Tell me, Melinde, the babe? Is he — "

"He seems strong, my lord, but I fear my lady is dying. The blood..." Her voice trailed off as she made the sign of the Cross.

"Do not delay then. Hasten now, and fetch a priest." Kicking the door open with one booted foot, Rolfe crossed to the bed where his wife lay, so pale and quiet he thought at first she had already passed from this earth. His heart heavy, he reached down and wiped sweat off her glistening brow. Cold sweat. He shuddered then regained control. "Elaine?"

Her eyes opened briefly, and she attempted a smile. "I have borne you a son. Just as we prayed for."

"Yes. I thank you for him. But do not tax yourself. I order you to be strong, to live for both of us." He chafed her icy hand between both of his, as though by sheer will he could force his own strength into her frail body. "I will not allow you to die."

"'Tis of no use to bluster, for we both know it is too late for me. Promise to take care of our son. And love him as I would."

'Twas as though those words, spoken with surprising clarity, sapped the last of her strength, for she closed her eyes and took one last shuddering breath. Laying her hand across her still chest, Rolfe blinked away the tears that threatened and turned his attention to the screaming babe. He had to take care of the child, honor his wife's last request. "Why do you stand there gawking? Damn you, woman, go and find a wet nurse for my son," he bellowed at the cringing midwife.

"My lord," she said, her hands shaking as she crossed herself, "the babe will need no wet nurse, for he's one o' *them*."

"Speak up, woman, or I'll rip your foolish tongue from your head. What mean you?"

"He's a blood drinker. A *vampir* born. Best ye drive a stake through his tiny heart now, ere he grows too powerful for the likes of us to kill."

"Kill? I'll have you burned as a witch if you breathe a word of this madness. Hand me my son." Rolfe lifted the baby. His only living heir. As he held the baby he understood what Elaine had meant. A feeling swept over him, one he'd never experienced before. Could that look he'd seen in his wife's eyes, the surprising strength in her voice as she uttered her last words as though not all the armies in the world could obliterate what she was feeling—was this love? If so, then for the first time in his life, he knew what it was to love.

The babe's clear green eyes seemed to hold the wisdom of the ages in their depths. His tiny body was full, well-formed. Rolfe laid him on the bed by his mother's lifeless body and watched him flail about, as though wanting...something. Then he noticed what the midwife had already seen. Fangs.

"See. I told ye." The woman crossed herself again when Rolfe gave his son his index finger and watched the infant pierce the skin. The babe's face pinkened as he sucked Rolfe's blood. This child was flesh of his flesh, blood of his blood. Rolfe would nourish him, watch him grow, teach him to be a warrior of renown, a leader of mortal men.

"His name is Alain d'Argent, and he will live."

* * * * *

Except for Claude, they'd all heard the story of their beginnings many times over the centuries, whenever Alain had called them together, rallied them to action in some worthy cause. Alina repeated the tale now for the benefit of her young uncle, for it was his first time to join in the Counsel.

Claude listened, his dark eyes focused intently on her, studying her face as she spoke. She knew what he saw. What they all saw. Alain's eldest granddaughter, thrust seventy-four years ago at an impossibly young age to lead an equally young clan. Claude had been an infant in his mother's arms, Alain's last son born mere months before his death. But he'd been nurtured on stories like these and knew he must follow in his father's proud tradition. Still Alina was terribly afraid, afraid of losing him. Like all the d'Argent males, Claude was a beautiful man, so darkly handsome he turned female heads, vampire as well as mortal. More important, Claude had a deep inner goodness—a trait they all valued but one she feared might result in his destruction.

The threat that put their clan, indeed all vampire clans, at jeopardy could easily catch him up, might even destroy them all. Alina hoped Claude would not take his mother's tales about Alain's legendary feats too seriously, for he was yet very young—not quite seventy-five in mortal years.

Not that the threat would treat Stefan and Alexandre more kindly, but they at least had been hardened in battle. Their formidable powers had been proven and were not in doubt. Alina counted on them to destroy the most potent enemy they'd faced in her lifetime. She hoped that in the process they might shield Claude from the worst risk as they went out to find and destroy the evil vampire who threatened the existence of all their kind.

Silently cursing the feminine weakness that had her longing for her grandfather now, some seventy-four years after his death, Alina got a lump in her throat. She dared not shed tears. Had to be strong emotionally. Once again the d'Argent clan must rally to a cause—this time, the protection of innocent mortal women from the evil of a single demented vampire, the current head of the infamous Reynard clan. Louis Reynard, known in vampire circles throughout the world as the Fox.

"I hate that I must ask you to take on Reynard." Alina looked first at Stefan then at Alex and Claude. "I hate even more that I am the cause of his vendetta."

"It's not your fault Louis Reynard is insane," Alex said, shaking his head. "No vampire in his right mind would take out his anger with you on mortal women. Not when doing so risks infuriating mortals into starting another vampire hunt, the likes of which no one has seen since the time of the Medici."

"No one doubts the Fox has lost his mind. Nonetheless, we're the ones who must stop him." Stefan moved toward a window, stared out over the narrow channel toward England. "I will take to the hunt myself. Claude is too young. Too inexperienced."

Alina noticed all eyes turning toward Stefan. He rarely ventured from this ancient castle except when called on to do battle for the clan, not since he'd inadvertently killed his mortal lover while trying to change her centuries earlier. Of all the d'Argents, Claude and Alexandre would go to whatever lengths necessary to spare their beloved elder cousin pain. So would Alina, but she had no choice now. After a long, silent moment, Claude spoke up.

"No, Stefan. You're needed here. I may be young, but I'm not afraid to fight."

Alina turned and looked at Claude. He'd spoken in a voice she'd not heard before, as a force to be reckoned with. Their young uncle had always amused them with his ability to defy vampire physiology by snacking on pizza, brioche—an interesting combination of various mortal foods, washed down with soft drinks or the occasional beer. And her heartstrings tightened over the image as only a loving relative's heart could, even as she realized Claude had the maturity as well as the inborn right to fight for the honor of the d'Argent clan.

This wasn't the laughing young vampire who inspired indulgent sighs from the others of the clan. A warrior stood before her, galvanized to earn the honor promised by his birthright. In Claude's eyes Alina saw the raw courage of her grandfather...his father. The same fierce determination to fight evil wherever it lurked that had driven all the d'Argent males to champion freedom right up until the moment of their own destruction. "For now, Stefan, let us leave the pursuit to Alexandre and Claude. You will remain here and coordinate the hunt." She paused, then looked Claude and Alex in the eye. "Both of you, take care. I do not wish to have to tell your mothers you became reckless one too many times."

Chapter One
The present day, Miami Beach, Florida

ഒ

The night had always been his friend, but it closed in on him now, choking him in its sultry, damp embrace. A starless sky met the black expanse of the Atlantic, the horizon seemingly without beginning or end. Only the slapping sounds of waves kissing the shore punctuated an uneasy silence.

A silence Claude d'Argent had not experienced since that day two weeks ago when he'd come close to dying at the hand of the killer vampire for whom he now lay in wait. This strip of beachfront wouldn't stay silent for long, because the clubs would be opening soon. Claude sighed. Miami Beach hardly held a candle to his favorite haunts in the Marais district of Paris, even when it was buzzing with teeming bodies bent on finding pleasure…and courting danger.

But a vampire could mingle unnoticed here, stalking his prey. A killer like Louis Reynard might mingle with crowds of tourists once night fell, stalking his next victim. Having so recently encountered the Fox face-to-face, Claude would know him, recognize him. Hopefully be able to confront him and destroy him before he could kill again. He still woke in cold sweats, remembering the hot blonde in Buenos Aires that he and Alex hadn't been able to save, the night Reynard had practically destroyed them both.

I'd sense his presence if he were here. Wouldn't I? The killer had an uncanny ability to fuck up his vampire radar. That radar was kicking in now, warning Claude of trouble even as neon signs began to flash across the way, their garish messages luring patrons to sample barkeepers' wares, indulge in mortal vices under a moonless sky.

Fronds of tall royal palms swayed like so many dancers in the night as the wind rose, brought dissonant sounds of music to Claude's ears from the clubs across Highway A1A. His gaze drifted toward the sign that featured a hot-pink neon stripper doing her thing in lights above the sign advertising a place called, unimaginatively, The Strip. His hotel loomed large and opulent, its pink stucco façade commanding the scene directly south of the section of beach where he stood.

Claude rubbed at the still tender scar on his chest—a reminder of the wound from Louis Reynard that had come close to destroying him. Damn the bastard anyhow. If not for him, Claude would have been enjoying the Paris nightlife instead of acting as lookout here on the off chance Reynard had picked Miami Beach for the site of his next gruesome murder. Or, even better, chasing the Fox in a more active way instead of staking out a place where none of his elders seriously thought Reynard would seek out his next victim. Knowing this assignment had been handed out more to take him from his amusements and facilitate his recuperation than because of any real need for him to stake out the beach here didn't set well—but then he was used to his elders in the clan cosseting him as though he were no more than an infant vampire.

The way the neon dancer's hips undulated reminded him of a certain woman he'd enjoyed in Paris—the enthusiastic way she rode him while he tugged on her massive enhanced breasts. She'd had her moves down, for certain.

Claude's cock ached. It had been too long—much too long—since he'd had a woman. He even had a painful hard-on from staring at the stripper flashing him from the neon marquee across the highway. He scanned the deserted beach once more before he let his gaze drift back to the neon sign.

What the fuck? Angry voices floated into Claude's hypersensitive vampire ears. Strolling casually, he crossed the highway toward the club—and the sounds. When he strained his eyes, he made out the silhouettes of two men in the alley beside the club. Shit. They apparently were threatening a petite woman who, from the sound of her voice and the way she had a hand raised up over her head, was giving back as good as she got.

But she was no match physically for one, let alone two grown men. Incensed that the bastards dared gang up on a lone woman, Claude headed for them. He'd save the woman, and he'd work out some of his frustration by kicking some mortal ass.

"Bloodsuckers!" she spat out, terror evident in her voice despite her loud defiance. When she shook her fist at the larger of her tormentors, he laughed, said something in rapid Spanish and turned away.

"You've had it, asshole." Claude took to the air now, determined to punish the attackers, but by the time he reached the alley, they'd disappeared as if by magic, and the woman herself had disappeared through the stage door to the club. Claude cursed fluently, hated the weakness that must still be lingering after his encounter with Reynard. Fuck, he should have been able to overtake the two mortals without breaking a sweat.

He recalled what the woman had called them, let out a chuckle.

Bloodsuckers the two men might very well have been, but he was satisfied that neither of them was a vampire—Reynard or otherwise. From the snippets of conversation he'd understood, he gathered some drug deal must have gone sour—and that the men were shaking down the woman. Vampires, even villains like the Reynards, didn't sink so low as to deal in the stuff that enslaved so many mortals. Too bad he couldn't have translated faster. He might have learned where they were going and meted out some vampire justice. He shrugged, making a mental note that he needed to improve his Spanish vocabulary.

As much as he'd have loved to chase them down, he was here on a mission to find and destroy the Fox before he killed again. Scanning the beach and the sidewalks outside the clubs for any sign of his prey and finding nothing, Claude made his way inside The Strip. If Reynard were there, they'd fight…if not, he'd enjoy an hour's entertainment before resuming his vigil. Perhaps he'd even see the woman from the alleyway, talk with her, find out how he might help…

* * * * *

"Five grand, pretty lady. Your brother cheated the patron. *Pay up, or the little cocksucker dies."*

"B-but I don't have that much."

"Get it, or Raul dies." Marisa shuddered when she remembered how the larger of the *patron's* messengers had slashed his finger across his throat, at the same time shooting a condescending grin her way. *"I give you two days. Forty-eight hours. We see you here, same time Thursday."* As quickly as they'd come, the two thugs who did the drug lord's dirty work had evaporated into the blackness of the night. But she had no doubt they would be back as they'd said they would.

Marisa Delgado shivered in the dingy dressing room at The Strip. The air-conditioning blew cold, but she doubted that had much to do with her feeling chilled. She'd felt the same outside, despite the damp warmth of the summer night.

God, but she hated drugs, had done her best to talk Raul out of using them. She'd warned him against getting caught up in the circle of using and dealing, selling coke in order to feed his growing habit. More and more using, more and more dealing until the cops or the drug got you and destroyed your life. She might as well have saved her breath.

Worse, she hated the thought of having to reimburse the *patron* for the cocaine the police had confiscated when they caught her brother selling and charged him with trafficking. *It wasn't my coke. It shouldn't be my problem.* But it was Raul's problem, and if she didn't pay his debt, her young brother would die. It didn't matter that she'd had nothing to do with those drugs or with Raul's business of selling enough of them to support his filthy habit. All that concerned the drug lord was getting back the money represented by the cocaine her brother had lost.

Dios. There's only one way I can get that much cash that fast.

No! She'd sworn on her mother's grave that she'd never sell her body. But she couldn't see any other way. Much as she hated Raul for getting them into this mess, she knew Mama wouldn't have wanted her baby boy to die. *She* didn't want her brother to die. And the drug lord Raul had gotten himself indebted to was known for making good on his threats.

She had about a thousand left in savings after bailing Raul out of jail two days ago. Maybe if she worked double shifts both days… No, she was dreaming. If business was good she might earn a thousand, even two, giving lap dances to the customers. No chance she could earn all she needed in The Strip, not in time to pay off the *patron* and save Raul's life.

Whatever happened to the avenging angels, gargoyles and other fanciful creatures her mother had read stories to her about all those years ago? The ones with supernatural powers who would swoop down from above and destroy the evil people here on earth? Then she remembered. Those avengers, even the fearsome ones like gargoyles and vampires, only saved good boys and girls. And as she looked at her face, painted in a garish whore's makeup, she knew she was far from that. That decided it. She clenched her jaw.

There was only one way she could make the remaining four thousand dollars in two days and nights. Her cunt tightened at the prospect of picking some temporary sex partners and doing whatever it took to please them. Anticipation or dread?

It has to be dread making your pussy twitch. This isn't about sex, it's about necessity. About money.

So...she'd become the *puta* she'd promised Mama she'd never be — but then she'd also promised Mama before she died that she'd take care of Raul. Perhaps she'd have to keep on hooking, because if there was one thing her boss at The Strip wouldn't put up with, it was having his dancers soliciting the customers for sex. If he found out, she wouldn't have her job. Tears stung her eyes, but she blinked them back. It did no good to grieve over something that hadn't happened yet, might not happen at all.

Even if she had to make a permanent living as a whore, it wasn't as if she'd be the only girl from the *barrio* who'd given up on the idea of making it inside the law, let alone in keeping with the morality the priests talked about in the confessional.

Marisa shrugged out of her robe in the shadows of the stage curtains and tried to push away the fear that still quivered in her belly. She'd figure it out. But first she had to do this job.

"Get your ass out there, baby. You're on," the stage manager whispered, punctuating his order with a smart slap on her naked butt as the opening strains of her signature salsa music blared through the club's speakers.

It was time. As she'd done a hundred times before, Marisa strutted into the spotlight and began to gyrate to the distinctive Latin beat. She smiled, enticing the crowd, getting into the beat, twirling the tassels on her pasties, enjoying the mild arousal that came from feeling the erotic brush of silk on the bare skin of her rib cage, her belly. Like a lover's touch, almost...enticing her, as if she were stripping for a special man, dancing only for him in his garden or out on the beach where moonlit waves undulated behind her. For a few moments she forgot the hundred or so pairs of lascivious eyes that glowed eerily through the multicolored floodlights pulsating all around her. As she did each time she performed, she managed to escape the club's sleazy surroundings for the erotic fantasyland of her mind.

But she couldn't set aside her woes for long or forget what she had to do. It wasn't that she didn't like sex. She did. She'd dreamed of a white knight finding her, sweeping her off her feet, taking her to a world where there was no poverty, no *patron*, nothing but indulging the senses, celebrating the beauty in each other. But this wasn't about fulfilling fantasies or even about pleasure. It was about surviving alone, clawing her way out of the Cuban *barrio*, dragging Raul along for the ride. About using her body to buy her way to freedom, respectability. Strutting around the stage, Marisa eyed the crowd of customers and settled on a dark, dangerous-looking man whose gaze seared her with its intensity. She sensed something about him, felt an erotic charge in the air unlike any she'd felt with other customers on other nights. If she had her way, he'd be her very first john.

* * * * *

When the next dancer came onstage, Claude clenched his glass of cola. Blood slammed into his cock, leaving him dizzy. As dizzy as he'd have been before his injury if he'd tried to handle something heavily alcoholic instead of the beer or soft drink he'd always been able to enjoy without ill effect. Had the sultry creature who exuded sexual invitation been the same one he'd seen at the back entrance moments earlier, trembling while the two bullies had issued her some sort of ultimatum? It had been too dark for him to see her clearly, but she was about the right height. Tiny, like the woman outside. She wouldn't even come up to his shoulder.

For such a little thing, this dancer packed one hell of an erotic punch. His fingers itched to dig into that tousled mane of ebony, find all the erogenous places there…to trace the pulsating vein in her throat. He'd tug at her reddened, pierced nipples that poked impudently through gold shields that lent their glow to satiny olive skin, and then move lower to tweak her clit and find her cunt that even now filled his nostrils with the heady scent of sex.

24

Other customers smelled it too. He could tell by the slackening in their jaws, the shifting of legs to accommodate sudden arousal. It made no sense, yet Claude couldn't help wanting to chase them away. Not just the customers, but the men who might have been threatening her out in the alley. They'd wanted something, they'd wanted it now, and they hadn't been inclined to take no for an answer. He'd understood that much of the conversation, smelled the fear and sensed the terror she'd been trying so hard to hide. This was the same woman.

He had no reason to be so certain, yet he was. Although she showed none of that fear now as she enticed him and every man in the place to fantasize they were fucking her, he sensed a desperation beneath her smile, the come-on sway of her hips to the beat of that Latin tune. She wanted something, needed something beyond a few dollars tucked into her G-string.

He wanted something from her too. Steamy, sweaty sex. Sex the pretty Latina was blatantly peddling from a few feet away on the stage. Swirling lights made her sequined pasties and G-string sparkle, inviting his gaze. His balls ached with anticipation when he looked beyond the glitter to her full, firm breasts. Her dusky, silky mound. Around him equally attractive women in similar states of undress offered lap dances to the patrons, dances he imagined would be delivered in the privacy of the VIP rooms every strip club had.

But it was the woman dancing onstage who intrigued him, the soft look of innocence barely visible in her dark eyes that belied her blatant come-on when she rolled her hips his way to the sultry beat of a conga drum. Claude gasped when the delicate tip of her tongue wet her painted lips. He could practically feel those full lips surrounding his cock, sucking out his come.

Oh, fuck. He wanted to sip the glistening sweat from her brow, her ass, her flat, tanned belly. His fangs itched penetrate the creamy column of her throat and sip ever so gently from a vein he saw pulsating there. What was it about this woman, this night, that made him desperate to have her…to taste her blood while he fucked her glistening little cunt?

Her female musk swirled in the air, the aroma tempting yet elusive across the distance between them. Though he'd felt instant lust before, he'd never wanted a stranger so strongly, never been compelled to have her, master her, give her the pleasure she silently requested with each sultry move of her hips, every come-on gesture. Each upward curve of blood-red lips as she tempted him and every other patron in the club. It was as though destiny had brought him here, to her, on this night in this place in time.

A nearly naked blonde sidled up to his table, a huge smile on her beautiful but too-heavily made-up face.

"Buy me a drink, honey?" she asked, bending until her cleavage was in line with his face so he got a good look at her naked breasts. Breasts so perfectly round and firm they had to have been created by a plastic surgeon's skilled hand.

She straightened, giving him an eyeful of her shaved pussy, naked except for a jeweled G-string that helped display instead of hide her considerable charm. "Like what you see?"

Unfortunately for her, she reminded Claude of the blonde Reynard had killed in Buenos Aires, and that did almost as much as an icy shower toward squelching his libido. "You're very pretty." Wanting to let her down but do it easy, he smiled. "I'll buy you a drink if you'll take a message to the dancer who's onstage now. Tell her I'd like to see her when she finishes her act."

He pressed a folded bill into the woman's outstretched hand. "Marisa? Ha! If you're looking for a good time, better pick me instead, handsome. The best you'll get from the Madonna's a half-assed lap dance."

A ten-minute lap dance from her would be worth an all-night fuck with you. Claude liked to do the hunting rather than being the object of such blatant pursuit. "No offense, but I'll take my chances." Peeling another bill off the roll in his pocket, Claude tucked it into the blonde's G-string before she pivoted and headed off in search of a more promising customer. "Thank you."

He leaned back in the chair, imagining how Marisa's firm, shapely legs would feel around his waist. His balls tightened. Hell, he didn't want a lap dance, he wanted to fuck her until they both were spent. Then he wanted to fall asleep with his head pillowed on her full, lush breasts.

His mouth went dry as though he needed to feed, although he'd partaken less than a day ago of life-sustaining blood. Maybe one of the prefab pizzas he'd seen at some of the other tables would take the edge off. Quickly he denied that temptation, for since his injury he'd practically lost his taste for mortals' junk food. Sighing, he took another sip of the cola, now watered down with melting ice. Thankfully the club didn't serve alcoholic beverages, an oddity he'd learned resulted from an ordinance that prevented sale of booze in clubs that featured nude entertainers. If it had and he'd given in to the temptation to drink some, his head would have been spinning. His cock was painfully hard already, but it began to throb insistently as he watched Marisa toss her sparkly pasties into the audience. He managed to raise a hand in time to catch the tiny G-string he'd imagined tearing off her with his fangs.

The drumbeat accelerated. Totally nude now, she straddled the pole at center stage, humping it to the accelerating beat of the music. The small hoop in her clit sparkled against her glistening pussy, beckoning Claude as clearly as a whispered invitation. Hopefully he was managing not to show his fangs, but he wasn't certain.

He felt need in the air—his own for her, but more. For scant seconds she met his gaze, and behind the façade of sensual abandon he sensed her desperation, her need not only for sex but for help. A need he'd be damned if he'd let another of the ogling customers fulfill.

* * * * *

Once again Marisa eyed the dark, gorgeous, prosperous-looking customer who stared at her from a front table as she writhed against the pole at center stage. He was a tourist for sure, probably a European or South American like most of the strangers who came to Miami Beach for sun and fun. But this one looked *muy macho*. Even tougher than the mob goons the *patron* had sicced on Raul and Raul had passed along to harass her instead. The customer's white teeth gleamed when he smiled, his very prominent incisors giving him a menacing look.

Menacing but oh-so sexy. This man would be able to take care of himself with the likes of the *patron's* enforcers. *Sí*, this man was the sort she'd want to have as her protector from those thugs—the sort of man she'd want to fuck for free if she didn't need the money so much.

She peeled off her G-string and tossed it his way. Totally naked now, she wiggled her ass so the little bell on her clit ring swayed invitingly, in concert with the ones dangling from her nipples and colliding with the gold nipple shields she always wore beneath the tasseled pasties she'd discarded.

If he would take her bait, she'd give more than the lap dance he undoubtedly expected. Much more. Her cunt clenched when she imagined the dark, delicious things the stranger would do once she'd enticed him to take her not to one of the VIP rooms in back but to his hotel room. Though she'd never laid eyes on him before, she sensed a connection — a pull that had as much to do with raw sexual attraction as with her dire financial situation. She also perceived an aura of power surrounding him, as though he could take on any mere mortal...and win.

Who knows? Maybe he does possess supernatural powers.

He definitely was no angel, avenging or not. And no one as beautiful as he could be a gargoyle. But maybe—yes, he could be a vampire. He certainly looked like some of the ones she'd seen in movies. If he were, he could... *Marisa, do not wish for the impossible. He's a man. Not some supernatural creature. Hope only that you can please him.* But try as she might, she couldn't let go the notion that this stranger might be not only her john but her salvation.

In the fantasies and dreams she'd once had as a girl, her man had possessed special powers. He would have been strong enough to find and destroy the nameless, faceless drug lord who supplied the cocaine her brother had proved yet again he couldn't live without. Her dream man would have destroyed the *patron*, erased Raul's debt and rid the Hispanic community in Miami of a scourge who'd ruined the lives of countless people. People who'd sought pleasure and found misery instead.

Dream on, Marisa. Think of the man as a customer, not the white knight of your wildest fantasies. Don't delude yourself that he's anything more than mortal.

As the music faded, she slithered down the pole and off the stage, moistening her lips as she strutted, unashamedly naked, toward the beautiful man. As she moved toward him, his gaze followed her, moving over her body like a caress. Suddenly the vulgar gyration of hips she'd intended became a languid dance of its own, a sensual beckoning, not just from desperation for her brother but for the desire in herself.

When she got to him, he rose and reached out his hand as if he were helping her down from a carriage. As he sank down into his chair, he drew her onto him, suddenly in control, guiding her actions. She'd intended to straddle his lap, but now he compelled her to do so.

Remembering her goal, she ground her pussy against the hard bulge of his cock. "Let me entertain you, handsome. I can show you a real good time."

* * * * *

Claude's balls tightened. His fangs itched. His cock throbbed and hardened more each time the woman ground her satin-smooth cunt against his fully clothed groin. Reflexively, he gripped the rounded flesh of her ass cheeks and began to move.

For a moment she moved with him, a sensual mating dance. Her mouth went slack, her eyelids fluttering shut against her creamy skin. Then, as though she suddenly realized where they were, she lifted her hands off his shoulders and looked him in the eye. "Not here, *por favor.* Whatever you want, I will give you, but we must go somewhere else." Her voice wavered the tiniest bit, just enough to give Claude second thoughts.

"What's your name, beautiful?" He knew because the blonde had mentioned it, but he wanted to hear it from the woman's gleaming red lips.

"Marisa. Come with me, lover." Reaching down with one hand, she cupped Claude's cock. "You're *muy macho*. You will give me a good time too."

"How much?"

"All night? Two thousand dollars. I will give you whatever you want, however you want it. All night long." Obviously Marisa wanted him—at least she wanted the money he'd give her. Beyond the come-on, though, he perceived the same desperation he'd sensed earlier while she danced onstage. And he could practically smell the fear that lay barely beneath the surface of her lush, naked body. Though she hadn't said a word, he knew. She was the woman in the alley. Though she hid it well, the fear those bastards had put in her an hour earlier had to have been driving her actions now.

"My hotel is right across the street." Although Claude wasn't in the habit of paying for sex and found the prospect of doing so vaguely insulting, he wanted to wipe away the thinly veiled terror in her dark eyes, put an end to whatever threat it was she faced. He also needed release. From her, not from just any attractive female. Hell, his cock was about to burst out of his pants. He desperately wanted to bury it inside this small, dark-haired woman with sun-kissed skin and a shy smile that seemed out of place with her blatantly seductive actions. "Come, little dove," he said, lifting her off his lap and standing.

"Meet me at the stage door. I must dress, gather up some toys..."

"All right. Five minutes. No more. I'll be waiting." He hoped his painful hard-on wasn't as evident to the customers he passed on the way out as it was to him.

Chapter Two

** හ**

When Claude got her to his hotel room, Marisa didn't bother wasting time.

"What do you like, *señor*? I will provide any form of pleasure you desire." Slowly, as if she were stripping again but this time just for him, she peeled off the surprisingly demure pink dress she'd worn from the club and stood, her delectable body highlighted in the moonlight that flooded through the window of Claude's oceanfront room. Half seductress, half innocent, she gave him a shy smile while undulating her body just enough to make the bells on the rings in her nipples make tinkling contact with the nipple shields she'd worn during her act and apparently left on for his pleasure.

Claude couldn't take his eyes off them or the jingling bell on her clit ring. Couldn't stop looking at her, wanting her. And though he knew he must be crazy, he couldn't beat down the intuitive voice in his head that said this woman—a prostitute he'd agreed to pay two grand for a night's fucking—was the soulmate every d'Argent vampire eventually encountered. His soulmate. The woman he'd love for the rest of his long, long existence. Yeah, his injury must have thrown his mind off-kilter.

Fumbling in a way he hadn't done since he'd been a child of fifteen years about to fuck a woman for the first time, he worked the buttons of his shirt loose...shed it...tackled the fastenings of his khaki slacks and shoved them down along with his underwear. Blood surged to his cock, leaving him lightheaded as he stepped out of the pants and stood there, aroused by her scrutiny.

Her gaze had settled on his raging hard-on, and that tongue of hers was touching her lips again. The way she looked at him...damn, it made him feel ten feet tall. He grinned, not caring if she noticed his fangs. "Do you like what you see?"

"*Sí, señor.*" She sank to her knees before him. "Would you like for me to suck your cock now?"

Damn stupid question. What working girl wouldn't know his cock was aching to feel the touch of those lips? But then maybe she wasn't one. Another indication she was new to her trade. Maybe she wasn't a hooker at all, only a desperate woman in dire need of the money he'd agreed to give her.

What the fuck? Why she was doing this didn't matter now. Nothing mattered but having her, absorbing her warmth, burying himself in her and chasing away loneliness that had been dogging him since he'd left friends and family in Paris on what was beginning to seem like a never-ending hunt for Louis Reynard.

Claude reached out, stroked her flat, taut belly. So soft, so tempting, she sighed when he drew her into his arms. "Yeah, I want you to suck my cock. I want you to suck it 'til you make me come. First, though, I want to taste you. Lie down, *señorita*, and let me show you how a Parisian vampire makes love."

Her eyes widened as she looked up at him, even though he didn't doubt she'd suspected, considering the way he'd been gaping at her in the club, fangs hanging out for all to see. He smiled, deliberately showing her those fangs, making them elongate enough so they grazed his lower lip.

"*Dios mío.*" For a moment she trembled, but she recovered quickly, squared her shoulders and shot him a dazzling smile. "I know I should be afraid, but—"

"You've no reason to fear me, for I fed only yesterday and have no need for sustenance—only for release of the ache you've caused in my cock and balls." Claude gathered her in

Ann Jacobs

his arms, retracting his fangs and wishing he hadn't made her tremble. "I only want to devour your sweet honey."

"It's all right."

But it wasn't. Claude sensed her fear, fear incongruous with her stated occupation. His instincts had been right. Marisa was no prostitute. That knowledge made him unreasonably happy, even more aroused than he'd been before. He smiled, making a conscious effort not to bare his fangs this time. "Truly, my mama would be most angry if she thought I'd frightened a beautiful woman like you. She would tell you the vampires of our clan don't make a habit of lurking in coffins or attacking unsuspecting mortals for sustenance."

"I believe you, señor. It is only that you are the first vampire I have met—in person."

"My name is Claude. Claude d'Argent. Come and let me show you how well a vampire can satisfy a woman."

She bit her lower lip. The smile that followed looked forced. "It is my job to give you pleasure, not demand it for myself."

Scooping her up in his arms, Claude nibbled her earlobe, being careful not to break her tender skin. When she sighed with apparent pleasure, he moved lower to sample the satiny skin of her tempting, olive-tanned throat, the upper curve of her full breasts. "It will be my pleasure to seduce you," he said, answering the invitation of the turned down bed and laying her at its center.

Marisa's heart pounded in her chest, whether from fear or desire she could not say. Part of her wanted to run and hide, for a voice inside her warned this man—this vampire—would steal her will, make it his own. A stronger voice in her head urged her to stay.

She didn't want to stay only because he'd promised to pay her. Deep inside, she wanted to savor the sensations of sex with Claude d'Argent. This sexy vampire bore no resemblance to any of the evil creatures Buffy had battled in the series on

34

TV, or any of the vampire villains she'd seen portrayed in movies. Instead he was the epitome of all the lovers in her wildest fantasies.

Would her lover's kiss—no, not her lover's but her mark's, she reminded herself as reality intruded with the intensity of a chilly wind on a warm Miami day—make her skin tingle, her belly do flip-flops? When she looked into his dark eyes, she saw no menace, only passion whose heat contrasted with the cool, smooth texture of pale skin stretched over rippling muscles.

"Open to me." The deep sound of his quietly uttered order surrounded her, heated her skin. Wanting him more than she feared losing herself, she spread her legs, giving him silent approval to touch and taste her pussy.

But he didn't. He made no move to cover her but touched her only with exploring fingertips that lulled away her misgivings, aroused her so much she almost forgot she was a prostitute to this man—this gorgeous vampire. That she'd sold her body to him just as she'd handed over her soul to the devil. Her cunt clenched and her honey began to flow.

She took his hand, drew it between her legs. "Do you like that I grow wet for you, *Señor* Vampire?"

"I like it a lot. I like you a lot." When he found her clit and began to circle it with his finger, she felt her flesh harden around the clit ring. Her body apparently didn't care that she was selling it for money, for it eagerly responded to her john's skilled touch. She sensed he was looking up at her and met his glittering gaze. "You don't do this often, do you?" he asked.

"No." *Madre de Dios.* Imaginary vampires she'd heard about had psychic powers, but… Could real ones hear mortals' silent thoughts? *Dios*, how she wanted her vampire to know she wanted him to fuck her—with or without the money he'd agreed to pay her. The warm dampness of his mouth contrasted with the coolness of his hands when he shifted and drew her clit between his teeth. "*Señor*, I want…" Her mouth watered to taste the hard, sculpted length of his cock, to run her tongue over his satin-smooth ball sac.

"Call me Claude."

"Claude." She liked the unusual name, liked everything about him.

"Is this what you want?" He turned, his movement graceful as he straddled her face. His rock-hard thighs framed her cheeks when he leaned over her pussy, the warmth of his breath on her slick folds filling her with anticipation. "Touch me, Marisa. Torture me as I intend to torture you."

His cock and balls were big, rigid, as pale and hard as marble. Cool to her touch. Yet when she wrapped her fingers around him, he pulsed with life, and his testicles tightened further at her touch. His flesh warmed as though absorbing her own heat. "I like it that you have no hair down here." She ran her tongue along the vein that pulsed along the underside of his shaft. His thick cock tasted good. Clean. It throbbed and twitched when she took its broad, thick head between her lips and licked away a drop of pre-come that had settled in the dimpled slit at its tip. Her nipples tightened against their rings when he spread her pussy lips and inserted first one then two long fingers into her dripping cunt. She took him deeper, swallowed.

Claude let out a groan. "Don't stop now." He blew on her wet pussy, the playful act contrasting with the tightness of his muscles, the guttural tone of his voice. "Vampires don't have hair except what's on our heads. I like it that you keep your cunt smooth too."

"Mmmm. You taste good." Marisa licked along the vein that ran the length of his swollen cock then sucked his cock head into her mouth.

"So do you. You know, when I first saw you dancing, I hoped you'd wrap those full, red lips around my cock and suck it the way you're doing now. When I watched you dance and imagined you taking me in your mouth, I got so hard I hurt. The reality is so much better." His pelvis jerked, forcing her to take him deeper. "Don't stop," he begged, his tone desperate. "Take it all."

She wanted to. *Dios*. He was so huge she had to tilt her head back to take the length of him down her throat. With one hand she cupped his tight balls, caressed them with her fingertips as she sucked and swallowed. With the other she stroked around his asshole in a circular motion, pressed a finger against his anal sphincter until it gave way and let her in.

Claude's groan when she caressed him there came out sounding like something between a purr and a roar. So. It was true. Marisa hadn't believed it when the girls at work had talked about how many straight men enjoyed anal play. Encouraged, she began to move her finger in and out, imitating the rhythm of sex — until he reached down and stilled her hand.

"Where did you learn to do that? No, don't answer." The possessiveness in his tone made her tremble. It hurt when she reminded herself it meant nothing, that she was only hearing what she wanted to hear, acting out the wishes in her head.

He fucked her with his fingers and tongued her clit while she sucked his cock and explored his tight asshole. His hard-ridged belly brushed against her breasts, abraded them and caused her nipple rings to tug deliciously at her flesh. The unfamiliar coolness of his satiny skin did nothing to alleviate the heat coursing through her veins.

Hot. She felt so hot. Heavy. She couldn't have moved even if the *patron* himself had been stalking her. Not now. Every nerve in her body tingled at Claude's touch. Every swipe of his velvety tongue on her swollen clit, each stroke of his fingers in her cunt, her ass, turned her blood to liquid fire. *Madre de Dios*, the sensations took her breath away, left her teetering on the edge of ecstasy. Her climax began as just a twinge in her clit, growing in intensity, bursting into a thousand nipping fingers of flame that spread through her body and left her weak. Her cunt sucked in his fingers, contracted around them, wanting more. Wanting him.

His cock swelled more against her throat. She sucked harder. His balls tightened in her hand. When he let go and flooded her mouth with his come, she swallowed. Wanted to take him into her body, consume him. She wanted to give her vampire lover all he'd given her and more. Wanted to give herself to him. All of her.

It was crazy, as though he'd placed a vampire spell on her, as if by some act of magic he'd invaded her heart as well as her body. Marisa clutched his hips, held his still-pulsating cock between her lips. She couldn't bear the thought of letting him go. Claude d'Argent was not just a night's fuck for money, but a master of her senses — and her emotions.

Chapter Three

✖

Claude lay back, spent, his head resting on Marisa's shoulder. Her throat lay mere inches away, the large vein pulsating with life, tempting him. If he turned his head a little, he could sink his fangs into her flesh. Change her. If he did, whatever mortal problems plagued her would be over.

But he could not. Dared not. He remembered his cousin Stefan trying to turn a lover, failing and destroying her instead. Stefan hadn't been all that much older than Claude was now. That thought made him clamp his mouth shut, banish that dangerous temptation. He didn't want to follow Stefan's footsteps and exist alone in one of the d'Argent bastions of antiquity, never daring to look again for a soulmate.

Idiot. She's not your lover, she's the woman you hired to fuck you for the night.

Claude moved back, took a good look at the woman who was affecting him much more strongly she should. She'd given him the best fuck of his life, never mind she was a whore, albeit a first-time one. But Marisa was a stripper, so he couldn't deny she sold sex for a living. A twinge of self-disgust took the edge off his satisfaction, but only for a moment.

So she was fucking him for money. So what? Claude hadn't come so long, so easily in all his seventy-five years on earth. At this moment it didn't matter that he was the baby of the d'Argent vampires, much too young to think of settling down with just one woman.

I want to turn her, keep her for all eternity.

You don't even know for certain how to turn a mortal. And you barely know Marisa. What the fuck gives you reason to believe she'd want to become your dhampir lover? Disgusted at the direction his thoughts were taking, Claude stroked her silky back, cupped her firm ass cheeks and drew her closer. Protected her from himself, his own impulsive desire.

His cock twitched. She shifted, let him in between her firm, silky thighs. Her honey wet his flesh, its heat and dampness showing him the way to her deliciously tight little cunt. "Would it please you to fuck me now?"

Right now he wanted to talk, needed to find out for certain if she was the woman he'd seen being threatened in the alley. "Later. If what I read in your mind is right, you're afraid of something...someone."

"It's not important." When she tightened her firm thigh muscles, her flesh caressed his cock, and his resting sex grew instantly hard. "I promised you all night. Now all I want is to feel your long, thick cock inside my cunt." She cupped his cheek with one soft hand as she looked into his eyes. "Not because you're paying me, but because you've made me hot and wet...for you."

Claude couldn't resist her pleas, not when his usually quiet heartbeat was accelerating, when blood was pounding through his body, settling in his cock and balls, making his head feel light. "All right. But we *will* talk later."

"*Sí, Senor* Vampire. We will talk later, but fuck me now. Please."

"Oh, yeah." Wasting no time, he rolled Marisa onto her back, positioned himself, and mounted her. "Do you want my cock in your hot little cunt?"

It shocked him when she shoved him back, hard, gripping his shoulders. He saw what looked like panic in her eyes. "What's wrong? Did you decide we need to talk after all?" One thing he'd learned during his relatively short lifetime was that females could be mercurial.

"Oh, no. It would please me very much for you to fuck me. But you need to use a condom. Please. If you do not mind." She reached on the floor and fumbled in her bag, finally finding one and handing it to him while mumbling apologies.

He was in no mood at the moment to explain that vampires didn't get or carry STDs and rarely impregnated their partners, not with her steaming flesh caressing the swollen tip of his cock. He'd wear the condom because it obviously would put her at ease. "Put it on me."

"Yes, sir." Her fingers trembling against his hard-on, she hurried to sheathe him. "Whatever you wish."

He'd never felt so hot, wanted a woman so much. "Take my cock in your hand. Rub it against your tight little asshole."

She shifted, drew him to her, circled the tip of it around her rear entrance. "Do you want to fuck me here?"

"Later. Do you mind?"

"It will be my pleasure to serve you. However you wish."

She sounded like a true submissive. Like the fantasy women who'd fueled his daydreams of mastery for longer than he could remember. Claude grew harder and hotter, impossibly aroused by the possibilities. Possibilities he had to explore.

Deliberately he made his voice deeper, more authoritative. "On your hands and knees, now. I want to hear these bells ringing while I fuck you." Slowly, though without hesitation, he slid his hands up to cup her full breasts, jiggling them and making the bells that hung from her nipple rings jingle in the silence of the night.

"Like this, *señor*?" She rolled over instantly and knelt, head down, her pretty shaved cunt exposed, her ass in the air as though inviting his attention.

"Yes. Exactly like this." He slapped her ass cheek smartly, watched with satisfaction as it turned pink and her cunt glistened with a new burst of lubrication he caught on his finger and used to lubricate the hard little bud of her clit. "You like it when I spank you. I can tell. I want to hear this bell

41

ringing too." He tweaked the one dangling from her clit, enjoyed the high-pitched sound of the tiny clapper as it resounded against the gold bell.

Yes, she was a sub. She liked giving up control. That was obvious from the heat and wetness of her swollen pussy, the rough cadence of her breathing. Knowing she wanted him to master her had him so hot he thought his cock would burst.

He bit back a groan when he got a whiff of her female musk. Couldn't wait. Had to bury his cock inside her cunt and feel her heat. "I'm going to fuck you now. Will you like that?" he asked as he went on his knees between her widespread legs and rubbed his sheathed cock along her sopping slit.

"Yes, please. Please fuck me. Fuck me hard."

"It will be my pleasure." Oh, yeah. When he found her cunt and plunged inside, he let out a yell. "You're so tight, so hot. So wet. Yes, squeeze me. Squeeze out my come."

His balls lay against her clit, making the little bell ring over and over, sounding out every stroke. His cool flesh absorbed her heat, her honey, drove him crazy. He loved the way her inner muscles milked him, as though they wanted to take his essence and make it her own. Grasping her hips, he controlled the movement. Her cunt was a perfect fit, tight and wet. Her hard breathing let him know she was on the edge, and he was ready to take her over.

"Squeeze my cock. Harder. Oh, yeah, do it again." Her tight cunt gripped his cock like fingers of fire.

"*Dios mio*, I'm coming!" Her words dissolved into whimpers of pleasure as her cunt began to spasm around his cock.

Instinctively he bent over her, angling his head so his fangs aligned perfectly with his lover's golden throat. He slammed into her cunt again and again. Pressure built in his balls. In her too. He felt her passion in the clenching muscles that held his cock inside her, heard it in the little moans and breathy entreaties please to fuck her harder, take everything she had to give. Her blood pounded through her veins as the smell of sex filled his nostrils. He had to come.

But first he had to taste her. The temptation of her creamy flesh throbbing with life and passion beneath him was too much. He had to see her face, feel her tight nipples boring against his chest. "Turn over," he rasped, withdrawing briefly as he issued the order then joining their bodies again. She felt incredible, especially when she raked her nails across his back and inclined her head, as though to give him better access to the irresistibly throbbing vein in her throat.

Claude opened his mouth, aligned his fangs with her pulsating jugular vein. He'd take just a sip. No more. She clenched him harder with every thrust. He was about to come. Sensations rushed through his body, tightening his balls and making him gasp for the breath of cool air his body didn't really require.

"God yes," she hissed, her buttocks tightening as she reared up against him as if to consume every inch of his pulsating cock.

"Have to taste you. Oh, baby." His spurting climax triggered by her own, he bit her, let himself savor the salty, metallic taste of blood on his fangs for a mere second before moving away from temptation—away from the risk of taking enough to make her lose consciousness, and turning her. Or draining her blood completely and causing her to die, he thought, once again reminded of Stefan's life-altering mistake so long ago.

* * * * *

His love-bite still stung when Marisa came down off the incredible climax that had left her limp. After going to the bathroom to relieve herself, she lay on her side facing her vampire lover. Curious, she reached over and stroked Claude's cheek, her gaze locked on his sensual mouth that now hid those prominent fangs.

Ann Jacobs

"Did you turn me into a vampire too?" She didn't feel any different, but once the thought came in her mind she began to think of vampire movies and the erotic vampire romances she and the other girls often talked about during breaks at The Strip.

His gorgeous green eyes opened and he smiled, deliberately displaying his fangs. "No."

She didn't know why that disappointed her, but it did. "But you bit me—"

"I nipped you. You tasted so sweet it was hard for me to turn away, but I did. Do you trust me?"

Marisa had to think. He was a stranger—a vampire yet—but she'd felt compelled to offer him her heart and soul. She had no reason to trust the man—vampire—she'd agreed to fuck the night away with for two thousand dollars. Creatures of his kind were said to destroy mortals in the most horrible of ways. That poor woman in Buenos Aires a few weeks ago…according to accounts on cable news, she'd been drained of every ounce of her blood by what the reporters hinted might have been a killer vampire. Marisa shuddered as she recalled reports of other such grisly murders of women in various spots around the world.

But when she looked into Claude's eyes she saw no evil, only goodness and concern. And desire, more intense than any she'd experienced before. Though she had every reason not to, she trusted Claude. Besides, according to the accounts she'd read, the killer vampire or vampires chose only blondes. If Claude had been the killer in the news, surely he'd have chosen Donna, her co-worker who'd come on to him at the club. "I believe you wish me no harm, *Señor* Vampire, although I do not understand why."

Claude laughed. "I am a trustworthy sort, peace-loving. Not like the two men I saw you talking with outside The Strip. I do not threaten women, and I don't go looking for fights."

44

"You found one, though. What happened here?" Marisa traced the healing scar on his chest, shuddering at the thought of how badly someone must have hurt him.

"Yes. A few weeks ago my cousin Alexandre and I fought an evil vampire in Buenos Aires—Louis Reynard is his name. Even with our combined strength, we were unable to destroy him or to prevent him from killing yet another beautiful woman." Claude's expression clouded.

"You—you were the ones who tried to take down that serial killer—the one who targets blonde women."

"Yes. We will get him next time. Alina, our vampire queen, has commanded it. It is because of her that Reynard has gone on his murderous rampage."

"What is your life like, really? I've read about vampires, seen them in movies and on TV, but—"

"Our life's not so much different from your own." When Claude smiled, his expressive deep-green eyes sparkled. "Except that we live for centuries, sustain ourselves on blood...and possess uncanny abilities as fighters and lovers."

"You don't sleep in coffins or melt if you get into the sunlight?" Some of the more scary scenes from vampire movies Marisa had seen replayed in her head.

"Hardly. I prefer a big, soft bed to a cramped coffin any day. That rumor must have started about the time Count Dracula started raiding tombs in Transylvania. Not a single vampire from the d'Argent clan would dream of taking a snooze in some mortal's final resting place." This time he laughed out loud. "We're all sensitive to light to some extent, but I've never heard of the sun melting even one of us. It is true, though, that a stake through the heart will destroy us...and that our bites can be deadly."

Somehow those things didn't seem as frightening as they might if someone other than Claude had said them. "You said you're from Paris. I always wanted to see the Eiffel Tower," Marisa commented, hoping he'd tell her more.

"I live there now, in the *Marais* district. But I was born in Normandy, in a castle my grandfather built more than a thousand years ago." He smiled when she gasped at his comment. "Rolfe was mortal. He died in his bed when he was hardly older than I am now. His son, who was my father, was born a vampire. He'd likely still be alive today if he hadn't gotten caught up in trying to save people from Hitler's holocaust."

That would have made Claude what? At least sixty-five or seventy years old? Maybe centuries older than that? "Just how old are you?"

"Seventy-five. Practically a baby by vampire standards." He grinned, his expression turning self-conscious when he apparently realized his fangs were showing. What she noticed most, though, was the angry scar that stood out on his chest.

Marisa couldn't help herself. She had to touch him. When she traced the length of the scar, the cool, firm feel of his smooth pale skin began to arouse her again. Him too, she guessed when he shot her a feral smile and laid his hand over hers. "Don't worry about me, *cherie*. I am back in fighting form, and Alex is recovering quickly in Paris. If my guess is right, the Fox now lies in some hidden lair recovering from his wounds."

"So you say you are a peaceful sort, yet you fight and injure your beautiful body?"

"When I must. I'd much rather make love." When Claude reached over and soothed the small bruises his fangs had left on her throat, a jolt of fiery sensation coursed through Marisa's veins.

Against a mortal, Claude would be invincible. *Sí, muy macho.*

Not even the *patron's* best fighters would have a chance against her vampire lover. It made her cunt cream, sensing the extent of Claude's powers. How surprising that the aura of menace surrounding him made her hot—hotter than she'd ever been before. Suddenly she wanted him to take her, change her, transport her to his world where she'd be safe. If only he would... "The men you saw with me..."

"I know they wanted something from you. I'm afraid my Spanish isn't good enough that I could figure out exactly what it was that they wanted, or why. Something to do with your brother, I thought."

"*Sí*. It was about my little brother. Raul. He's only eighteen. He—he's had some trouble. Drugs. He owes the *patron*—the drug lord down in the *barrio* where we live—much money for what the cops took from him when they arrested him. Now the police watch Raul, and he can't make the money back fast enough to satisfy his boss. The bastard."

"So this drug-peddling boss expects you to pay your brother's debt?"

Claude's muscles tensed, reminding her of his strength— and her desire. "Yes." But Marisa didn't want to think about that now. What she wanted—craved—was to forget Raul, the *patron* and his goons. She'd put everybody and everything from her mind but Claude, and enjoy all the delicious sensations that filled her mind and body, chasing away every mortal concern.

For once in her life Marisa was going to do exactly as she wanted. *El Diablo* take her brother and his problems, if only for the moment. "Never mind. I'd rather make love with you again for now."

"Rest easily. I will take care of your problem. But not until daybreak. Until sunrise, you will fulfill my every fantasy."

"And what might your fantasies be?" She shuddered with anticipation, sure that whatever he might command would bring her pleasure.

"Lie face down on the bed. Put both pillows under your hips." His words, softly spoken but with the take-over authority she needed, gave her no choice but to obey—to eagerly await the ecstasy he promised with every touch, each light nip of his fangs on the sensitive skin of her buttocks.

"Good. Now close your eyes, grasp the bedposts and don't move. Trust that all I do will bring you pleasure." His words reverberated against one ass cheek before he began to nip her there...on the other cheek. "Trust me, period. Now and always."

No other lover had ever taken her out of herself, into a world where all that mattered was the touch of his hands, his mouth, his long, thick cock.

Something wet and warm and satiny—his tongue—ringed her vulnerable asshole, and the sensation made her grow wet with anticipation. "Open for me," he murmured against her most private flesh, and she could not say no.

"So soft...so hot. So tempting. I'm glad you thought to bring your toys along with the condoms." He finger-fucked her cunt, then lubed and inserted the large gel dildo he must have taken from her bag while she used the bathroom. "Do you use these often?"

Marisa's cheeks grew hot when she realized he might reasonably assume she used them in her vocation as a prostitute. "Sometimes I like to play when I'm by myself. And once in a while I use them in my act at the club. I've never...had a man use them on me the way you're doing."

"Good. Someday I'd like to watch you turn yourself on with them, but now I want you to relax and enjoy the ride."

When he turned on the vibrator mechanism, the motion started the bell on her clit to tinkling. *Dios*, but that felt delicious. Tiny explosions of sensation slithered along nerve endings, over her ass and up her spine until they collided in an erotic tango.

"Oooh." The vibrations made her shiver, or was it his fingers, spreading her ass cheeks and finding her last virgin hole? She opened her eyes and lifted her head, wanting to look at the man who had every cell in her body begging for his attention.

He nipped her ass cheek with his fangs as he used his well-lubricated fingers to stretch her asshole. "I told you, don't look. Don't talk. Don't worry, I put on another condom. And don't move unless I command it. Feel me inside you, on you, taking you higher than you've ever been taken, driving away the memory of all the lovers who've gone before."

There are fewer of them than you think.

She wanted to tell him she was no whore. That she'd had a handful of clumsy boyish lovers, none of whom had ever made her burn the way Claude did. But Marisa realized she was lying to herself. She *was* a prostitute. She *had* sold herself to him for money, never mind that she'd done it to save her brother's hide. "You have. I think of no lover but you."

He slapped her with the flat of his palm and she jumped, her ass burning in more ways than one now. "That's good, my beautiful little one. But you forget. I told you not to talk."

When he knelt between her legs and nudged her asshole with the slippery head of his rigid cock, she gasped. "Forgive me."

Claude replied by turning up the speed of the vibrator inside the dildo in her cunt. She couldn't help it. She let out another little whimper at the delicious sensations that coursed through her body. "I'll forgive you, but I'm going to fuck your pretty ass."

He was going to possess her. Own every orifice in her body. She started to murmur a weak protest, then clamped down her lips. He'd told her to be quiet, and he intended for her to obey.

As though he sensed her worry, he bent over, nipped the back of her neck. "Yes, I'm going to fuck your ass. And I command you to relax and enjoy it. You liked taking my fingers. You'll like my cock even better." He paused. "Don't be afraid, my sweet. I know you haven't been ass-fucked before."

How did he know? Was she that transparent? "I'm not afraid."

"You are, but I want you to relax. Let me in." He ringed her asshole once more with his fingers, then replaced them with his cock and found the tiny opening at the center. "It will hurt a bit at first, but then you'll feel incredible pleasure."

She wanted to let him invade her here, claim her in a way no man ever had. Marisa let out the breath she'd been holding, concentrated on the buzz of the vibrator in her cunt, the steady pressure of Claude's cock pressing against her rear passage.

It hurt when he pressed past her anal sphincter, but she breathed deeply and made her muscles relax. Sensing a whine would displease him, she bit her own tongue to hold it back. If this gave him pleasure, she didn't mind. *Madre de Dios!* The initial pain was nothing compared to the delicious feeling of fullness when he slid his cock head, then his shaft, ever deeper within her rear passage. Through the thin wall of tissue that separated the two holes, incredible sensations converged. The rocking motion of his cock in her ass, the vibrating dildo in her cunt, the incredible feel of his cool, dry skin against her back, his large hands cupping her breasts, flicking the sensitive tips of her nipples with his fingers, tugging the bells on the dangling rings... *Dios.* Nothing could have been more erotic than this. She wanted it to last forever.

"You're mine. Mine." His choked words dissolved into deep groans that reverberated against the back of her neck, made the hair at the nape of her neck shift against her skin.

She knew then that was what she wanted. Total submission. Enslavement to her vampire lover. "You are my Master," she whispered, "just as I'm your slave." She wanted him to bite her, drink her blood, make her his forever. But he'd told her not to talk, so she clamped down on her lips, squelched the words.

"Oh, yesss. Yes, Master." His balls nudged the dildo, set it to buzzing faster, harder. "May I have my Master's permission to come?"

"You like being ass-fucked. Like taking my cock up your tight little ass. Knew you would... Oh, yeah, my precious slave, use those muscles. Let me feel them milking my cock. Come for me. Now."

Great waves of pure sexual pleasure washed over her, one after the other, so fast and hard that they merged into one huge tsunami and crashed her into oblivion. When he shouted out his own release and rolled to his side, taking her with him, the aftershocks of her climax were still transporting her, keeping the incredible sensations coming, slowly now, like smooth, sweet honey. For a long time she lay in the secure safe haven of his arms, basking in the unfamiliar tenderness she sensed as he stroked her hair, her cheeks, the spot he'd nipped earlier in the curve of her throat.

She should have felt invaded, for the dildo still whirred in her cunt and his half-hard cock still filled her ass. But she didn't. A sense of fullness and contentment warmed her from the inside...contentment that came from the oneness she felt from her vampire Master.

Marisa shifted, wanting more of the sensation of her heat against his coolness, the bite of his strong fingers on her nipples, her clit. As though he knew she needed more, he pressed two fingers between her lips.

"Suck my finger, slave. Pretend it's my cock. Pretend that with my vampire powers, I can fulfill all your erotic fantasies at the same time." Her Master's deep, mellow voice washed over her, a soothing balm to her troubled thoughts. Her thought that this was a one-night stand for money and he was not her Master but her hooker's mark.

I can't take his money. Not now, when he has given me far more pleasure than I could possibly have given him. That wasn't it, at least not entirely. Marisa couldn't bear the thought of being a whore. Not in her Master's mind or heart.

Chapter Four
ະ

"May I get up for a moment, Master? There is something I must do."

She raised her head but made no effort to move, obviously waiting for permission. He liked that, liked how easily she handed over control to him. "Yes. But you need not ask. I may be your Master, but I'm no ogre who'd keep you from taking care of mortal necessities."

"Not that. This." She went straight for her purse, removed the twenty crisp American hundred-dollar bills he'd given her and laid them on the table beside the bed. "I cannot take money from the man who has become my Master."

Claude had known it from the moment he'd looked into Marisa's guileless brown eyes that they reflected desperation, not greed. Now she'd confirmed it. He made no move to pick up the cash, for it didn't concern him. She did.

Her eyes downcast, she spoke through trembling lips. "I am no prostitute, in spite of what I must seem. I fucked with you because I wanted to. And I received more pleasure than I've given you, Master."

That he doubted, but he let it pass for the moment and took her now empty hand. "Why then did you offer to fuck with me for money?" Claude paused, but when she didn't answer right away, he went on. "Did it have something to do with the two men I saw threatening you in the alley beside The Strip before you performed?"

She nodded, her eyes still focused on the floor. "As I told you, my brother, he owes much money to the *patron*. The men you saw with me—his enforcers—said they would kill Raul if I didn't pay up by tomorrow night. I have less than two days left now to come up with another four thousand dollars," she said, looking out the window at the rising sun.

Bastards. Mortal bloodsuckers who preyed on those weaker and smaller than themselves. Claude had read them right. "Your brother. Does he owe this money rightfully?" She shrugged. "You might say so. Raul ran cocaine for the *patron*. As I think I mentioned already, the police took nearly five thousand dollars' worth of cocaine Raul was carrying when they arrested him. Now he has nothing to sell on the street, no way to pay what he owes the *patron* for the drugs. The drug bosses don't want explanations about what happened. They just want their money, and they don't care what people have to do to get it."

"It seems to me this *patron* has it good. No matter what happens to his runners, he gets paid." Claude managed to hold back the string of curses that flooded his brain. This drug lord who apparently held Marisa's brother in a stranglehold with his own addiction sounded as evil in his own way as Reynard. Claude gentled his voice when he spoke again. "What does your brother say about all this, my pet?"

"I haven't spoken to him about it, but I am sure Raul would beg me to save his life, as he has done many times before. And...I promised our mama before she died that I would take care of him." Marisa sat on a chair by the window and stared out at the beach.

It infuriated Claude that such responsibility had been dumped on her frail, submissive shoulders. "If you will allow me the pleasure, I will take care of your brother and this *patron*."

Marisa's beautiful eyes widened, as though she had just realized that was exactly what Claude had implied. "*Sí*. I would like nothing better than to rid the *barrio* of... Surely, Master, you do not mean to kill them?"

"Only if I must. As I said, I'm really a peaceful sort."

Marisa nodded, her eyes downcast as a good slave's should be. He got the sense that she didn't like the idea of causing her tormentors' demise, but that circumstances were such that she felt she had no choice. "Show me then where I may find these bastards. I swear I will make them pay." For the first time in his memory, Claude wanted to protect a woman more than he wanted to fuck her. At last he was beginning to understand the emotion that had compelled Stefan to try to turn the mortal he had wanted for all time. The desire to have his lover for all eternity. To risk everything to make her his vampire mate.

He wanted to take her for his slave...become her Master. See to her safety and her pleasure and keep her from mortal danger and pain.

* * * * *

A half-hour later, while the morning sun still lay low over the Atlantic, Marisa walked through the hotel lobby with Claude. *Dios,* but he was one gorgeous Master, one she'd like to spend the rest of her life pleasing. Her cunt and ass still ached, reminding her how completely he had filled them and how much she wanted him to fill them again. Perhaps...

She imagined him taking her to dungeons like the ones she'd heard existed on South Beach, restraining her on a St. Andrew's cross, forcing her to reach for the outer limits of sexual pleasure. Tying her to his bed and invading every one of her bodily orifices over and over, until she screamed with her release. Using his fangs to nibble at her nipples and clit, then chasing away the pleasure-pain he'd inflict with the velvet touch of his tongue.

She'd kneel at his feet and suck his cock at his command, cup his heavy ball sac in both hands and weigh his testicles while he pushed her head lower, making her swallow the full length of his huge sex and drink his come. Her cunt and ass clenched at the prospect of him claiming them. Claiming her over and over through the years. The centuries.

What would it be like to be his vampire slave-mate? To feel the prick of his fangs at her throat, know he was ending her life as she knew it? To look forward to a future, roaming the world with her Master for centuries — perhaps an eternity? Marisa looked over at Claude, wished they could have stayed in the shelter of his room, fucking and sucking and exploring how their very different worlds might come together.

She wanted him to take her away with him, away from the *barrio* and the drugs and all the troubles they represented. *I want you to sink your fangs into my throat until you've made me one with you, forever.*

"Be careful of what you wish for, *cherie*, or you may get it." His warning punctuated her silent desire, as though he possessed psychic abilities and could read the thoughts she hadn't dared put into words. Perhaps he could.

"Can you read my mind?" she asked, more than a bit unnerved at the prospect that he'd known all the jumbled thoughts that had made their way through her mind last night…as well as the fantasies that had carried her away as they walked toward her car.

"Yes. Well, not if I'm concentrating on other things." He grinned. "Reading minds is a vampire skill that often comes in handy. Our psychic powers get stronger as we age. My nephews — who by the way are centuries older than I — are much better at it than I am."

Marisa figured she'd divulged very few secrets last night, since Claude had definitely been concentrating on other things, such as making her come until she couldn't come any more. Such as compelling her to wish for an eternity with him, in his world, although she'd certainly revealed that wish to him just now. "I wouldn't mind, you know. Master."

"You're thinking now how you'd miss your brother. Wondering where we'd live, whether we'd have a family. Your mind's churning with questions, but right now we need to take care of your immediate problem. Turning you would be one way to get you away from your tormentors, but it would leave your brother here to face unpleasant consequences."

Shame made Marisa hang her head. "You're right, I couldn't abandon Raul. Still…"

Claude's brow furrowed, and for what seemed a long time he focused his gaze on waves edging up the beach on a strong incoming tide. "Don't get me wrong. I'd like nothing better than to have you forever as my *dhampir* slave."

"*Dhampir?*"

"That's what you'd be. A vampire made from a mortal by the will of a vampire born." Claude paused a moment. "But turning you is not our only option. I can destroy your brother's enemies if that is what you want. Or I can try to spirit you and your brother somewhere far away, where you'll never have to worry about the *patron* or his enforcers again. What is it that you want me to do?"

What did she want, really? Marisa met Claude's sober gaze, held it, imagining as she did what the rest of her life would be like if she took that fateful step into her Master's shadow world. Reliving in fast-forward motion the years that already had passed her by, her few friends and family members who had gone to their rewards. The smaller number she'd leave behind.

"Marisa?"

"Oh, pardon me. I was thinking. Thinking that if I went with you I'd leave precious little of value behind."

Claude smiled, slipping a hand beneath her elbow to steady her as they climbed the short set of stairs that led to the public parking lot behind The Strip. "I could tell. Now you must tell me. Do we fight or do we run?"

Fight? Run? Those were her choices, weren't they? One fact stood out, crystal clear. Marisa wanted an eternity with her hero, her vampire lover who offered her freedom when all she wanted was bondage to him, a lifetime to service all his needs while he held her safe from harm. Although he might not agree to do it, she had to ask. "I want to go away. With you. I want to spend a lifetime as your slave. But I must try to get Raul away from the people who turned him from a good boy to a street punk. Could you..."

Claude stroked her hand. "Let me get this right. Are you telling me you want me to turn you and Raul into vampires?"

"Yes." As a vampire, her brother might live for centuries. And if he were a vampire he'd have no need for cocaine. As a mortal in the *barrio*, he was likely to die much too soon, either by the drugs or by order of the *patron*.

As though deep in thought, Claude paused and scratched his chin. "I'm not certain I can turn you. As I think I mentioned to you earlier, I'm very young as vampires go—less than a hundred years old. My powers are still developing. Perhaps it would be better if I destroyed all your brother's enemies then flew you and your brother to Paris, away from potential harm. I know I can do that."

"Oh, I want you to do that first. I want you to use your special powers to destroy the *patron* so he can never ruin another young life with his evil. Unless...unless by destroying them, you put yourself at risk."

"No mortal is a match for me," Claude said, laughing as if that idea amused him. "Guns and knives have little effect on vampires, and mortals have little or no defense against the simplest of our powers."

"B-but the police? Won't they chase you to the ends of the earth if you leave a string of bodies littering Miami?" Marisa wouldn't be able to live with herself if she caused Claude harm.

"If you say the word, the bastards will disappear without a trace. I'd never leave bodies littering the beaches. Trust me, I will leave no trail for the police to follow should they miss these vermin, which I doubt will be the case." He grinned then sobered as he met her gaze. "It is your conscience I worry about, little one. Can you live knowing you indirectly caused

Ann Jacobs

the deaths of these men?" Claude cupped her chin, made her look at him.

"I do not wish to play God or ask you to do so if it is against your own conscience," she said slowly. "But for the past five years I have watched the drug peddlers destroying lives, and there seems to be very little anyone can do to stop them. Yes, I know when the *patron* is gone, another will come in his place. But for a little space of time, people like my brother may be able to break free of the cycle, conquer their addictions."

"All right. I will try, however, to destroy the threat they pose without ending their miserable lives, for I sense that is what you want."

"Turn me first. Please, Master, let me help you." Marisa couldn't stand the thought of putting Claude at risk. Vampire or not, he'd be going up against not one but three men—maybe more—who had no conscience and no qualms about committing murder.

"I want to, but I cannot. I told you before. I've never turned a mortal." In hushed tones he told her the story of his nephew Stefan killing the woman he loved when he'd tried to turn her, admitting his own fear once more.

"Have you any older vampire friends who would turn me?"

"Not here. If I took you to Paris...but no, we don't have time for that. Your brother has such a short time left to pay up or die. Normally I could fly you both there through time and space, but I haven't regained all my powers since I was injured." He shook his head. "No, that would be much too risky. You don't know...there are things you'd give up along with your mortality. Things you undoubtedly would miss."

"Yes. I'm sure I will miss some things. The kiss of the noontime sun, the taste of familiar foods, the sense of my own mortality." The words caught in her throat, but she managed to look him in the eye and get them out in a hoarse whisper.

"Not as much, though, as I would miss submitting to my vampire Master. Please, bind me to you for all eternity. If you care to have me as your eternal slave."

"I want nothing more than to take you as my mate. But you must be sure, for once I make you my *dhampir* slave you can never go back. Never be mortal again." He turned her, held her, made her shiver from the chill of his body as she absorbed the slow, almost undetectable beat of his heart beneath his white polo shirt...the insistent pulsing of his rigid cock against her swollen pussy.

All Marisa's doubts disappeared. This was the Master she wanted. "I am very certain, Master."

Claude frowned, his doubt evident. "If that's what you truly want, knowing I might fail."

"Yes. That is what I want. Turn me and I will spend an eternity seeing to your every pleasure. Together we will destroy the *patron* and his henchmen and spirit Raul away. He will be better off anywhere but—"

"Dead? Because that's what you will be if I try turning you and fail. As dead as Reynard's victims, only you'll leave me behind, suffering because I caused your death. Or I could turn you successfully yet inadvertently kill your brother, and you'd hate me for that eternity you're talking about us spending together. I couldn't stand that." Claude held her fast, the rising sun over the Atlantic illuminating his face, showing her the depth of his fear, his uncertainty at his ability to do as she asked.

She recognized his dilemma...and her own. "Then let the blame fall on me, for I would rather be dead than live without you. And Raul will die anyhow unless we manage to save him." She paused, hoping...but he said nothing. "This is my car."

Her heart sinking for he simply stared at her, she laid the key in his hand. For a moment she thought she was mistaken, that he did not feel as she did.

"So be it." Claude kissed Marisa hard, driving her fears away before opening the door of the clunker car she'd bought years ago when she first had started dancing at The Strip. "I want you to know I'm doing this because you ask. But also because it is what I want more than anything. I know the elders of my clan would tell me no, to wait, to let you live with me as a vampire for a while before taking this final step. But I feel doing this now is right. For both of us." He slid into the car after her, turning sideways behind the wheel to face her.

Her heart beat faster. She laid her fears to rest when she looked into his deep green eyes that seemed more protective now than dangerous. "I want you for my Master. And I trust you to carry me safely to your vampire world."

Slowly, his long fingers fumbling with each of the buttons, he bared her to the waist, bent and laid soft kisses along the skin he'd uncovered. "I welcome you to my world, and if I succeed you'll never need to fear mortal evil again."

"Oh, yes." The gentle scraping of his fangs on her sensitive flesh aroused her unbearably. Threading her fingers through his thick black hair, she drew him closer, encouraged him to take her, accept her as his loving slave.

"I accept you completely. With any luck you will be my *dhampir* slave when you wake up. But in case I fail, I want you to know I love you. I've felt since before we made love that we were soulmates, fated lovers." Turning slowly toward her, Claude positioned his hands on either side of her head, his fingers threading through her hair, baring her throat to fangs that had elongated as he'd prepared her for the taking.

He clamped down on her jugular vein and began to feed. The sensation aroused her more than anything in her memory, made her lightheaded...dizzy. It was as though she was floating, half-cognizant, somewhere between life and death, aware only of Claude drinking her blood. Making her his— forever. As her consciousness ebbed, she felt Claude withdrawing his fangs, cradling her limp body in his muscular arms.

Chapter Five

෨

Had he followed in Stefan's footsteps and destroyed the woman he loved? Desperate, Claude felt Marisa's throat for a pulse, found none. No rise and fall of her chest. No heartbeat. Her skin felt cold, clammy, not vibrantly warm as it had been or cool and dry as his was—as all vampires' skin must feel. She lay in his arms, passive, making no sound, no movement to indicate she still lived.

Then he remembered. *He* didn't breathe spontaneously. Neither did any vampire he knew. Since his heart beat so slowly his mortal lovers had often commented about it, hers might slow appreciably as well. "Wake up, my *dhampir* slave," he ordered, but she didn't obey.

She did respond, though, with a long sigh. And she snuggled in his arms as though seeking warmth. Marisa was alive. Incredibly relieved to know he hadn't killed her, Claude stroked her pale skin, felt the dampness start to subside. "Hang on. I will take you back to the hotel." Apparently, he figured as he laid her under the covers in his bed and pulled the drapes shut to keep out the morning light, it would take her several hours before she'd recover from the changing.

Several hours, his vampire senses told him, would be longer than her brother had to live. Gathering his strength, he donned his dark glasses and took to the air. His instincts guiding him, he circled Miami's Cuban district, scanning the scene before him for...

There they were. The two bastards who'd threatened his lover. Working over a skinny young kid who was no more a match for them than Marisa, they paid Claude no mind as he swooped down on them, landing a pair of stunning blows before they knew they'd been discovered. Claude kicked their unconscious bodies into a heap and fell to his knees.

He'd thought the boy was in trouble, hurried to his side. But was he too late? Blood poured from a chest wound, gurgled out from his nose and mouth. Raul? Claude had no doubt once he got a look at the pale features that were so like Marisa's. "Don't you dare die on me."

Raul wasn't listening. His chest heaved twice then became deathly still. Claude felt for a pulse, found none. He had one choice, and he took it, not caring if someone saw him. For the second time that day he held a mortal in his arms while he drained the lifeblood from his veins. Satisfied that Raul might survive now as a vampire, Claude spirited him back to the hotel and laid him on the bed beside Marisa.

Returning quickly to the scene of the fight, Claude found the two goons where he'd left them, apparently trying to explain to the police officers who'd just cuffed them that they'd been assaulted by some otherworldly creature. Stepping into the shadow of a crumbling storefront, he concentrated on the larger one while the cops led the weasel-faced one to a squad car.

Humberto Majore. It came to him, straight from the reeling thug's mind. A name for the *patron* who'd ruined so many lives, who'd nearly turned his soulmate into a prostitute to pay her brother's debt. Claude concentrated harder, came up with the name of the store where the drug lord dished out his poison.

La FemmeFatale. A vintage clothing store by all appearances, with mannequins sporting club attire posed casually in the showcase windows. A pretty young clerk walked outside, crossed the street and entered a café with a sign in the window that said it specialized in black beans and rice.

The man he sought would be alone inside now. Striving for a casual look, Claude strolled inside, pretending to look at colorful gowns full of feathers and lace set out for display on crowded racks in the front of the store. He saw no one, nothing out of the ordinary. Had his intuition failed him?

He thought so until he spied a rotund man smiling from behind a counter filled with costume jewelry that had been fashionable when Claude was a child. It had to be Majore. The faceless *patron* of Marisa's nightmares. Despite the almost cherubic look about the man's expression, Claude knew. He smelled the aura of evil. Sensed it hanging heavy in the air.

Claude opened his mind, saw ghosts of this man's victims parading before his eyes. Innocents in death, though the corruption of this man's filthy products had tainted them, stolen their futures, their lives. The *patron* would have to go.

"How can I help you, *amigo*?"

"An ounce if you please. Raul Delgado tells me I can get my supply direct from you." Claude had to be sure, very sure, it was the right mortal's life he was about to take.

The angelic face turned purple. The black eyes flashed with fury. "You tell that son of a diseased whore he wants more stuff to sell, he gives me my money. Better yet, let your bullet-ridden body tell him." Moving fast for one so porcine, the *patron* pulled a snub-nosed .32 automatic and peppered Claude with a barrage of bullets.

They stung. But they didn't stop Claude. Majore's eyes bugged out when he saw Claude coming. "No. Your bullets will not stop me. Now you will experience vampire justice." Slowly, for speed wasn't necessary, Claude reached over the counter and snagged his victim. Consumed him until his existence was a mere memory, his mortal remains a million particles of dust caught up and disseminated in a silent gust of wind.

On the way out, Claude locked the door. The clerk who actually sold the vintage clothes might wonder what had happened to *Señor* Majore, but she'd never know. Neither would the police, if she cared to involve them in the *patron's* disappearance. His mission accomplished, Claude hurried back to his *dhampir* mate and her brother, his plans already in motion to take them home.

* * * * *

How long she'd been out, she had no idea, for when Marisa woke she found herself in a dimly lit bedroom, its dark wood furnishings obviously priceless antiques. Claude stood over her, a worried look on his handsome face. "Raul?" she asked, her mouth feeling unfamiliar—different than it had before.

He sat beside her and took her hand. "Your brother is recovering nicely from the turning, as are you. Just now my mother had to send out for a new supply of A positive. It seems Raul has developed quite a liking for it, more than for the finer vintages she normally stocks here in the house. Don't worry that he'll get in trouble here. *Maman* can be a stern taskmistress."

"How—"

"After I turned you, you slept for a long time, much longer than I'd expected. Once I was certain you would be all right I went to find Raul. The two goons who threatened you had him cornered, so I was forced to deal with them."

"They are—"

"Quite shaken from their encounter with a vampire, I assure you. At the moment I imagine they're cooling their heels in a Miami jail cell, thanks to the officers who came to investigate the fracas. I imagine by now they are spilling all they know about the operation of this *patron* who wielded so much power in the *barrio*."

"I assume you changed Raul too."

"I had no choice. One of the goons had stabbed him, and he was practically dead. I turned him and brought him to you in my hotel room. When I finished meting out justice to the *patron*, I came back to the hotel and made arrangements for a charter plane to bring us home."

"Justice?"

"The *patron* is no more. Once I realized how he'd used cocaine to enslave not only your brother but also so many other young boys in the *barrio*, I decided he had to go."

"I'm glad."

"It bothered me, seeking out a mortal to destroy him. In the end, though, I didn't have to commit cold-blooded murder. The bastard emptied a gun into me when I asked to buy some stuff and said Raul had sent me." Claude shrugged. "Hard to believe a mortal would dare go head-to-head with a vampire, but he did."

"The *patron* thought himself above the law...above retribution. I'm glad he is no more, but gladder that you killed him in a fair fight."

"Not particularly fair. Still it eases my conscience, knowing he'd have killed me first if he'd been able to." Claude sat beside her on the bed, lifted her hand and intertwined their fingers. "Let us forget the *patron,* may he rot forever in mortals' hell."

"Yes, let's." Marisa glanced around the room, saw nothing familiar. "This cannot be a hotel room. Where are we?"

"My home. Paris." He shrugged, his expression suddenly sheepish. "*Maman* scolded me for turning you without her having met you first, but she says you make me a lovely *dhampir* bride."

"*Dhampir?*" She thought he'd used the word, but she couldn't be sure.

"A vampire made by the love of a born vampire, *ma chere.* I do love you."

He'd said that before...before he transported her into his vampire world. Marisa looked at him, saw not only the Master who made her submission incredible pleasure but also a good man she could count on for a lifetime. A mate for more than

65

mating, more than protection. Claude d'Argent was a mate meant for loving.

And she did. "I love you too, my darling Master. Why are you sitting there, fully clothed, while I lie naked on your bed, awaiting your pleasure?"

His wide mouth breaking into the same toothy grin that had intimidated her when they'd first met, Claude began stripping off his clothes. She loved his body—so pale, so muscular, the skin as soft as the velvet hangings on their bed.

Her cunt contracted. Her nipples hardened. Her clit twitched so hard the little bell on it tinkled. She sensed her fangs growing with her arousal and wondered how she'd ever manage now to suck on her love's huge, pale cock. Eager to have him, she spread her legs and held out her arms in blatant invitation.

He sank into her wet cunt, filling her beyond full and baring his throat. "Bite me, my hot-blooded vampire bride. Don't be afraid, you will not hurt me. I want you to drink my blood, the way I fed on yours to make you mine."

When she sank her fangs into him, he groaned, a sound that spoke more of ecstasy than agony. The salty, slightly metallic taste of him fed her arousal, turned her cool body warm. It felt good, so good. Euphoria set in as he thrust harder and faster into her welcoming cunt, when he turned them where she was on top and directed her movement with big, powerful hands on her ass.

"Fuck me, fuck me hard," he rasped out, and she felt his cock swell and harden even more inside her. She sank down on him once, twice, three times more, mindless as delicious sensations washed over her. "Don't stop. Oh yes. Squeeze my cock. God yes, I'm coming." He bathed her womb in hot, hard bursts. Bursts that claimed her yet again. Made her know she belonged to him.

Long into the night under a new Paris moon they made love, two vampires dancing in the dark, sucking and fucking and sipping of the nectar of the life they'd share for an eternity together.

Ann Jacobs

Epilogue
A month later

so

Alina lifted her glass and sipped daintily at the fine vintage A negative that was her favorite, laced with a mere thimbleful of anisette. Then she met Claude's gaze across his mother's dining table. "I hate to disturb your honeymoon, Uncle, but we've traced Reynard to Chicago. I sense Stefan will need your help."

Claude clasped Marisa's hand, gave it a reassuring squeeze. "Of course. We will leave at once."

"Not we, Master. You. I've just learned we are to have a child, and that it's somewhat of a miracle that we've managed to conceive. Your mama would visit me with some awful vampire curse if I did anything to risk this baby."

When she laid his hand over her still-flat belly, Claude imagined he felt movement there. "A baby? So soon?" The idea thrilled him. It terrified him too, if he were to be completely honest about the feelings rumbling around his brain following his mate's announcement.

"Congratulations, Claude. It seems you must have inherited your father's potency. After all, he sired four children, and no other vampire in the clan has ever managed to produce more than one." Alina beamed with obvious joy. "Of course Marisa's right. She must stay here, take care of herself and my cousin." When she frowned, her brow wrinkled momentarily. "It is a cousin, is it not?"

"I guess." When one's niece and nephews were centuries older than oneself, relationships tended to get confusing. Claude figured "cousin" sounded as good a title as any for an uncle's offspring. Suddenly aware there must be some danger

68

in being pregnant, he turned to Marisa. "I don't want to leave you. Not now. Still, this is the best chance we've had so far to corner the Fox."

"I understand. The world won't be safe for any of us until he's been destroyed. Go. I'll be fine, getting to see all the attractions in Paris with Alina and your mama as a guide." Marisa smiled, her dainty fangs showing, reminding Claude she'd given him the gift of a lifetime by turning her back on her mortal life and choosing to join him in the shadow world.

A world where no vampire would be safe unless they destroyed Reynard soon. Unless they put an end to his senseless killing spree before he brought the wrath of all mortals down on every vampire on earth. Claude stood, ready to do his duty as his father had done nearly seventy-five years ago, even if duty meant destruction.

"*Au revoir*, my love" he said, giving Marisa a quick squeeze before taking to the air once more. "We'll get the bastard this time. And make a safe world for our child."

ETERNAL VICTORY

ಔ

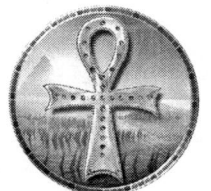

Trademarks Acknowledgement

ಬ

The author acknowledges the trademarked status and trademark owners of the following wordmarks mentioned in this work of fiction:

Sig Sauer: S.A.T. Swiss Arms Technology AG

Prologue

ॐ

The night cloaked him in moist black velvet. Wild waves pounded in the ocean below him. Rhythmic slapping sounds ricocheted off his ears as he propelled himself through humid air that became warmer as he moved south-southwest toward Miami Beach and the evil vampire who was his nemesis—and his queen's continuing nightmare.

I'd swear the old bastard never left his lair, but another body turned up on the beach last night with a white rosebud clutched in her lifeless hand. Alex heard the frustration in Philippe's voice, loud and clear even over the whistling of the wind.

"Fuck." The epithet slipped through Alex's lips, a guttural cry that echoed against the heavy air that surrounded him. *You're certain?*

Reynard landed right outside the gate to this deserted estate on Biscayne Bay and went inside. There's only one way out, and I've been watching it. I swear he hasn't gone anywhere unless he's found a way to slip through stone walls. But since he's been in Miami, three women have died. His work. I'm sure of it, though I don't know how he gets in and out.

Most vampires, Alex included, could move with stealth when circumstances demanded it. But Alex had been studying Louis Reynard since his pattern of serial killings began, and he'd never observed that the bastard could cloak his presence from fellow vampires—or that he could move through solid walls the way Alex and his clansmen could if they were sufficiently motivated. Still, the wily vampire had obviously managed to sneak out from under Philippe's watchful eye. Three times so far.

It became more evident every time Alex encountered Reynard that while he might have been old and battered, even for a vampire, he possessed an unequaled arsenal of powers. Alex shouldn't have been surprised. After all, Louis had been honing the supernatural abilities he'd been using for evil since centuries before Alex had been born.

What should I do? Philippe's tone broadcast his frustration, a sentiment Alex echoed.

It's all right, my friend. I should be there very soon—assuming the winds don't change direction. Damn. He, Stefan and Claude shouldn't have expected a made vampire, no matter how well Philippe was motivated, to be able to destroy Reynard or even keep him under surveillance once Reynard sensed his presence. They themselves had failed to end the serial killer's life, and they'd been three against one. Alex let out another oath as he broke through the clouds and zeroed in on the bright lights of Florida's Gold Coast.

No. Reynard still lived to wreak havoc on mortal women. And to horrify and terrify Alina, his cousin and the d'Argent clan's beloved queen. Alex concentrated hard, cut through the damp air with a satisfying *whoosh* and sped toward his destination with hardened resolve.

This time he wouldn't fail. Louis Reynard would die. And d'Argent honor would be restored.

* * * * *

Mara Leone woke screaming, drenched in her own blood. No, not blood. Sweat. It wasn't Dante returned once more from his grave, but another vampire, one exponentially more evil than the one who'd seduced her then been destroyed after having been caught feeding on the wrong mortal victim. Yes, as much as she hated to admit it, Dante had been a killer. But he'd gone berserk with bloodlust and taken one victim. One. Not three and counting.

She tamped down on bittersweet memories, concentrated on the here and now. All her instincts told her the bastard doing the killings on South Beach was on the hunt again, somewhere on her turf. Tonight, unless she missed her guess, another woman would become his victim.

And since he did his thing and promptly disappeared, there wasn't a thing she could do to prevent it.

But she could try, and she would. Moving quickly, she pulled on her clothes, ran a brush through the shoulder-length tangle of her hair and headed for the station. A crescent moon lay high in the ink-black sky, its light a faint beacon above the neon lights of the South Beach clubs.

The sort of sky she'd lain under with Dante all those years ago before he'd shed his cloak of humanity and reverted to the nature he'd no longer been able to deny. Fuck it, she had no business thinking of him. He'd been dead for years, destroyed by the vampire hunters who'd given him no chance for escape, no time to explain why he'd killed a mortal—if indeed there had been an explanation that might have saved his life.

Her responsibility now was to put a stop to this current rash of vampire attacks. If she didn't, she'd be busted back to beach patrol and spend the rest of her career handing out parking tickets.

Not her idea of upward mobility, she thought wryly as she hurried into the busy South Beach station.

"He's hit again, Lieutenant Leone," a uniformed patrolman called out as they passed on the stairs.

Why should she have been surprised? This wasn't the first night Dante had visited her in her nightmares...or the first time the nightmare had foretold tragedy.

Chapter One

ഇ

Another death by vampire. As she headed across the beach toward the site of the latest murder, Miami-Dade Homicide Lieutenant Mara Leone wished her bosses hadn't known about her long-ago liaison with one of the vamps who mingled, mostly unseen and unnoticed, among the humans on whom they depended for their sustenance. If they hadn't, she might have been able to escape revisiting so many old, painful memories.

But she'd had no such luck, and now she had a vampire serial killer to stop—as if she could do that with her very mortal team of detectives.

The beach patrolman who'd found the body had been right when he called the murder in as being another vampire attack. Mara stared down at the dead blonde illuminated by the harsh light of the patrolman's flashlight. Probably a showgirl, she surmised from the heavy makeup that almost but didn't quite manage to conceal the pallor of death. The marks on the woman's throat looked suspiciously as though they'd been made by the same vampire fangs that had punctured the other women's throats, but the pathologist would have to make that determination by measuring the angle of penetration and the distance between the two marks. What Mara found even more telling was that this woman, like the others, didn't appear to have been sexually molested or to have put up a fight.

Seduced by vampiric compulsion yet not seduced in the usual sense of the word. Strange. Her gaze settled on a freshly cut white rosebud the killer apparently had laid on the palm of the victim's outstretched hand. Its pale beauty provided a macabre contrast with spatters of darkening blood that marred its petals. Just as it had with the three previous crime scenes.

Mara had to turn away when bile began to rise in her throat, threatened to spill over and splatter over the crime scene. What the hell was going on?

This made four women found dead on the beach in less than two weeks, all apparently victims of one crazed vampire who drained them of their blood and left a fragrant, creamy rose as his calling card. Who knew when the killings would end?

Soon, if she wanted to keep her job. Her bosses had started getting nervous after they'd found victim number two. This pattern of similarly committed murders didn't do much to boost the tourist traffic on Miami's famed South Beach, and it was damn hard to keep a lid on such titillating albeit gruesome news as a spate of vampire serial killings.

"How long has she been dead?" Mara asked Joe Krill, the assistant coroner who'd arrived right behind her and now knelt beside the body.

"Not much more than an hour, I'd say. Body's still warm. Looks to me like another vampire bite."

Yeah, Mara had figured that out for herself, and she didn't have the letters "MD" behind her name. "Got any new ideas where we might find a vampire with a fetish for white roses and blonde bimbos, boys?" Not that she expected them to know. If any of the assembled cops had come up with a clue about where a suspicious-looking vamp might have been hanging out, they'd have been on him like stink on shit. Her team members were nothing if not devoted to their jobs. "Come on, don't you all start talking at once."

"Damn it, Louis Reynard's the vampire we're looking for. I don't care if everybody thinks that fiend who went around the world killing women on the full moon has been put out of commission. Or that our murderer isn't following a pattern of doing his dirty work only on the full moon. There are too many similarities. No signs of rape or attempted rape, or of the victim trying to escape. The white roses. He's at it again. Here." Rookie detective Ben Braunstein had an earnest look about him that kept Mara from ripping him a new one following his recitation of an opinion he'd held ever since he'd researched an unsolved killing that had taken place in Atlanta a little over a year ago, shortly after the first of their own victims had turned up dead.

Yeah, Ben had done his homework, but Mara had listened to him state his opinion at least one time too many. Especially since she was beginning to believe his hypothesis that the vampire serial killer might have miraculously recovered from injuries he'd supposedly suffered at the hands of three vampires from a rival clan, and settled down to wreak more havoc on her turf. "You've told me at least a dozen times that you think this killer is Louis Reynard. You've also mentioned that some of his fellow vampires damn near killed him in Chicago a couple of weeks after the Atlanta attack." She paused and riddled the rookie with a look she hoped would shut him up. "What makes you think Reynard might suddenly have recovered and settled in here?"

"How many vampires have the balls to leave their calling card?" Ben gestured toward the rose.

"I can't imagine him being able to do this if he was hurt as badly as Ben said." The coroner looked up from the corpse, his expression dubious.

Mara shook her head. "It's not outside the realm of possibility that it's Reynard. The creatures heal fast. And they can't be trusted." She recalled how Dante had drawn her in and made her trust him, back when she'd been on the force less time than Ben. She'd been so young, so fucking gullible. And so much in love that thinking about having lost him to those hunters still made her want to cry. "Watch out. If you should ever run into an actual vampire, he or she will charm you out of your autopsy tools before you can figure out what hit you."

Ben shrugged. "I've seen some. I even saw a vampire earlier tonight at a bar a mile or so down the beach, near the big hotels. He didn't strike me as the sort of guy who'd attack a female. Doubt he'd need to—the women were swarming around him like hungry mosquitoes who didn't know their potential victim was an even more effective bloodsucker than any of them."

Mara had learned the hard way that vampires had an uncanny ability to seduce mortals without putting forth any obvious effort. She supposed the fiend they were looking for possessed a knack for seducing humans to do things they ordinarily wouldn't have done. After all, he'd apparently found it sickeningly easy to lure his victims, including the blonde now lying at their feet. "So this vampire you met seduced you into thinking he's a good one? I'm not surprised. Come on, I want to meet this paragon with fangs before another woman turns up dead."

She turned to Joe. "Go ahead, transport the body. I'll want preliminary autopsy results on my desk by the time we get back to the station. The rest of you, secure the scene and comb the area for clues, in case the killer left some hint as to who he might be." Mara doubted he had. The other three crime scenes had been as clean as any she'd ever worked, and she was becoming more certain every minute that these murders were the work of the same out-of-control vamp that had left a string of bodies peppering the globe over the past couple of years.

That didn't keep her from getting annoyed with Ben every time he put forth the vampire-serial-killer theory. Or frustrated that she had no clue as to how they were going to bring the bastard to justice.

* * * * *

Apparently Reynard's near-death experience had fucked his mind up royally. According to Philippe, Louis had done in three blondes—two showgirls and a tourist—in the few days since he'd arrived and set up housekeeping in a previously deserted stone fortress on Biscayne Bay. Alex clenched his fists. Whatever it took, he'd put an end, once and for all, to the old bastard's murderous adventures.

Enjoying the kiss of a soft breeze off the Atlantic, Alex took up the same spot at an open-air watering hole for mortals that he'd noticed before checking in at one of the high-rise hotels dotting South Beach. It offered a convenient vantage point to scan up and down the beach, looking for a sign that Reynard had once again come out of his hole. Idly, he stroked the short Vandyke beard he'd cultivated back in Paris after his barber had shorn his usually longish hair into an almost military-looking cut a few weeks earlier.

So far, he'd had no luck. Philippe hadn't seen Reynard leave his fortress, and Alex hadn't spotted him hunting along the stretch of beach where blondes had been turning up dead. That didn't necessarily mean the sonofabitch was sleeping off his most recent kill, however. The Fox, as Reynard was often called, had always had an uncanny ability to slip past his observers.

Since Alex had spent months on end chasing the Fox around the world, he found the notion that Reynard would stay in one place and elude his hunters instead of meeting them head-on hard to imagine. But he had no reason to doubt Philippe's account of where the wily bastard was and what he'd been doing. The d'Argent clansman, who'd been stalking Reynard since he'd left his lair in the Carpathian Mountains, hadn't seen the killer at all after having observed him make a shaky landing on the shoreline of Biscayne Bay and hole up in a deserted hunk of stone overlooking homes of the rich and famous.

But since then, every few days another hot blonde had shown up dead on the beach, drained of her blood. Each one's limp palm had held Reynard's signature white rose. So Alex had no doubt the Fox somehow managed to slip from under Philippe's vigilant observation to get his nourishment.

Nourishment he seemed to need a lot more frequently than he had before Alex and his kinsmen had nearly destroyed him.

When the bartender slid his drink across the bar, Alex looked up. "Sorry, this is all we've got tonight. Don't get a lot of call for blood."

For a minute Alex watched the guy make his way down the bar. Claude had been right. On South Beach nothing much seemed out of the ordinary. Not vampires, and not the shaky mortal at the other end of the bar who snatched a tiny bag of white powder from the swarthy guy next to him as if it were a lifeline. The addict, like Alex and his fellow vampires, moved freely in a sea of cops and derelicts, of vacation-time pleasure seekers and those who preyed on them.

A sliver of golden moon hung low over the ocean, its light faint compared with tiki lights and neon signs that dotted the beach and blinked along the highway. Alex sipped the very ordinary but seemingly fresh A-positive the bartender had delivered. No one paid him any mind. Not him and not the man who now was snorting his own poison. It seemed that, in this place, the mortal patrons wore blinders to anything but their own needs, their own pleasures.

He doubted any of them would have their guard up enough that they might sense the presence of an evil vampire like Reynard. They'd become too blasé, too caught up in their own pursuits of pleasure to sense mortal danger in their midst. The Fox had picked an ideal place to disappear. A killing ground full of long-legged blondes with which to satisfy his hunger—and his madness.

Back in Chicago, he, Stefan and Claude must have come closer to destroying Reynard than they'd realized at the time. Alex was certain now that Louis no longer had the energy to wing it from city to city, taking out one victim then moving on. When Alex made mind contact with his two kinsmen, they agreed it was likely that the evil vampire had been damaged sufficiently that he'd never completely healed, and that he now had to hunker down in one place to feed an ever-growing appetite for blood.

That place was here. Miami's South Beach, where tourists came in droves for a taste of the forbidden. Where vampires could blend in with the locals — businessmen and undercover cops and drug lords — and attract no particular attention to themselves. A place where hot blonde showgirls and tourists out for a thrill could be found at every bar, on every stretch of the clean white sand. The hot pink neon exotic dancer sign that Claude had just mentioned with what sounded like fond memories, gyrated above a sign across the highway that said "The Strip".

The neon cast eerie colors over two undercover cops who were making a beeline for the bar. Idiots. The way they looked, they might as well have been wearing blues and badges. Anybody with eyes could make them a mile away. The nondescript guy's ill-fitting jacket did a piss-poor job of concealing a nine-millimeter semiautomatic in a shoulder holster. And his female companion, a short, skinny redhead, had on a beat-up blazer despite the warmth of the night air. Who the fuck but cops wore jackets in Miami — in July, yet?

Hey, what the hell? The cops were heading straight for him. Alex remembered having spoken to the man soon after his arrival at the bar, but the woman was new. From her body language, he gathered she was the one in charge. She wasn't the sort of submissive beauty Alex usually chose for his liaisons, but something about her — maybe it was that fall of silky auburn hair his fingers itched to fondle — made his cock twitch. He ordered it to behave and bestowed one of his best smiles on the little firebrand. "What can I do for you tonight, beautiful?"

"Cut the crap and tell me where you've been for the past three hours." When she perched her hands on her hips, her blazer gaped open, the tank top underneath it giving him an eyeful of surprisingly full, round breasts — and a very businesslike-looking Sig Sauer automatic in a black shoulder holster. As though she were laying down a gauntlet in challenge, she slapped a shiny badge onto the bar. "I'm Mara Leone, detective lieutenant, homicide division. Come on, spill it."

Something about her attitude made Alex pretty damn sure she wasn't inclined to believe him no matter what he might say, but he'd give it his best shot. "I've been sitting here for the past hour, watching the stars and nursing this draft. Before that I was traveling here from Paris, checking in at my hotel and resting up for a night of partying."

"What about last Thursday? Last Tuesday? And a week ago tonight? Where were you then?" She met his gaze, her lips set in what she must have thought was a menacing frown.

Oh, shit. She'd made him as a vamp—at some point he must have forgotten to take care and keep his fangs retracted—and from the direction her questioning was taking, he gathered she thought she'd just cornered herself a serial killer. He'd better talk fast, or he'd end up cuffed and hauled to jail unless he wanted to pull a vampire disappearing act. "Cool it. You've got the wrong vampire, baby. I was having a great time in Paris until three days ago, when I came here looking for the same bad egg who's got your ass bent out of shape. I'm Alexandre d'Argent." Smiling his sweetest, Alex extended his hand. "And by the way, you *are* beautiful."

She snorted, a sound that should have turned him off but didn't. "So are you going to tell me how you heard about these murders?"

This cop wasn't about to step aside, or to give an inch of control over her case to him—unless he used vampire compulsion to seduce her. It wasn't his usual method of obtaining bed partners, but he figured Mara would be better off at his side than on her own, impeding his own hunt for the Fox. He met her gaze, willed her to give in. "Members of my clan have been after Louis Reynard since he started on his killing rampage nearly two years ago."

He sounded sincere—too much so—but Mara had her doubts. The vampire sitting calmly at the bar sipping a draft of blood had her heart beating double-time. Not just because he had the most compelling smile, or because the twinkle in his deep green eyes seemed to be focused exclusively on her. It wasn't the ripple of powerful biceps that she sensed he did deliberately, just for her. And it wasn't only the impressive bulge of his sex that drew her eye beyond muscular jeans-clad thighs and between his casually spread legs. Nope. Alexandre d'Argent, if that was his real name, was the epitome of a vampire seducer...an expert at the art of vampire compulsion, so practiced he wouldn't need to exert conscious effort to draw a woman in.

Like Dante, who'd come and gone twelve years ago and hadn't bothered to give her back her heart. Mara glanced over at Ben, whose eyes had widened with undisguised interest when he heard the name "Reynard".

"Pity you haven't managed to stop him." She kept her tone deliberately noncommittal even though her clit swelled against her panties when she imagined how it would feel if he rubbed that short, crisp-looking beard and mustache against her there.

"Yes, it is. Which is why I'm here to finish the job." He picked up her badge and traced the raised numbers on the shiny brass with his thumb.

How would it feel if he used that thumb to trace along her cheek? Over her nipples? Mara's pussy clenched, oblivious to reason, to anything but the mindless desire this vampire kindled with such a simple gesture. *Stop it! You've got a job to do, and it won't get done if you get tangled up with Alexandre d'Argent.*

Wait. Mara suddenly realized she'd heard that name before. Ben. He'd said members of the d'Argent clan had gone against Reynard three-on-one last year. That was how Reynard had ended up so battered no one had believed he might live to kill again. "What makes you think you can come on my turf and destroy this vampire? We've got laws to take care of criminals. Prisons."

Alex reamed her with that emerald gaze. "Lieutenant Leone, there's not a prison on earth that can hold Louis Reynard. Like it or not, you need me."

Mara didn't want to need a vampire. Dante. No, Alex. She didn't want her pussy creaming the way it was doing now, when Alex met her gaze and smiled. She didn't want to bare her throat, feel the pressure of his fangs, the incredible sexual rush when he pierced her. And she certainly didn't want him to pump his big, hard cock into every orifice she possessed. So why was it she couldn't break this sensual spell?

"Boss?" Ben's concerned voice dragged Mara from a world where she'd sworn she'd never go again. "He's right. If we're going to take down Reynard, we need to work with him."

Vampire compulsion. She understood it. Ben didn't. He felt it, though. Mara sensed his capitulation in his voice, and in the way he looked at d'Argent with rapt interest. A picture came to mind of Ben's sweet young fiancée—Susan something or other, she'd never been able to remember the girl's name. "Go on back to the station, Ben. I'll be the one working with the vampire."

"But—"

"If you argue, Braunstein, I'll have you walking a beat in Liberty City."

"Damn it. I was the one who figured out we were looking for Louis Reynard."

Almost a head taller than Ben, Alexandre stood and stared down at him. "Good for you. Now go back and stick your nose into your computer. Solve another crime or two and leave Reynard to Ms. Leone and me. Mara, come with me." Like Ben, Mara felt the compulsion that flowed as smoothly as d'Argent's words.

Ann Jacobs

* * * * *

The eastern sky was beginning to lighten as they walked toward Alex's hotel, the velvety black of night transitioning to soothing tones of pale gray and lavender. The moon hadn't yet given way to sun, but dawn was breaking. Alex figured Reynard would be back in his hideout by now, sleeping off his latest overindulgence. He'd contacted Philippe, told him to find a way inside the old mansion, locate Reynard and not let their prey out of his sight.

"Where are we going?"

Alex squeezed the lieutenant's elbow. "To my hotel. Might as well get some rest before we go after him again. He won't be going anywhere for a while. Sunlight hurts Reynard even more than it does most of us vampires." Her muscles tensed beneath his fingers, as though his touch confused her as much as his own compulsion to take her perplexed him. Despite her silky auburn hair—his favorite color—Mara Leone wasn't his usual type of bedmate.

Idly, he delved into her mind. She'd had a vampire lover a long time ago, one who'd left her emotionally bruised and bitter. Fuck. That explained why she'd sent the young detective away, to protect him from the disillusionment she felt was inevitable if he stayed and joined them *en ménage*. "I'm not like any other vampire you may have known, sweetheart. We'll get the bastard before he kills again. I promise."

"We must."

The strain evidenced by her tone of voice made him want to take her in his arms, soothe away the tension...replace it with tension of another, sexual kind. It also engendered a need in him that he didn't quite understand—a compulsion to wrap her in his protection, keep her from harm. And he wanted her to do it on her own.

"Trust me," he coaxed, but he knew asking wasn't going to cut it. The walls of hurt and suspicion Dante had forced her to create for herself somewhere along the way were way too

86

tough for a mere request to break through. Alex grasped her chin and tilted her face where she had to look at him. Without the slightest bit of conscience he looked into her solemn brown eyes and put her under a vampire spell.

In his room he closed the curtains then undressed her as though she were a child. First the ugly blazer, then the shoulder holster. "You know, this thing's pretty much useless against one of us," he commented as he laid it on the bedside table.

"So I've been told. I've never been on a vampire hunt before. Guess I'll have to requisition some silver bullets and wooden stakes." She sounded softer, compliant now that she'd shed that tough cop veneer.

He ran his hands up her arms, tracing the veins, feeling the toned muscles that didn't begin to compensate for the fragility of the bones beneath them. "Scratch the silver bullets. I already tried using them on Reynard. They didn't faze him."

"You mean that's just legend, that silver bullets kill vampires?" When he connected with her mind once more, he learned she was thinking about her lover, who'd succumbed to a barrage of them from a team of mortal hunters. Alex regretted having stirred her hurtful memories.

He laughed, not wanting her to know he'd read her mind. "There are vampires...and then there are vampires. Some go down like sitting ducks when you pump them full of silver bullets. Others don't. There are only two certain ways to destroy almost any sort of vampire."

She looked up at him, her eyes wide as he spread her collar and tackled the buttons down the front of her sleeveless white blouse. "And those would be?"

"I think I'll keep that information to myself, sweetheart." Her skin felt like silk beneath his fingers as he slid the blouse off her shoulders and slid down the shoulder strap of a surprisingly seductive white lace bra. "You're not nearly as tough as you try to sound, are you?"

"Yes. I am." She didn't sound all that tough, not when she was gasping for breath as he cupped her breasts and ran his thumbs over the hard, pink nipples. "Please."

The word came out between little moans that were driving Alex crazy. So crazy he released the vampire compulsion that had been holding her. He wanted her to want him because she wanted him, not because she had no choice. "Please what? Do you want me to hurry? Rip this skirt and whatever you're wearing under it off, and nibble your clit? Suck these beautiful breasts? Or would you rather have me sink my fangs into your inviting little throat and give you a vampire kiss?" The tiny scars he could barely see annoyed him, a lasting reminder he wouldn't be the first vampire to have claimed the feisty redhead.

"Oh, yes. Please hurry. I want to be naked. I want you naked. I want to suck your cock."

Chapter Two

ॐ

"Hush. I'm already so hard I'm about to burst." Alex slid his hands down, fumbled with the waistband of her skirt. Gave up. "Sorry, I'll get you a new outfit," he said as he ripped the thing off with one furious tug.

His usually quiet heart pounded in his chest when he looked at her, all pale and creamy and — fuck it — sexier than any of the Parisian club dancers who frequently entertained him for a night or two. His cock strained against his jeans.

He could take her now. Her female musk had filled his nostrils the moment he dragged her plain cotton panties down her legs, and a fine sheen of sweat dampened her brow. It was the small tremor in her hands that made him hesitate, ignore his own need, delve into her thoughts and dreams and…

Fuck. She was still thinking of her other vampire lover. Missing him. Wanting Alex, but afraid. Alex clenched his fists as though the intruder to her mind were in the room, in the flesh, so he could pummel him the way the dead vampire's memory was pounding at Mara's heart and mind. "Say my name," he ordered, reaching out and taking those hands, stilling their nervous movement. "Tell me you know who's making love with you tonight."

"Alexandre." Barely a whisper, the word came out like a prayer. An admonition he read clearly in her frightened eyes. *Please don't hurt me.*

This brash, no-nonsense mortal had turned to a quivering mass of nerves once stripped from the ugly armor of her trade. Instead of scooping her up and claiming her right now, with no foreplay and none of the niceties as he'd intended, he knelt at her feet and gently spread her legs.

"I won't hurt you, I will only make you feel good." Leaning toward her and drawing her hips forward, he caught her clit between his front teeth and flailed it with his tongue. Conscious of his own need but determined to drive the ghost of some vampire of long ago from her memories, he stroked along her inner thighs with both hands, pausing to claim the sweet spot behind her knees then moving downward to encircle her slender ankles, soak in the mortal heat that emanated from every inch of her delectable flesh. She shifted, widening her stance, giving him room to move in closer, nudge away her neatly trimmed auburn pubic curls and lick the pearly moisture from her swollen slit.

His balls ached. His cock was ready to explode. Still he took his time. Before he took her he wanted her hot, so hot for him that nothing of that faceless vampire's memory stood in the way of her pleasure. With him. He found her wet, hot cunt and tongue-fucked her there, all the time touching, caressing, listening as much as he could in this painful state of arousal to the words she was thinking but wouldn't say.

The love. The trust. The loss that had turned her against males, mortal as well as vampire, for a long, long time. The desire to open up, experience all the sensations she'd suppressed beneath that prickly veneer. If Alex could have, he'd have gone after the vampire named Dante and destroyed him again for what he'd done to Mara.

But he couldn't. All he could do was show her there didn't have to be pain or fear—that she need not resist falling under his vampire spell. That he wouldn't seduce her then walk away. When he felt her first climax surge through her, he stood and laid her on the bed.

With an economy of motion she hadn't seen since Dante, Alex undressed and stood before her, his pupils distended, his shapely lips tight. He was pale—vampire pale, almost like alabaster yet so alive. Powerful muscles rippled beneath skin as smooth and unblemished as ivory satin. His sex stood straight up against his flat belly, ready to take her in whatever way he chose. It pulsated, long and thick and darker than the rest of him, a blue-veined column tipped with a fully exposed pink crown. So hard, yet so smooth and soft she longed to take it between her lips. His testicles were drawn up in their wrinkled sac, twin orbs that looked strangely vulnerable, not hiding like mortal men's in a nest of pubic hair. A small ring swung beneath his scrotum, its brilliant gold tone a startling contrast against his pale vampire flesh. A *guiche*, she thought the piercing was called.

Though seeing he was pierced surprised her, his lack of body hair didn't. Vampires only hair grew on their heads and faces, Dante had told her. She'd loved the smoothness, the clean feeling of flesh on flesh when she'd shaved herself for Dante. Loved the incredible sensations when she'd run her hands over every inch of him. But Alex looked even more perfect than the picture of Dante that she carried in her memories, for by all appearances he was more than capable of taking her with his body as well as his mind. Mara held her arms out, the gesture an entreaty she dared not make aloud.

He answered. Without hesitation, without a hint that he, not she, should be the instigator of all things sexual. When he stretched out on his side, his cock nudged her thigh. He raised his head on one elbow and looked down on her, his emerald gaze full of vampire heat. With his free hand he traced the pair of scars on her throat, and his expression turned dark. "If I ever mark you this way, you'll never leave me. And I will never leave you, either." The surprised look on his handsome face let her know his statement came out without conscious thought, and that made her shiver at the prospect.

But she quickly shoved her own reaction away. What he'd implied was only a bunch of words. Nothing meaningful. It was just a vampire wooing a woman, keeping her in his bed with charming, seductive visions of forever.

His touch as light as a feather, he made his way down her body, circling one nipple then the other before laying his large palm over the curve of her belly and using his fingers to sift through her pubic curls. "Did he make love to you first?"

"N—no." Why did that matter? She was no virgin, and Alex had given her no indication he expected her to be. "He was a vampire, like you."

"Not like me, sweetheart. I'm a born d'Argent vampire. From what you've told me—yes, baby, I can read your mind— your other vampire was made. Impotent, unable to find a measure of sexual pleasure except by giving a vampire kiss."

Mara reached up and stroked his chin, liking the scratchy feel of his neatly trimmed short beard, imagining how it would feel when he rubbed it against her throat...her nipples. "Made?"

"A mortal who was turned. With a few exceptions, they can only get off sexually by drinking blood from its source. Fortunately most don't take it as far as Reynard and leave all their victims dead."

A shudder surged through her, and Alex gathered her in his arms. "Easy, baby. I'm not like them. I was born a vampire, nearly three hundred years ago. I don't need blood to come, although I admit there's no bigger rush than to feed from a lover instead of a glass. Trust me. I'll give you pleasure now. We'll sleep away the day. Then, when the sun begins to set, we'll go on the hunt for Reynard. And you'll let me destroy him before he can kill again."

She couldn't do that, because if she did she'd be ignoring every rule of law that had been part of her since she joined the department right out of college. But now wasn't the time to go into a discussion of mortals' ethics, not when he was touching her, eliciting her trust, at least so far as it related to him bringing her that pleasure, filling the emptiness inside her. "Yes, I trust you." The slow beating of his heart beneath her hand...the insistent prodding of his cock seeking a home between her legs...the soothing yet arousing sensation of him molding her ass cheeks with his calloused hands, holding her with a pressure that was strong yet light. "Fuck me, Alex."

He rolled her to her back and rose above her, a magnificent male god come to life. His fangs remained retracted as he fit their bodies together and plunged inside, the delicious friction from his penetration eased by her own juices yet still significant. He stretched her, a sensation of mingled pleasure and pain and incredible fullness when he sank deeper, when the blunt head of his big cock pressed against the mouth of her womb.

Their mating was a dance of seduction, his penetration slow and deep. She absorbed the sounds and smells of sex, her own soft moans, the slow beat of his heart and the slapping of hard male flesh. The cool metal of his *guiche* ring along her hot, wet slit reminded her he was of another world. A world that fascinated her and aroused her incredibly as he brought her along. Pressure built in her womb and radiated throughout her body, sensation about to burst in a conflagration of heat.

She wanted it all, wanted the feel of his hot semen bathing her, the extraordinary release he promised. But not yet. Not until she experienced it all, the press of his fangs at her throat. The taste of her own blood on his lips as her pussy spasmed around his rock-hard cock. "Bite me. Please."

"Not this time, sweetheart. Concentrate on feeling me fucking your tight little cunt for now." Sliding his hands down to cup her ass, he fucked her harder, faster, his testicles ramming hard and tight against her pussy with every stroke. His cock jerked once, twice inside her, setting off the explosion of sensations she'd tried to hold back. "Oh, yeah, that's it. Come with me." His words trailed off, and the only sounds she registered were his fast, shallow breathing, her own little scream of satisfaction that he muffled with a soft, gentle kiss.

How she'd missed it, the strength of a Dominant male vampire, the sense of being taken. She'd gone with him partly from compulsion, yet of her own volition as well. She'd believed she could handle the passion, savor having Alex as the living shadow of Dante's memory, but Alex hadn't let her do that. He'd made her focus totally on him, pushing Dante into the deep shadows of her past.

As Mara drifted off to sleep, it was Alex—not Dante— whose remembered image fueled her dreams.

* * * * *

Riinngg.

What the hell? Alex blinked. Light poured through the window, telling him it was much too early for any self-respecting vampire to be awake. Squinting, he located the source of the noise and picked up Mara's cell phone.

"Yeah?" It was Mara's shadow, the kid detective.

Ben's worry flowed through the sound waves even before he managed to ask, "Where's Lieutenant Leone?"

Good question. The bed was still warm where she'd been curled up next to him, but the sound of water running in the shower gave Alex a pretty good hint. "In the shower. Shall I have her call you?"

"Yes. She's all right, isn't she?"

Alex shut his eyes, pictured the way Mara had come apart in his embrace. "She's fine, kid. Want to tell me what's on your mind?" When Ben hesitated, Alex concentrated hard, projected vampiric compulsion with his next words. "Tell me, Ben. We're in this together. You want Reynard put out of business as much as I do."

"One of the Key Biscayne private cops spotted a vampire last night over on the grounds outside the castle—that's what folks call a deserted estate over there. We're going over there to have a look."

Just what Alex needed, a bunch of mortal cops spooking Reynard and witnessing his destruction. "Don't do it. I know where our killer is. I have one of my clansmen inside the ruin of that old house, watching him. As a matter of fact, it was probably Philippe they spotted, not Reynard. Let it go. I intend to get him. I don't need any interference."

"I can try to keep them away." The kid's thoughts were as transparent as anybody's Alex had run into lately. Ben didn't have to say it for Alex to know he understood Reynard must meet with vampire justice. And that he approved. "Good luck."

"Thanks." Alex would need all that luck and more. Mara walked out of the bathroom, her only garment an oversized bath sheet, and took the phone as he was about to set it down. The mutual concern the two cops had for each other was evident in the way Mara reassured the young detective.

When she hung up she turned to Alex. "You say you have a clansman watching Louis Reynard?"

Alex nodded then grasped her hips and drew her onto the bed beside him. "Philippe had been observing the only way in and out of the castle—he thought. Apparently Reynard found another exit, either that or he's learned to slither through solid stone and concrete. When Philippe contacted me last night, I told him to get inside the place somehow, and not to take his eyes off the bastard."

Mara pursed her lips, as if considering the situation. "This vampire of yours. Philippe. Do you trust him?"

"Completely." When Alex sensed Mara's doubt, he went on. "He and his mate were chosen years ago by d'Argent clan leaders to guard our queen. One of Reynard's henchmen poisoned them both. Jacques, Philippe's mate, was destroyed."

"My God."

"Yes. Philippe had loved Jacques for as long as I can remember. I can think of no one who's more determined than Philippe to see Louis destroyed."

She gathered her clothes, shaking her head at the ripped disaster that used to be her good black skirt. "I can't walk out of here in this."

"Sorry. I'll have some things sent up." Though he didn't say it, he thought anything the concierge could scare up from one of the boutiques in the hotel would be an improvement over the drab outfit she was clutching in her hands. Before she could protest, he called downstairs and arranged for some clothes to be sent up for her. "I'll want some toys as well," he said, recalling the adult bookstore he'd seen among the shops across the highway from the hotel. "If you'll give me the phone number, I'll call the store across the highway and have them send over the items I want. One more thing. Have room service send up lunch. Some meat. Fruit and vegetables. And something chocolate. Nothing she can't eat with her fingers. I'll take a half pint of blood. O-negative if it's available."

Mara looked down at him, a confused look on her pretty face when he hung up. "Don't you need more blood than that?"

"Not for another day or so. I fed last night, before you and Braunstein came on the scene. I just ordered a bit so you won't have to eat alone."

"You know, I might have some preferences of my own," Mara said, dropping the bath sheet and giving him a great view of curves she managed to hide so well under her working clothes. "And I might not like hanging around this room all day, stark naked."

"I like the view just fine..." Alex let the words trail off, using his gaze to convey what he had in mind. He knew what she liked...what she wanted. And he wanted to be the one to give it to her. This thing he was feeling for her was more than lust, more than the natural protective instinct for someone smaller and less powerful than himself. Love? Never having experienced that emotion before, he couldn't say for certain.

Chapter Three

❧

Pamper me. Treat me the way you would a woman you want for your mate. Tell me I'm beautiful and make me believe it. Crack the shell I've kept around my heart since Dante left me.

Mara didn't have to say the words. Alex heard them in his head, and they touched his heart. This woman seemed so self-sufficient, even dominant to a degree. Inside, though, she yearned to give her heart...to submit to a lover's will. His will.

He flattened his palm over her auburn bush, felt her heartbeat accelerate, heard her breathing grow ragged. "Go make yourself as smooth as I am," he told her. "By the time you're finished, your lunch should be ready."

Her quiet assent humbled him. Not that he cared whether he buried himself in satiny skin or soft pubic curls, but for some reason she cared. That was what was important. After calling in his toy order, Alex cracked the curtain and winced a little at the stream of sunlight that bathed the room. That sunlight would reassure her, remind her she was with him and not the vampire named Dante, who'd apparently stolen her self-confidence and left her with fear of males, both mortal and not.

A discreet knock on the door drew Alex out of his thoughts. Wrapping Mara's discarded bath sheet around his hips, he swung the door open. After peering inside the bag of clothes from a designer boutique whose name he recognized and seeing a smaller toy store bag inside, he signed for its contents. By the time the bellman who'd brought them moved away, a waiter appeared. Alex stepped back so the man could wheel in a small table draped in white linen and topped with dishes under silver domed covers.

"Want the table by the window, sir?"

"No. Here, by the bed." While Alex could tolerate sunlight better than most vampires, he wouldn't deliberately place his naked body directly in the path of Miami's fierce summer sunshine. He glanced at the plates of sliced meat and shellfish, chopped raw vegetables, fruit and an interesting collection of chocolate truffles. The candies' gold foil wrappers caught sunlight, called attention to the way they'd been artfully arranged on their plate in the shape of a small pyramid and topped with a maraschino cherry. Alex smiled at the hotel chef's attempt to bridge the difference between mortal and vampire—a bottle of sparkling water on ice in a silver bucket beside his snack of blood. "Thank you." Suddenly eager to be rid of the waiter and check on Mara's progress in the bath, Alex handed over a generous tip and watched until the door had swung closed.

When he opened the bag, he fished out the toys, and saw and found clothes designed more for a vacationing socialite than a homicide detective. He liked them, imagined them showcasing Mara's petite, well-toned body. It took very little of his vampire perceptive skills to figure she'd pitch a fit, though. The clothes were going to cause an argument. He had no doubt he'd win, but not now. Checking to be sure she hadn't emerged from the bathroom, he hung up the sundress in the closet and set the bag that now contained only underwear and a pair of high-heeled sandals below it on the floor. He'd deal with that when it was time for them to leave and go find Reynard. Meanwhile, he stashed an anal plug, some condoms and a vibrating dildo in the drawer of the table beside the bed.

"Lunch has arrived," he yelled over the sound of the shower spray. "Need some help?"

The shower stopped abruptly and she stepped out, all rosy and pink and dripping onto the bath mat. "Like me now?"

Yeah. He liked seeing her cunt smooth as a vampire's...or a baby's. He was certain he'd like tasting and touching that impudent little clit that peeked out from the pink folds, even more than it aroused him to look at it. "Yeah, I like." He reached for a towel and blotted a drop of water from between her legs. "Come on, your sustenance awaits you."

As if they were clothed and dining in a fine restaurant, he seated her in the lone side chair and unscrewed the lid on the sparkling water with a flourish. Pouring two glasses—his less than half full—he slid the full one beside her plate before mixing the small portion of blood into his own. Smiling at her, he fished a strawberry from the plate of fruit and brushed it gently over her closed lips. "Try this first."

Her tongue darted out between lips still bruised from his kisses, its smooth texture and dark pink color contrasting with the berry's tiny black seeds on bright red flesh. When she sucked it into her mouth and bit down with small, white teeth, Alex imagined her going down on him, using suction to coax his climax. When he pictured her tugging at his *guiche* ring with her teeth, playing with it while she sucked his cock, he got so aroused that he hurt.

Piece by piece he fed her the finger foods, observing every expression that crossed her face, reading thoughts that had his cock about to burst. Lifting her glass to her lips, he zeroed in, determined to learn the fantasies her previous vampire lover had left unfulfilled—and satisfy them now, before he let her go.

If he let her go.

Where the hell had that thought come from? Alex mulled over the unfamiliar emotions Mara had wrung from him since...since she'd walked up to him last night in that bar all bristly cop, prepared to cuff him up and haul him off to jail. In less than twenty-four hours, she'd managed to engage his feelings, unlike any of his previous lovers. He wanted to protect her from all the dangers she faced, in a way no cop's weapon could. But more than that he wanted to hold her, use all his vampire powers of seduction to drive out the memory of that long-gone vampire who'd hurt her. All the tender emotions he'd denied with success for his entire, long life had suddenly come to life, the feelings so strong he doubted he could walk away. He wanted to make her smile, drive away the doubts and fears that made her vulnerable, protect her from every man, mortal as well as vampire, who would cause her pain.

Was he in love? He didn't know, but he certainly wanted to make her every fantasy come to life. "Here, try one of these," he said, lifting one of the chocolates and holding it to her lips as he looked into her dark eyes and delved into her mind.

Mmmm. So good. She wasn't thinking about the chocolate truffle she'd just bitten into, but of Alex...and a shadowy figure, a man. Mortal or vampire? Alex didn't know. It didn't matter, though. He concentrated, closing his eyes and joining his lover's dream.

She spread her legs, an offering he couldn't refuse. In slow motion, he went to his knees, opened his mouth over her baby-soft pussy. Flailed her clit with his tongue and rubbed his bristly chin along her slit while she moaned softly. Her fingers fluttered then tunneled into the clippered hair at the back of his head, the pressure feather light yet incredibly arousing. Almost as arousing as the taste of her cream and the mind-picture in her head.

She lay on her side in bed, her sweet pussy exposed, needy. A naked male with a shaved head and a ring in his penis knelt near her face. She took his cock, first in her hands. Slow and easy, she stroked the shaft, squeezing, circling, dipping down to weigh his heavy testicles then returning to her task. The ring intimidated her, kept her from taking his plump cock head between her lips.

She shifted her head, laid it on his massive thigh, licked and nibbled at the base of his shaft instead as another male—Alex— joined them and began to tongue-fuck her.

So she wanted a ménage. If she became like him, a permanent part of his life, she'd experience ménages and more, on a regular basis. The more he thought about it, the more he believed Mara's destiny might be with him, in his vampire world where there were no restrictions, no constraints on sexual activity among the clanspeople. When he imagined her on her knees above him, his cock throbbing in her cunt while his kinsmen claimed her ass and mouth, he got so hard he hurt. Yet he continued to lap her honey while she writhed in the chair on the brink of climax.

I want a vampire kiss. Please.

Alex wanted nothing more than to give it. To feed on her until he took her mortality...gave her new life as a d'Argent vampire. But he wouldn't do it. While she might beg, he knew she wasn't ready to commit to a long lifetime in what to her would be an alien world. For that matter, he wasn't certain of his own readiness to mate for eternity with a virtual stranger, no matter how strong his feelings might be today. He nipped her thigh instead, before ringing her tight rear entrance with his tongue. "On your knees on the bed, sweetheart."

His command was just that—an order, not uttered as the vampire compulsion Mara expected...wanted. Compelled or not, she wanted to obey, longed to let go and experience all the tender emotions that bubbled to the surface whenever Alex touched her. Rising on shaky legs, she did as he'd said while he opened a drawer of the nightstand and looked inside.

"What?" she asked.

He laughed. "You were daydreaming about a ménage. I'm about to provide you with the next best thing." The drawer shut with a soft thud, and he was behind her, the coolness of his vampire flesh a shock against her own heated skin. His big hands cupped her bottom, spread her ass cheeks, his fingers delving into her wet, sensitized slit and spreading the lubrication from her swollen pussy to her rear hole. "Feel good?"

It did. Anticipation built as he petted her, made her tingle wherever his nimble fingers touched. "Oh, yes."

"I'm going to fuck you here," he told her, inserting first one finger then two past her anal sphincter and moving them rhythmically.

Her pussy clenched with anticipation. It had been so long...too long since a lover had taken her there. Since Dante. But he'd used a... She clamped down on her thoughts, certain Alex could and often did read her mind.

"I'm going to use my cock, sweetheart. But I'll put on a condom first if that's what's worrying you."

Any doubt Mara had about whether her lover was privy to her thoughts flew out the window. But it didn't matter, not now when he was arousing her to a fever pitch.

When he withdrew the hand he'd been using to tweak her clit, she nearly cried out, but then he came back and worked a dildo into her pussy. When it began to vibrate, she shuddered at the twin sensations of his fingers and the large toy working together, building pressure...and anticipation for when he'd replace his fingers with his big, rigid cock.

God, but it felt good, better than anything she'd ever experienced. Her pussy contracted, grew wetter. "Hold on, now. Think about how good this is going to feel. I'll be right back." He gave a last sensual stroke to her rear then rose and went to the bathroom.

The sound of water running...then silence. It seemed like forever, but it couldn't have been more than a minute before he came back and knelt behind her. When he rubbed his sheathed cock head along her slit, stopping to probe her rear entrance, she gave out a little yelp. Was what she was feeling fear, or anticipation?

A little bit of both. Sensations inside her built, causing pleasure so great it nearly erased the pain when he began to move against her, probing and stretching until he passed the barrier of her anal sphincter and slipped inside. The only way she could have felt fuller was if he'd also been feeding his cock down her throat. He must have read her mind because he reached up, brushed her lips with an insistent forefinger and slipped it between her teeth.

"There, sweetheart, let go. When this is all over, we'll have our real ménage. Squeeze me. Oh yeah, like that. You've got the tightest little ass. Made just for me."

The slightly salty taste of his hand made her think of the surf kissing her face while she lay in its warm embrace. But this was so much better. She panted, trying to hold back the waves of delectable feelings that sped through her body and carried her over the edge.

Vaguely, she heard him shout out his pleasure, felt him gather her in his arms. As she lay there quietly against his chest, she felt his heart race then slow to an almost imperceptible beat, as though he had found the same contentment he brought to her. Mara fell asleep, thoughts of Louis Reynard and his evil washed away for the moment in the arms of a vampire who'd just made one of her wildest fantasies come alive.

* * * * *

Damn d'Argent clansman who's been watching the door got inside here somehow. Louis deduced the persistent vampire was not one of the clan leaders, since he apparently hadn't fully mastered the skill of stealth.

Damn, it was too early to be wakened from a sound sleep. Louis cracked an eye open, shuddered at the strength of the noonday sun that was seeping through tightly closed shutters. He felt every one of his nearly one thousand years, each of the lacerations and fractures inflicted on him by those three bloodthirsty relatives of the d'Argent queen he'd wanted for his bride.

Louis felt the other vampire's presence but couldn't locate him. Fuck, it wasn't only his body that was broken and bruised beyond healing. His powers also had taken a beating. Although he'd gorged himself last night, he felt the hunger returning. The compulsion to go out and feed. To kill again no matter how great the risk.

Going out to hunt tonight wasn't that dangerous, he told himself. He'd fought off three born d'Argent vampires and survived. This lackey they'd sent to watch him would be no more than a pesky flea on a dog's back, if he dared to follow and try to stop the inevitable. Louis admitted he'd been battered, and that he might not possess quite all the physical powers he'd had before.

But he was still Louis Reynard, leader of his clan. He was still one of the most powerful vampires on this earth. Whatever it took, he would have his vengeance on Alina and all the beautiful women of the world. No d'Argent clansman would have a prayer against him. Especially not just one. Not even one of the vaunted d'Argent leaders, the born vampires who helped Alina rule the clan, could go up against Louis Reynard and survive.

Louis closed his eyes and hunkered under the covers. He'd take his rest, ignoring his enemy's malignant presence until night fell and he could hunt again. If the vampire intended to attack, he'd have done so before, while Louis had slept.

* * * * *

Mara snuggled against Alex's broad chest, sated sexually in a way she hadn't been since…since ever. Compared with Alex, Dante came up in her memories not as the standard she'd set for lovers in the past, but as a poor substitute for the vampire who even now was stoking her fires.

But time was ticking away. The sun was sinking toward the Everglades, and Miami's night people were stirring, getting ready to open the clubs and tiki bars along the beach. Mara stroked Alex's muscular chest, her touch evoking a lazy smile, the slow opening of those sexy deep green eyes. He reached out a hand, but she caught it in midair.

"We need to talk," she said. And there was no way she could think when he was touching her. Quickly, before he could stop her, she slid off the bed, dragging the top sheet with her and wrapping it toga-style around her body. "But first we both need to get dressed."

He yawned, his gaze raking her as though he could see right through the sheet. Maybe he could. "Your new clothes are in the closet," he said as he felt the five o'clock shadow on his chin. "Go ahead, use the bathroom first. There's some makeup in the bag with your underwear and stuff."

"Don't you..." Of course he didn't have needs common to mortals. He was a vampire. It was just that he seemed so human. So like the sort of man she'd dreamed of back when she still indulged her fantasies.

"Not with any degree of urgency. I'll trim my beard and shave while you're getting dressed." When he smiled and showed her his small but lethal-looking fangs, she leaned over and brushed her lips across his cheek.

"All right." She liked his short, neat beard, though the fact he had one surprised her since she'd never before seen a vampire who let his facial hair grow.

Steam rose in the shower, surrounding her in a cloud of moist heat. Mara closed her eyes and tried to clear her head. Now wasn't the time to fantasize about vampire lovers or imagine herself becoming one of them. Not when Louis Reynard was running free, destroying victims with alarming regularity.

Neither could she ignore all the rules ingrained in her since she'd been a rookie cop, and leave the destruction of Reynard to Alex, even though she liked the idea of destroying the killer rather than leaving him at the mercy of the courts. She'd go with Alex, find the killer, notify her team and let them deal with arresting Reynard, hopefully before he killed again.

Alex's words echoed in her head, coming through loud and clear over the shower spray. *There is no prison on earth that can hold him, Mara.* Alex probably was right about that, but she hadn't signed on as an assassin.

The door opened and Alex stepped inside, magnificently naked. His playful grin when she let out a little yelp touched her heart. It almost made her forget she was about to deceive him, save him from the inevitability of mortals' punishment by taking the destruction of Louis Reynard out of his hands. "Get out of here. If you stay, we'll never have that conversation."

"Is that a bad thing?" Alex smiled, his fangs gleaming in the fluorescent lights as though the task ahead were no more hazardous than going out for an evening's entertainment.

"Reynard is no joking matter to me." Mara stepped around him and toweled herself dry. When she really looked at the underwear Alex had provided, she shot him a look that would have sent most rookie cops running for cover. "Why did you bother? You couldn't see any more if I were naked."

Alex laughed as he came out of the shower. "Not guilty, baby. I told you I'd get you clothing, and I did. The boutique apparently thought you were as hot as you are and sent up stuff they thought would suit a—"

A hooker. Or one of the showgirls who frequently augmented their already substantial income by turning a trick or two with affluent tourists. "All right. I get it. I didn't look yet at what they set up for me to wear on the outside. Am I to assume the vice squad will likely pick me up once we step outside?"

"I kind of doubt it. I saw a woman on the beach yesterday afternoon who had on less than those lacy pink things."

Mara glanced down at the see-through bra and thong panties. She couldn't imagine any woman daring to go out on the beach in less. "Okay, I guess I can wear these, but I'll reserve judgment on the other things until I see them." Showing Alex her back, she stepped into the bedroom and opened the closet door.

"Like them?" he asked, following her out into the room.

The silk sundress was as pretty as anything she'd ever seen, all tones of pink and orange and lavender that reminded her of a summer sunset. It had a swirly skirt and a sleeveless top cut on the bias. The short white jacket would work fine to ward off a cool night sea breeze, but it would hardly work to conceal her Sig Sauer. Not to mention, it had a price tag that would have eaten up the better part of one of her biweekly paychecks if she'd had to buy it. "It's very pretty. Hardly appropriate for a homicide cop, though."

"Consider it my contribution. After all I was the one who tore your skirt."

Mara smiled. "You did, didn't you? Well, let me get this on. You do know I can't let you kill Reynard."

Alex's expression tightened. "I don't know how you plan to stop me."

Arrogant bastard! "I'll toss you in jail if I have to."

He came closer, cupped her chin and forced her to meet his gaze. "You can try. Look, sweetheart, no mortal's a match for Reynard. And no mortal can put him out of business. I know it bothers you to break the laws you've sworn to uphold, but trust me. If you want this bastard stopped, you're going to have to accept that he must be destroyed. And that I'm the vampire to do the job."

She had in mind to persuade him somehow that they must do it her way, but then Alex's cell phone rang. When he answered and listened, his expression turned fierce. "We've got to go. Reynard is on the move. Philippe believes he's gone out to feed again."

"Feed?"

"Make that kill, because the bastard doesn't ever take a sip or two and walk away. He drains his victims until they're dead, beyond redemption. Beyond turning. D-E-A-D." He dressed faster than anybody she'd ever observed, slipping bare feet into deck shoes before she could retrieve her weapon from the nightstand. "Come on!"

Mara followed, but not until she'd contacted Ben and sent her team onto Reynard's tail.

"Why did you do that?" The frustration in Alex's voice made her feel she'd betrayed him.

Perhaps she had. "I had no choice. It's mortals this bastard's been killing, mortals I swore to defend and protect." She took his hand, squeezed it. "Maybe between us, we can stop him."

"Maybe." His doubtful tone made her wonder if she should have followed her instincts and kept her team out of the hunt—at least for now.

Chapter Four

∽

"Sun's still pretty high for Reynard to be out and about." Alex rested his arm on Mara's shoulder as they made their way through the hotel's courtyard toward the deserted strip of beach where the bastard had killed before. "I hope old Louis isn't leading Philippe up a blind alley."

"You and me both." Mara strained her eyes looking for signs of Ben and the others up farther along the beach, but she saw nothing. "Where were they coming from?" Ben had told her Biscayne Bay, but she didn't notice anyone coming onto South Beach from that direction.

"Reynard has been holed up at a deserted estate on Biscayne Bay, which I'm sure your fellow cop told you."

Of course he knew what Ben had told her. Alex's ability to read her mind was damn inconvenient. Sighing, she did her best to mask her thoughts. Damn it, she hated to have Alex think she didn't trust him, but she dared not let him take over her case. Not for the first time, she considered how much simpler some decisions would have been if mortals would just let vampires police each other. Yes, there was something good to be said for vampire justice, she thought, remembering a time last spring when one of them had neatly rid society of one vicious drug lord. The vice division had been trying for years to stick that piece of slime with a charge that would have sent him away for a long time before deporting him back to his native Colombia. "Mortals have to follow mortal rules."

He stopped in his tracks, listened as though somebody was talking inside his head. "Fuck your half-assed rules. Your team of idiots has just arrested the wrong vampire. They've got Philippe. Now Reynard's pretty much free to do in another victim. Philippe said Reynard had headed into The Strip. Come on, maybe we can get to him in time to prevent another killing."

So much for having tried to make her mind a blank. Although he never raised his voice, Mara felt Alex's fury. Part of her didn't blame him. "Your friend Philippe must have attracted my team's attention."

"You're right there. Hold on." Before she could complain about the indecently tight embrace he'd just put on her, he took to the air, circling slowly over the area. She held on for all she was worth, imagining as she did what a drop of fifty feet or more onto the damp sand would do to her. "Trust me, I'm not going to let you fall."

She hoped not, for they were descending now. Palm fronds fluttered in the breeze they made as they sped by toward the beach below. "Do you see Reynard?"

"Not him. His victim."

As soon as they landed, Alex set Mara down. The acrid smell of blood filled her nostrils as he knelt by the glassy-eyed corpse and felt for signs of life. "Can you turn her?" she asked.

"No. He killed her. Irrevocably." Alex eyed the white rose, curled his lip in obvious disgust.

She looked down at the victim, said a silent prayer for the soul of the woman who'd just become the serial killer's fifth victim in less than two weeks. Nausea practically overwhelmed her, and she couldn't seem to stop herself from shaking with the frustration of it all.

Alex had been right about keeping her team out of this, even though doing it would have challenged everything she'd been taught—everything she'd believed in. Seeing the result of her following the protocols that had been drilled into her since she'd been in law enforcement made her feel as if that work she'd committed herself to had been pointless. Mara looked down at the dead woman, the rose. At Alex who knelt beside her, fists clenched in righteous anger.

Did it really come down to the fact that to get any kind of justice, you had to resort to vigilantism?

Alex stood and dusted sand off his jeans. Then he took her hands and looked into her eyes. "Sometimes it does, sweetheart. Especially when you're dealing with a vampire as evil as Reynard."

When he stared down at the dead woman once more, Mara saw raw emotions cross his ruggedly handsome face. Anger, yes. But she saw undertones of sadness, resignation...reluctant understanding that she'd done what she'd had to, as a mortal cop. "You'd better get on your cell phone and tell your people we just found another victim. And that they've got the wrong vampire." He raised his gaze, the unnatural brightness in his eyes the result of unshed tears.

As she tried to steady her hands enough to drag her cell phone from her purse, guilt washed over her. What if she'd trusted Alex before and ordered her team to stay away? *If you had, the woman at your feet might still be alive.* "Ben? While you and the others were locking up Alex's clansman you caught when he was tailing our killer, Reynard struck again." Her voice broke, and she sank to her knees as she told them where to come.

Two mortal women, one pale in death, the other vibrant with life. Alex looked down at them and concentrated on visualizing the killer. Louis was close by, sated with the blood of his latest victim yet cunning as the fox for which his clan had been named some time lost in antiquity. Intuitively, Alex knew Louis wouldn't return to the so-called castle where he'd been spending his sleeping hours. But where would he go?

"Alex?"

Mara's voice broke his concentration. "What?" he snapped.

"They're releasing Philippe. Do you want him to come here with the crime team?"

"He might as well. Maybe he'll have better luck than I, sensing where Reynard might have gone to ground." Louis could have been in one of the nearby clubs or shops, mingling with unsuspecting mortals. Or he might have walked in and rented a room at one of the aging motels anywhere along Highway A1A. The bastard could have gone almost anywhere. One thing for sure, he'd be surfacing again tomorrow night to feed an increasingly voracious appetite for mortal blood.

A warm sea breeze caught the palm fronds above them, made them sway in a macabre dance. In the distance, sirens wailed. The sounds grew louder as blue and red lights emerged from the darkness, the colors muffled by the humid night air as cars drew into the nearly deserted parking lot adjacent to this public beach area. With Ben in the lead, the detectives converged on the crime scene with an air of futile urgency Alex fully understood. Philippe followed, his long dark hair catching the breeze and framing his face, emphasizing his intent expression.

"I'm sorry, Alex." Philippe inclined his head, a typically submissive act that seemed incongruous considering that he had all that hair while most of the male submissives in their clan kept their heads shaved. Still, Alex understood his clansman's grief and recalled his vow not to cut his hair as long as his mate's death lay heavy on his heart.

As the cops scurried about, stringing up yellow crime scene tape and snapping photos of the body, Alex considered his options. It was obvious both he and Philippe needed to restore their vampire powers…

And the best way to do that was with sex. Uninhibited vampire sex, not the conventional though incredibly satisfying joining he and Mara had enjoyed earlier. She stood beside him now, her attention focused on her team and what to do about the growing collection of bodies now filling the department's morgue. Alex didn't understand why she couldn't accept this wasn't a job for mortal cops. That Louis Reynard would keep on killing until he met a vampire stronger than himself. As much as he hated to use his supernatural powers on his lover, Alex slipped into Mara's mind. *Send them away, baby. Leave it to Philippe and me. Reynard has to be destroyed, finally and completely.*

As he'd known she would, she sent the cops away. She watched the ambulance pull out, its lights and siren silent now. Turning to Alex, she stood before him and Philippe, her dark eyes glistening with tears. A woman. His for the night and coming day, to pleasure and protect.

And more. Though he wasn't ready to go on his knees and declare his eternal love for Mara, he felt compelled to include her in the ritual of reinstatement that he needed — the ritual he knew Philippe needed, as well. Whether or not she'd admit it, she needed it, too, the affirmation of life, the restoration of strength…the security of loving and being loved.

Alex's cock swelled in his jeans as he imagined dominating not only his grief-stricken clansman but also the delectable cop who needed a few hard lessons in obedience. In obeying the Master who controlled her sexual responses, not the rules of her profession that were meant for humans with their human limitations.

* * * * *

The air seemed charged tonight, its damp heat caressing Mara's bare shoulders as they floated along high above the sandy beach, hands clasped. Sexual energy radiated from Alex on one side, his clansman on the other, warming her flesh that had grown cold from fear and revulsion as she'd worked yet another crime scene.

This time she wasn't afraid. She trusted them to carry her along safely. Yes, she knew when he was compelling her, like a few minutes ago when he'd had her send her team away. Part of her was angry at his arrogance, but mostly she accepted he'd only been challenging her belief as to what action would be best to stop Reynard. And he'd been right. The best — the only — way to catch Reynard would be to play by Alex's rules.

And her wary acceptance of that was almost as frightening as the rapid growth of her feelings for him.

A gust of wind caught them up, deposited them in Alex's room. It looked the same yet somehow different. A maid had laid back the covers, revealing snowy linens and jewel-toned pillows…and silky-looking restraints. Light, fragrant smoke from incense smoldering in a silver holder on the table swirled around them, binding them together as if with those silken cords. The lightweight sundress that had seemed so insignificant suddenly chafed Mara's skin, made her want to discard it along with all her mortal inhibitions and step into her lover's world.

As though he'd read her mind—perhaps he had—Alex skimmed the silky fabric off her shoulders, over her breasts and waist and hips. "Step out of it now," he ordered, his tone as smooth as the material.

Nothing could have made her disobey him, not even the knowledge that this encounter would be purely carnal. Vampire sex, where Alex and Philippe would both bring all their seductive skills into play to give her pleasure. Pleasure and submission to their collective will. No. To Alex's will. He hadn't had to say so for her to realize the third party in this ménage was submissive by nature and would bow to a Master's will.

Just as she would.

She stood there in the scandalous undies Alex had bought her, her nipples puckering and poking against the see-through lace bra cups. Matching thong panties did nothing to stem the flow of juices from her pussy—nothing but increase her arousal by brushing against her swollen slit. His touch, featherlight on her shoulder as he slid the bra strap down, sent shards of need through her, made her raise her face to his, silently begging for his kiss.

"Not yet. We're going to give you pleasure like you've never experienced before. Both of us."

Anticipation made Mara's pulse race when Alex's softly spoken words registered in her passion-drenched brain. Anticipation that trumped the very human, very mortal reserve that whispered sex was a couples' event, not a team sport. His calloused fingertips chafed her sensitive skin, reminded her of his strength—his undeniable masculinity.

"Give me your handcuffs." He handed over the black tote bag that looked so wrong with the clothes she'd been wearing and waited while she dug inside and brought out a pair of standard police-issue cuffs. "And the key." Digging in once more, she brought out a key ring and put it in his hand.

Would he restrain her? A shiver went through her body at the thought, a little bit of fear that the pleasure might be more than she could bear mingled with heightened sexual awareness, knowledge he was in charge and could ravage her helpless body the way he'd already destroyed her will to resist.

He did nothing but set the cuffs on the nightstand by the bed. And stand there, deliberate in his motions as he toed off his deck shoes and shed his jeans and boxers in one graceful motion. His sex stood straight up, its thick head glistening with lubrication, his smooth scrotum drawn tight against his body. "Come here. I know you want to play with this." He flicked the gold ring that had drawn her gaze then ordered Philippe to take off his clothes.

Her tongue darted out, moistened her lips. Even that small touch of her own flesh excited her. "Oh, yes," she hissed, moving so close that she felt Alex's slow, deep exhalations against her cheek when he bent and took her mouth in a long, slow kiss. Following his orders, she reached between his legs and set the *guiche* ring to swinging in slow motion.

"Oh, yeah. That feels fantastic. Stop it now, before I forget we're not alone."

She dropped her hand to his thigh, not wanting to give up the connection completely. He took it, brought it to his lips, moistened the back of her hand with his tongue. Then he set her hand over her navel.

"I want you to watch. Before night comes again you'll know Philippe's touch as well as you know mine." Alex settled her on the bed and laid a hand over her mound. A possessive gesture, she thought, even though he'd ordered her to watch his clansman bare a body equally muscular, equally smooth. An inch or so shorter than Alex, Philippe was paler, his skin a startling contrast with all that dark, shoulder-length hair. His blue eyes fixed on Alex, Philippe stripped, his movements practiced as if he'd repeated them a thousand times. Perhaps he had, for the mate who'd died. For countless vampire orgies he'd indulged in over the years.

"Philippe's a made vampire. A submissive. Hurry up, my friend, our mortal lover is growing anxious." Alex slid a finger under Mara's lacy thong, rubbed her clit in a circular motion as though to prime her for what was coming.

"Omigod." She couldn't help the exclamation of surprise when Philippe revealed his sex. Only half hard, his cock was huge, as was the heavy ring that pierced the shaft horizontally, just behind the bulbous head. His balls hung low, swinging slightly as he stepped out of his pants.

"Like what you see, baby? Philippe, come join us." Alex found her swollen pussy and massaged it, pushing her damp thong out of the way. "I want you to get our friend here hard. Use your pretty mouth and hands."

Could she take them both? She had no choice. Alex had stolen her will, primed her for the vampire pleasure she'd once yearned for with Dante. The lifetime of pleasure he'd denied her after giving her a glimpse of sexual paradise.

Alex pinched her clit, hard. "I command you not to think of him. Put those memories to rest and make new ones with me. With us."

How did he manage to intercept her every thought? Mara didn't care at the moment. She couldn't think at all, not with

Alex finger-fucking her pussy and Philippe playing idly with the lacy cups of her bra. She lay back, stroking Philippe's muscular belly while Alex ran his free hand up and down her spine. Foreplay times two.

Alex kissed her, an almost chaste kiss that had him tracing the seam of her lips with his tongue. Philippe shifted, bringing his cock into her hand. "Gods yes," he muttered when she began to milk his cool, smooth flesh.

"Open for me," Alex said against her mouth, and when she did, he claimed her. A second and third finger stretched her pussy while he tongue-fucked her and she stroked Philippe.

She felt heavy. Lethargic yet so sexually charged she thought she'd burst if they didn't stop toying with her and bring her to climax. The lace of her bra cups cut painfully into her swollen nipples, and her sopping thong dug into her rear entrance, reminding her she had another hole aching to be filled. Desperate for satisfaction, she sucked Alex's tongue, hard.

"Not good, baby. You're supposed to submit, not try to dictate the pace." He nipped at her lip then shot her a stern look. "Now you'll pay the price."

What price? She figured that out quickly enough when Alex deftly caught up the silk cords and tied her ankles to opposite ends of the footboard. "Now for these," he told her as he clamped her own handcuffs to her wrists and ran another cord through the chain and secured the cuffs to the headboard. He straddled her, the tip of his erection brushing her chin. "Do you want me to put my cock in your hot little cunt?"

"Oh, yes. Please."

He laughed as he shoved pillows behind her head. "So polite. But it won't do you any good. You'll have to wait your turn. I've been sadly neglecting Philippe."

He was going to fuck another man—another male vampire?

"Don't get so indignant, sweetheart. Did you think you were going to have all the fun?" Alex slid off her and took two condoms from the drawer. "Philippe, suit up and come to me."

It should have seemed unnatural, watching two magnificently muscled males locked in an embrace, kissing, running calloused hands through each other's hair then down to squeeze tight asses and play with their respective anal openings. But it didn't. Once Philippe joined them on the bed, Alex took charge, straddling Philippe's hard body and setting the pace, holding back when Philippe would have hurried, reaching between them first to caress Philippe's burgeoning erection and tug at the hefty ring whose shape stretched the latex receptacle at the end of his condom.

"Fuck me. Please." Philippe's plea conveyed an air of desperation, of need too long unmet. Mara watched the two, one Dominant, the other submissive, as they danced the dance she imagined predated modern civilization. Loving one another, celebrating all the senses. Vampire kisses that barely broke skin filled the room with a not unpleasant smell of blood. Touches, first soft then tinged with barely controlled male violence, made her long for them to use their magic hands on her as well, staunch the desperate desire that made her writhe against her bonds. Grunts and growls conveyed lust and need and something more she couldn't quite name.

Seeing them like this made her feel she should turn away, yet she could not. Their passion held her as firmly as her bonds, stoking her own lust to a fever pitch. Alex shifted and positioned Philippe on all fours, his eager ass in the air. Using his saliva to wet his hand, Alex lubricated the condom he wore. Then, surprising Mara, he withdrew a large anal plug from his lover's ass and replaced it with his own sheathed cock.

Philippe's expression was one of ecstasy when Alex plunged in up to his balls and slowly withdrew only to penetrate again, harder with each thrust. Her own look, she imagined, was one of longing, for it seemed unfair for her to have to watch Alex do to Philippe what she wanted both of them to do to her.

Their muscles bunched and strained. A vein throbbed in Philippe's thick neck, teasing...inviting. Alex leaned over, never missing a stroke. Fangs extended, he clamped down on Philippe's flesh, sucking his blood. Philippe screamed, a sound not of pain but of long-denied satisfaction. When Alex raised his head and met Mara's gaze, his deep green eyes glowed as he licked away the bloody residue that tipped his fangs.

Chapter Five

ം

I want you to bite me that way.

Mara's unspoken words resounded in Alex's head. He didn't know what it was about her, but he wanted to claim her as his own, not for a few hours' pleasure but forever. Lying there, restrained from moving by those silken cords that held her legs apart and her cuffed wrists above her head, she was temptation personified...temptation that could almost divert him from his goal.

Philippe slumped beneath him, sated for the moment yet not satisfied. His grief surrounded him like a shroud that kept out the heights of sensual satisfaction he'd found only with his dead lover. Keeping his eyes on Mara, Alex gathered Philippe in his arms, offered a clansman's love...and temptation for Philippe to set aside his grieving and participate fully in the ménage, despite his long-held preference for sex with other males.

Stripping off the condoms from his own cock as well as Philippe's, Alex drew him to Mara's side, laid his hand against her satiny cheek. Then he worked the ring out of Philippe's half-hard cock and sheathed him with a fresh, well-lubricated condom. "Help me show Mara how d'Argent vampires pleasure their lovers."

Cool. Soothing. Philippe's touch was tentative, as though it had been a long time—centuries—since he'd touched a woman to raise her passion. Looking down at her, he smoothed back a strand of hair behind her ear then crushed a handful in his fist. "Soft. I like it."

His own unbound hair brushed her shoulder when he lowered his head. Vaguely aware of Alex burrowing between her spread legs and blowing gently on her clit, she turned and accepted Philippe's kiss. Gentle at first, he suddenly claimed her mouth with a smooth thrust of his tongue. He nibbled at her lips while Alex tongued her clit. Their combined assault made her arch against them, demanding more.

She wanted release. Needed to let loose the painful pressure that built low in her belly with every carnal thrust, each slick abrasion of male tongues on her most sensitive flesh. Straining, she sought release — the satisfaction she knew would only come with her vampire lovers' massive cocks buried deep inside her. "Please," she begged, her voice muffled by Philippe's busy lips.

Alex reached down, unfastened the restraints from her ankles. As though in concert, Philippe freed her cuffed hands from the headboard. Alex lifted her and impaled her on his rigid erection as Philippe moved into position behind her and slid the head of his cock past her anal sphincter. Alex controlled the pace, lifting and releasing her, obviously taking care that the pleasure of their joint penetration exceeded the stretching pain.

Sandwiched between her two vampire lovers, Mara reveled in the heat...the passion...those rampant emotions that bombarded her, sending her tumbling over the edge to a place she'd only dreamed of. As she came she bared her throat, wanting it all. Wanting to belong to Alex and Philippe in their vampire world.

When it didn't happen she tried to shrug off her disappointment, tell herself it was too soon. But she knew it wasn't.

* * * * *

Everything outside looked normal. A brilliant blue sky dotted with a few white clouds. The hot golden sun drifted slowly toward the western horizon. Bikini-clad girls played volleyball on the beach outside the hotel while strippers and other club employees began straggling into the businesses on the other side of the beach highway known as A1A. A few dozen tourists were drinking beer and sunning themselves by the salt-water pool.

Alex got up quietly when he woke, and stood at the window, mulling over his options. There didn't seem to be a lot of them. Pity he didn't know exactly where Reynard had gone last night, because he'd have staked the bastard without a second thought if he'd been able to catch him sleeping off his most recent feeding.

Or maybe he wouldn't have. Attacking a sleeping vampire—no matter how heinous a villain he might be—wasn't Alex's way. Besides, the thought of explaining to a bunch of zealous mortal cops why he'd attacked and destroyed a sleeping, unarmed man didn't appeal.

One thing for certain, he wasn't about to let Mara set herself up as bait, the way she'd suggested doing earlier, after Philippe had gone to sleep. She'd wanted to talk about why Alex still refused to mark her, but that question had stayed inside her head. Good thing, because he could no more have explained that than he'd been able to justify his anger at the thought of her putting herself in harm's way.

Still, Alex chided himself because he'd hurt her feelings, pointing out that while Mara was a hell of a lover, she was no drop-dead gorgeous blonde like the ones Reynard had victimized in the past. The minute the words left his mouth, he'd regretted saying them because the hurt in her dark eyes had been unmistakable.

What they needed to do was find the bastard. Night would be falling soon, and Alex had a sinking feeling Louis would be killing on a daily basis now, since that had become his pattern over the past few days. He glanced over at the bed, then moved closer and shook Philippe's shoulder.

"Get up, both of you. It's time to go hunt down a vampire."

Philippe rubbed his eyes then tossed back the covers. "Both of us? It seems Mara has already left."

"Fuck." The expletive came out between tightly closed lips as Alex stared at the neatly arranged stack of pillows he'd thought was Mara. "Hurry. We've got to find Reynard before she does."

* * * * *

I'll show him. Standing in front of the mirror in her apartment, Mara adjusted a blonde wig on her head, almost losing her balance as she did. Damn, but standing up on these six-inch platform stilettos apparently took practice — practice she'd never had. Balancing precariously, she slipped into a skintight black dress. It would have to do, because she intended to be out trolling for Reynard before too many authentic hookers came out looking for a john.

Her pussy and ass still throbbed from the tandem fucking she'd enjoyed earlier. And her ego still stung when she thought about Alex telling her she'd never pass for a hooker, adding that she looked more like a cute little girl than a sex bomb. Of course he had finally let her feel the bite of his fangs after ordering her not to do it — not to even *think* about setting herself up as a trap for the serial killer.

She'd been so aroused she'd begged him, and he'd given in and satisfied her. He'd barely pierced her before lifting his head and looking her in the eye. His words echoed in her ears. *Reynard wouldn't stop with a little taste, baby. He'd feed on you until every drop of your blood was gone. Behave or I'll tie you to the bed and wake Philippe. Between the two of us we'll keep you so preoccupied with pleasure that you'll abandon your foolish plans.*

She'd behaved — at least she'd pretended to give in until he drifted off to sleep. She'd then slid out from between her two vampire lovers, arranged pillows in more or less the shape of her body, thrown on clothes and left them. Now she had a job to do.

Get a killer's attention before he hits on another civilian who doesn't deserve to die.

Sitting for a minute to take the pressure off her aching feet, Mara called the station and briefed Ben on her plan. It didn't make her feel better when Ben warned her that ambitious state attorney Sierra Sienna had been nosing around, making noises about following due process, warning them all to wait and catch the vampire serial killer in the act unless they wanted to be brought up on criminal charges.

Mara hung up and checked her weapon, stashing it in the small satin purse she'd dug out of the bottom drawer of her dresser since her "hooker" dress had no place where she might conceal it. The solid feeling of the Sig Sauer gave her a boost of confidence, even though she suspected Alex had been right when he said the gun would prove useless against their enemy.

Sighing, she got up and teetered out to her car on the fuck-me shoes she'd borrowed from the stripper who lived next door. Now she had not only Reynard to seduce, but also the mortal laws to heed in bringing him to justice.

* * * * *

He'd been wrong. Perched on a stool at the end of the poolside bar, a drink in her hand, Mara looked exactly like a prostitute or stripper trolling for a man. If it weren't for her expressive dark eyes and the swollen lips he'd kissed and nibbled on hours earlier, he might not have recognized her even with the small puncture marks that marked her as his. "Little fool," he muttered when he saw Louis Reynard take a seat beside her and start up some meaningless conversation.

"Wait, Alex. Let her lure him away from here. Don't try to take him now." Philippe laid a restraining hand on Alex's forearm, but Alex shook it off and stepped forward. "There. They're leaving. Let them get out of sight of this crowd."

"I don't care. He's going to fucking kill her. I won't let him."

"Neither will I." Philippe's declaration was no less lethal-sounding for being uttered quietly. "Come on."

Tiki lights sparkled in the dark, lighting the stretch of beach next to the hotel. A plaintive jazz tune floated over them, its source one of the clubs across the street. Alex strained his eyes, saw Louis drape an arm around Mara's slender shoulders. "I'm taking him now," he ground out between clenched teeth.

"Wait."

There'd be no waiting. Louis Reynard wasn't going to touch his woman. Alex wouldn't let Reynard lay his filthy hands or fangs on Mara. Not that he'd have let the bastard destroy any more women if he could help it. But Mara? His feelings for her were different. Stronger. No time to think about that, though, not now. Moving more quickly than he ever had before, he came up on the two, Philippe at his back. "Get Mara away from him now," Alex lunged at Reynard, caught him in a chokehold and wrestled him to the ground.

Weakened as he was, the ancient vampire put up an amazingly tough fight. But he was no match for Alex. Bloodlust consumed him when he thought of what Reynard had planned for Mara. Over and over until his own knuckles were bloody, Alex pounded his opponent. Bones cracked, the sounds satisfying beneath his fists. About to call for a stake to end it, Alex realized they'd drawn the attention of a crowd — mortals whose horrified expressions told him they didn't much care for his method of subduing an opponent.

Alex didn't give a fuck. Reynard was going to die. Grabbing the bastard by the neck, he dragged him into the shadows, out of the crowd's view. In that second or two, Reynard drew on some inner reserves, for he was fighting now with superhuman power, biting and gouging at Alex's eyes, struggling to get free.

His hands slick with blood, Alex struggled to hold on, but Louis somehow managed to break free. When he did, he let out an obscene cackle and bolted toward Mara.

"No!" Vaguely Alex saw Philippe shove Mara behind him, protecting her with his own body. But Reynard shoved Philippe aside and lunged at Mara. His bony hands dug into her shoulders, tearing at the fabric of her dress. He'd bared her breasts and extended his fangs by the time Alex tackled him from behind and brought him down.

"Die now, bastard." Ignoring the blood streaming down his face, Alex hoisted the wooden stake he'd kept tucked inside his shirt and drove it through Reynard's black heart.

Finally the Fox lay defeated and destroyed, his remains dissolving into a fine gray dust that blew slowly out to sea.

"Cuff him. I believe I have enough witnesses that the lack of a body won't cause problems with the prosecution." The words came not from Mara as Alex had expected, but from a dark-haired beauty standing next to Ben. A lawyer unless he missed his guess.

His expression apologetic, Ben moved closer and snapped handcuffs on Alex's wrists. They looked like the ones Alex had put on Mara last night, he thought when he looked down at them. Ben cleared his throat. "You have the right to remain silent…" Miranda Rights, Alex thought they called the words Ben recited now from memory. Alex had heard them before from a sheriff in Montana and now assumed they were part of the ritual involved in arresting someone here in the United States. "Sorry, man. Reynard needed killing," Ben offered at the end of his recitation, without the slightest change in his bored monotone.

Yes, Louis Reynard certainly had needed killing. To Alex's credit, the evil vampire now was dead. To his shame, nearly two years had passed since he and his kinsmen had first set out on the hunt—a year, twenty-five unfortunate mortals and thousands of miles later. As he let Ben push him into the police cruiser, he watched Philippe take to the air.

Alex knew where his clansman was going, and he had no doubt that Stefan and Claude would be arriving soon. Meanwhile he'd sit in jail and nurse his wounds. Might even con his jailers out of a feed to make up for the blood he'd lost.

No need to burst the mortals' bubble too soon by shedding the cuffs and flying away.

* * * * *

Mara couldn't get the picture of Sierra Sienna's self-satisfied smirk off her mind as she sped to her apartment to change. Why the fuck had her homicide case had to draw the personal attention of the most bulldoggish prosecutor in Dade County, a woman whose only apparent purpose in life was making a name for herself in the local media? Mara tossed off her disguise, scrubbed the makeup off her face and threw on brown slacks and a jacket. No time to primp. She ran a brush through her hair and tied it back with a rubber band before running to her car and hurrying to the station house.

Damn it, the last thing she'd wanted was for Alex to end up in jail. She had to talk to him, make him know she hadn't had anything to do with his arrest. With any kind of luck they wouldn't have transported him to the county lockup yet.

"Where's d'Argent?" she asked the desk sergeant as she scribbled her name on the sign-in book.

"Braunstein's interrogating him. Room 2."

Good. Alex still was here. Even better as far as Mara was concerned, Sierra was nowhere to be seen — a good thing since the woman had no qualms about sticking her nose in and fucking up investigations at every opportunity. Mara went inside, ordered Ben out and closed the door with a satisfying thud. "I didn't do this," she whispered as she sat next to him and removed the cuffs when she noticed he was holding his hands in an awkward position.

"I know." He curled his fingers around her hand, his movement uncharacteristically clumsy. "I think I broke a bone or two on the bastard. Don't worry, I'll heal."

It was uncanny how he read her thoughts. "Do you need to feed?"

"Your pal Ben gave me some when I first got here. It was enough that I'll survive, at least for a few days." He reached up and cupped her chin, forcing her to meet his emerald gaze. "Go away, baby. Leave me alone. I'm not in the best of moods." He stood, turning toward the barred window and staring out.

She'd get him out of here. Get Philippe to help hide him away so he could heal. Fuck it all, her magnificent vampire lover was a hero, not a criminal to be locked away. Maybe...maybe he could seduce Sierra, use his powers to sway a jury.

"Don't even think about it, baby. Remember what I told you, that no prison could hold Reynard. There's none that can hold me long, either." With what seemed like great reluctance he reached out and drew her to him, cradling her head on his shoulder, a silent gesture that seemed frighteningly like good-bye. "You need to go now. Please."

"I want to stay." What she was feeling was more than lust, more than the vampiric compulsion that had drawn her to him in the first place. "Please," she said, tilting her head back to look into his eyes—and baring her throat in a blatant offer of submission.

Alex glanced at the door where someone was rattling at the lock. "Not now. You think you want me now. I want you, too, but it's too soon. Get out of here before you get in trouble for helping me. And think about what you want. I'm going to get out of here soon, but I'll come back."

"How?" She gripped his shoulders, but she knew now she didn't care how he planned to escape. "Take me with you."

"Not now, sweetheart. Trust me, though. I'll be back."

She did trust him. But she didn't want him fighting vampire hunters...didn't want him meeting the same fate as Dante.

"There's no vampire hunter around who'll go after me unless it's to give me a medal," Alex said, bending as he did and brushing his lips across her cheek. "Hang in there for me."

Just then two dark, compelling vampires who closely resembled Alex entered through the barred window, swooped him up and disappeared with him the way they'd come. Mara was still looking out the window when someone broke down the door and Sierra burst in.

"Where is he? And why was the door locked?" The lawyer's gaze settled on the handcuffs on the table. "You let him go," she said, pointing at the open handcuffs. "Arrest her!"

Toby Cruz, the uniformed patrolman who'd trailed in behind Sierra, shot Mara an apologetic look, but she had no doubt he'd do the prosecutor's bidding. After all, she *had* let Alex go—not that he wouldn't have escaped without her, or that she could have stopped him if she'd tried. "The man's a vampire, for God's sake," she told the other woman, as if that would have done any good.

Sierra stepped closer as her companion cuffed Mara's hands behind her back. "Instead of staking him when he tried to escape, you took off the cuffs and let him go. For that you'll do some hard time. Read her her rights," she ordered Ben, who'd just come in the room. The lawyer's cruel smile projected her satisfaction at having found someone to put away in connection with the serial killings, however loose the ties might be. "Then take her over to the Women's Detention Center. I doubt she'll be bonding out."

Mara wouldn't be, not if Sierra had anything to say about it. Even if she was nothing except a grandstanding media hound when it came to grabbing cases to prosecute, the woman was a skillful advocate for the State when it came to getting defendants denied bail at initial bond hearings. "Get me a lawyer," she said when Ben finished telling her what she already knew.

"I will. We won't let the witch lady get away with this."

Chapter Six

✍

"I still say we should get you out of here and back to Paris," Stefan argued. "Reynard managed to get in a few good hits on you before you finished him off."

Not to mention that his cousin worried that Alex's disappearance would have set off a major vampire hunt by the Metro-Dade cops. But Alex didn't care. "I'm not leaving without Mara."

Claude turned back from where he'd been looking out the window of this new hotel across the highway from the club where he'd met his own mate a few months earlier. "Are you sure she wants you?"

No. He wasn't as sure as Claude had been that his woman really wanted to trade her mortal existence on Miami Beach for an eternity in his vampire world. After all, Mara had a good job—a good life—unlike Marisa, whom Claude had rescued from a miserable world where she hadn't been able to pull her brother out of the deepening schism of drug addiction and involvement with the mob. "I'm sure I want to find out."

They had Philippe nosing around the station, hoping to see Mara and bring her here without catching the attention of her coworkers. But Alex had an uneasy feeling that became acute when the room phone rang a few minutes later.

"Do you know a cop named Braunstein?" Stefan asked when he set the phone down.

"He's one of the men who work for Mara." While Alex understood Stefan's concern at having been located by the local police, he was more concerned with why Ben might have called. "What did he say?"

"That your woman has been arrested for letting you go. Stupid mortals, thinking you couldn't escape on your own. He says they're charging her as an accessory in Reynard's *murder* and for facilitating the killer's escape. That *killer* would be you, cousin."

Claude laughed, but the sound didn't convey much humor. "Stupid mortals indeed. If they had half a brain among them, they'd realize there are times that call for vampire justice. Where do they have Alex's lady cop locked away?"

"The Women's Detention Center. Braunstein just took her there."

"Fuck." Alex had to swallow a scream when he forgot and grabbed his cell phone with his broken hand. But he wouldn't admit to major pain, not now. They had to get Mara, take her out of what had to be a hellish situation. Having spent several days in a Montana jail cell, he had a pretty good idea of how miserable being locked up could be. He imagined it would be many times worse for Mara than he'd experienced on his brief stay, because she was a law enforcement officer tossed in among several hundred women she might have helped put there. "I've got to call *Maman*, tell her I'm bringing home a mate and that she needs to have a maid go over and tidy up my apartment." The gods only knew what souvenirs might still have been around after the farewell party those three female d'Argents had thrown for him before he took off after Reynard.

"Are you sure?" Claude asked.

Alex had meant to wait, give his own feelings as well as hers the test of time. But he didn't have that time. Not now. Besides, he'd known the minute he saw Mara that he'd found his mate, he just hadn't wanted to admit it. There was no time to waste. He had to rescue her and claim her as his own.

She might not be too thrilled at first to become a vampire, but she'd learn to love it. Claude's Marisa had and so had Stefan's Julie. Even Sam Quill, despite all his protests that he didn't want to change, had settled in nicely as Alina's mate.

Especially now that Alina had turned the clan leadership over to Claude and could reveal her submissive nature to one and all. "I'm sure. Let's go, break her out of that hole she's in."

"You know you're going to have to turn her there, and you're likely to have a very interested audience." Stefan shot Alex a doubtful look. "You don't look well enough to fight off half a dozen or more women desperate to get out and find a fix."

"I'll leave that to you, my friends. The only prisoner I'm interested in springing is Mara." Trying not to think about his aches and pains, Alex stood and made for the door. He knew, no matter how much they might protest, Claude and Stefan would always be at his back.

* * * * *

The Women's Detention Center might as well have been a dungeon, if only it had been below ground instead of above. She imagined the only reason it hadn't been built that way was because Miami's topography didn't lend itself to belowground construction. Seeing it inside, up close and personal, made Mara wonder if she really should have brought ninety percent of the women she'd arrested over the years to this hellhole.

She had six cellmates in a boxlike room designed for eight, surrounded by concrete block walls that had recently been painted an ugly shade of gray. No window, and only a barred opening in the locked metal door. From the look of it, the other women were sleeping off drunks or drug highs, except for one snarling psycho who looked as if she was trying to decide which one of them to attack. None of them smelled any too clean, but then the orange jumpsuit they'd given Mara didn't exactly feel or smell as if it had just come out of the laundry, either.

Where the hell was the lawyer Ben was supposed to have found for her? She wanted to see him, not that she figured he'd be able to do much for getting her out of this place. She knew the ropes. They wouldn't even hold a bond hearing for a couple of days, no matter how loudly her lawyers screamed. Taking a seat on one of the two unoccupied bunks, she took a deep breath and tried to relax.

Easier said than done, when the psycho was eyeing her with what seemed like intent, unnatural interest. Mara stared her down the way she might have done a suspect, and finally after what seemed like a long time the woman gave up and flopped back on her bunk.

Mara might have gone to sleep, but a mental picture of Alex kept getting in the way. A murderer? Never. So far as she was concerned, her vampire lover was nothing less than a hero. Because of him, Louis Reynard would never victimize another. And that made the world a safer place.

She couldn't help thinking about how he'd touched her mind as well as her body. How she'd responded to him sexually as she hadn't for many long years. As she'd never responded to any mortal. *I guess Dante spoiled me.* Instinctively she knew Alex would spoil her more. Her hand went to her throat, and she felt for the small puncture marks he'd left. Gone. Just as he was gone.

But he'd told her he'd come back.

As if she'd conjured him up, there he stood, in the cell no one had unlocked. The two vampires who'd rescued him were at his back. Shock, yes, but the thrill of seeing him overshadowed her disbelief. "How?" she managed to ask, surprised she was still able to talk.

"We're vampires. That's how." Alex took her hand, looked into her eyes. "Come with us now. Be my vampire bride."

The psycho jumped up and screamed, "Get these wackos outta here. I'm trying to get some shuteye. Guard!"

"Shut up, bitch," one of the other women growled. Then she apparently noticed Alex and his two companions. "Oh, my, any of you guys can fuck me any time you'd like."

Alex laughed as he reached out and cupped Mara's chin. "Well. I'm waiting. Isn't this the time you're supposed to throw your arms around my neck and say, 'Bite me'?"

Mara guessed it was, but she was still too shocked to move. Hours earlier she'd wished he'd taken her with him. It wasn't that she'd be spending her life in prison. No jury in its right mind would convict her. This was just Sierra's ego trip, and it would be over as soon as Mara's lawyer explained what had gone down to a judge. But did all that really matter?

She wanted Alex. Wanted him more than she'd ever wanted anything in her thirty some-odd years. *Mara girl, for once in your life do what you want to do. Take a chance.* She looked him in the eye and smiled. "Bite me, baby. And please, for God's sake, get me out of here."

When she bared her throat, Alex laid her back on the bunk and sank his fangs into her tender flesh. Not even the hysterical screaming from her cellmates detracted from the incredible high. Like sex, but better...almost. The sensations were indescribable, out of this world, transporting her to a place where she'd find true happiness with the vampire she loved.

Vaguely, as if from a great distance, she heard guards' boots pounding on the concrete floor, keys clanking and cellblock doors slamming open and shut. She felt Alex lifting her, had a sensation of drifting free, flanked by the other vampires as they made their way through barred windows. Then she felt nothing. Nothing but her lover's arms holding her safe and warm.

* * * * *

She'd lain limp in his arms as they crossed the Atlantic, and now that morning was breaking and they'd finally reached Paris, Alex tried not to panic as he strode past his clansmen who'd come to greet them. He placed Mara's cool, pale body in the center of the huge bed that had been the site of more than one d'Argent vampire orgy. Willing her to open her eyes and greet him as her mate...her Master, he went on his knees beside her, bent his head and brushed his lips across hers.

Nothing. He couldn't detect the first sign of life. Had he done as Stefan had so many years ago and destroyed his lover? No. Mara was too vital, too full of life to be dead. Alex remembered her sassy comeback when he'd said to tell him to bite her, considered the stubborn streak that had made her go out on her own to face Reynard. "Mara? Baby?"

"Let me." Alina placed a hand on Alex's shoulder, drew him gently back from the bed. "Wake up, Mara. Meet your new family."

Alex's gaze locked on Mara's face, searching for any sign she was coming around. Had she blinked at the sound of his cousin's voice? He wasn't sure. One by one, his kinsmen surrounded the bed, talking to her softly, touching her cheek, brushing lips across hands that were too still, too pale even for a newly made vampire.

Ass. You didn't even think that by saving her, you might destroy her. Alex cursed himself for his ego, his damnable confidence that no task might be beyond his ability. When he turned away Stefan embraced him. "She's not gone, cousin."

"Stefan's right." Her consort in tow, Alina turned into the circle of her cousins' arms. "What I believe Mara needs is a dose of our own life forces. Julie, you should join Stefan."

Claude joined them, dragging his heavily pregnant mate Marisa into the circle. "A vampire welcoming ritual?"

As they all shed their clothes, Alex felt the combined power among them, power unequaled by any other vampire clan on earth. Hope restored, he crawled onto the bed beside Mara and gently stripped away the ugly jail clothes she'd had on before she was turned. He did the same with the equally ugly white underwear, baring her completely to his family's eyes. "Join us?" he asked, wishing to all the gods he'd ever heard of that this were just another vampire orgy…just another time for sharing pleasure among his loved ones.

As head of the clan, Claude came first, sitting at the head of the bed beside Alex. He lifted Mara's head onto his lap and ran his fingers through her tangled auburn hair, his touch confident. Marisa came up behind Alex, resting her head against his shoulder. He felt life—the strong motion of Claude's child nudging him in the back. Alex laid a hand on Mara's cheek, passing along Marisa's energy…and the baby's.

Stefan and Julie took their places at Mara's side and began to stroke her cool, dry skin. Was Alex being hopeful or had some color come back into her still body? When Sam opened Mara's legs and ran his hands along her inner thighs, and Alina rested her cheek on Mara's flat, soft belly, Alex was certain he saw her eyelids flutter.

A sense of magic filled the room. Warmth surrounded her. She heard voices calling her, but she couldn't answer. Tired. So tired.

And hungry. Desperate to feed, not on mortal food but on blood. Vampire blood. She felt the sting of Alex's fangs, the incredible pleasure when he'd drained her. The sensation of floating…of a transformation from her world into his.

Mara rubbed her tongue across her teeth, found sharp fangs she'd somehow known would have been there. Hands touched her. Alex's. His two companions. Another male who now was rubbing his thumb over her clit. And females. Three of them, with gentle hands and long hair that brushed her skin, all murmuring soft words of encouragement.

She reached for Alex—her master. Drew him to her. Bodies shifted. Suddenly he rolled her on top of him and sank his hot cock into her well-primed pussy. "Bite me, baby," he said, baring his throat. "Yeah, like that. Feels so fucking good."

The women petted her with soft, gentle hands while she rode Alex and drank his blood. One at a time the men probed her ass first with their fingers and then with their hard cocks. Pressure built inside her, threatened to implode. She came and came and came, the salty taste on her lips incredibly arousing. She'd never felt so full. So sexually fulfilled. So loved, not only by her master but by her new vampire family.

When she felt certain she couldn't come again, Alex caught her hips and slammed her down on him. With a triumphant shout he flooded her with his seed as the other males left her and began to fuck their own women.

Later Alex introduced her to his family and explained who went with whom. His very young-looking uncle, Claude, had found his pregnant mate Marisa at a South Beach strip club, while Stefan had met Julie in Chicago when Reynard had singled her out for his next kill. Sam, the rugged older Dom who'd wakened her, was Julie's father whom Alex's cousin Alina had turned after one of the Fox's henchmen had ended his mortal existence. She lay back on the bed and held out her arms for her own vampire mate. "What did you do with Philippe?"

"He's with Sam and Alina. Do you miss his big, pierced cock?"

She grinned. "It *is* mighty tempting. Seriously, he seemed so sad."

Alex stretched out between her legs and licked her mound. Good thing she'd no longer need to shave it, because she loved the tickly, tingly feeling of his mustache and beard against her sex—almost as much as she liked the way his perfectly smooth cock and balls slid sensuously against her own hairless pussy. "He hasn't gotten over losing his mate. You know, they were together like this for over a hundred years."

"Like this?"

"Well, not exactly. But close enough." His movement more fluid than any other male Mara had ever seen, he straddled her face. "Like this. Suck my cock, my precious baby vampire. You'll need a lot of practice before the next d'Argent family orgy, keeping those pretty fangs retracted."

He tasted good. Very good. Mara would miss her team—especially Ben—but she was pretty damn sure she'd never regret having fallen for Alex, or opting to trade her mortal existence for a long, lusty life with Alex and his dynamic family.

ETERNAL SURRENDER

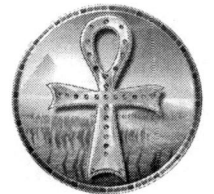

Prologue

☙

In the shadows of ancient oaks festooned with Spanish moss, an intruder lurked, observing silently. Watching vampires cavorting with mortals at a wedding celebration that had begun in Chicago and moved en masse here to New Orleans, Wim Reynard seethed at the indignity of his assignment. His hatred for the fallen leader of his own vampire clan kept growing by the moment. Too sick now to fight, Louis Reynard had refused to let anyone else end his mad quest for vengeance. Instead he had sent Wim as though he were some toothless lackey, with orders to observe the vampire queen who had spurned the old vampire's amorous advances.

Alina d'Argent didn't seem to be fighting off the attention of the mortal father of her cousin's bride. Not at all. Stroking the mortal's muscular arm, she looked into his eyes like a simpering mortal being seduced by a lover. The bride and groom stood, holding hands, chatting with a group of tasty-looking young women, presumably the bride's close mortal friends. Alexandre d'Argent joined the group, soon steering one of the women into the shadow of an ancient oak tree draped with concealing festoons of Spanish moss.

The abundance of goodwill that abounded between his clan's enemies and the cream of New Orleans' mortal society made Wim want to gag.

It took no genius to see why Alina stole male hearts, even the rotten black excuse for emotion that belonged to his leader. Her beauty had been renowned for centuries, her goodness remarked on for as far back as Wim could remember—for most of his nearly four-hundred-year existence as a Reynard vampire. Seeing Alina, he almost believed the rumor that she could restore the virility of vampires she had made. He understood why Louis had believed that folklore and decided to propose to the d'Argent queen. Tonight her pale hair glowed in the light from a hundred torches—he had amused himself by counting them—as she swayed to a haunting jazz tune, her hands resting on the broad shoulders of the party's host as she gazed not at the pulsating vein in his neck but into his gray eyes.

Wim glanced at Sam Quill, the affable host of this event. The mortal projected power. Dominance. He didn't appear the sort to play consort to a vampire queen. Still Wim sensed an aura of sexual awareness surrounding the two, radiating like the sun's rays, reminding him that unlike himself, the d'Argents were vampires born, able to mate and procreate.

Damn it, he didn't even have the memories of coupling that some of his clansmen recalled with more than a little nostalgia. Wim gritted his teeth, drawing a drop of blood from his lower lip. Why had he been turned when he'd been a mere child, too young to have experienced mortal pleasure? For the first three hundred years or so, being a vampire hadn't been unpleasant because he'd always had a warm bed with his blood mother and ready sources of nourishment, something he'd never enjoyed as a street urchin in Brussels. But then he'd hit puberty and discovered the carnal urges he could never satisfy.

He shook off the envy that threatened to overcome him. It was stupid to grieve for something he'd never known. He glanced around at the crowd, at mortals dancing with d'Argent vampires, other vampires sipping blood daintily from fine crystal stemware while mortals dined on local delicacies whose exotic aromas tickled his nose.

The surreal scene made Wim uneasy. In his world vampires viewed mortals as potential meals, not likely lovers. He zeroed in on a dusky-skinned beauty standing beside the bar. She had an enticing habit of baring her throat whenever she laughed at something her companion said. A potentially fatal habit. Wim's fangs itched at the prospect of sampling the salty taste of her lifeblood, his sustenance, though her grizzled vampire companion seemed interested only in whatever it was she was saying.

Because he'd fed earlier today on a homeless creature in the ruined Ninth Ward of the city that bore no resemblance at all to Sam Quill's Uptown neighborhood, Wim wouldn't need sustenance again for several days. It made no sense for him to stand here salivating over the wench. He couldn't have fed on her anyhow, even if he'd been starving. Like the others of Sam Quill's guests, she was strictly off limits. Louis Reynard's instructions had been crystal clear on that subject, and one didn't defy one's leader. Not if one valued his existence. Resting his back against a tree, Wim kept his eyes on the wedding party—especially the queen of the d'Argent vampires and the father of the bride.

I will tell you when it is time. Until then, watch and wait. Do not allow the d'Argents to sense your presence. Defy me and I will destroy you. Louis' words echoed in Wim's head as he recalled his recent meeting with the clan leader, gravely wounded from his encounter with the d'Argents and recuperating in an isolated lair deep in the Carpathian Mountains.

The power of age. The aura of single-minded omniscience fueled by madness. Even in his present debilitated state, Louis had projected both. Wim glanced at the newly married Stefan d'Argent and his cousin Alexandre and noted the absence of their mutual uncle, Claude, who apparently was nursing wounds too severe to let him travel to join in the marriage celebration. Too bad the three d'Argent warriors had botched their most recent attempt to destroy Louis Reynard. When the time came, Wim would succeed where they had failed.

First he would destroy Alina to demonstrate his power. Afterward he would persuade his fellow clan members to help destroy Louis, and he'd take over as leader of the clan. Though much of Wim's determination was fueled by greed, he had another equally important motive. He shuddered, recalling his leader's cruelty toward his own kind. Wim's blood mother. He'd burst into her thatched-roof hut, seen the results of Louis' torture and realized she'd never again tend his wounds, cradle his head on her lap and sing him to sleep as the sun began to seep through cracks in the flimsy walls. She was gone. Beyond help. Wim bit down on his lip, tasting his own blood as he renewed the vow he'd made that day. He would destroy his leader, and when Louis Reynard was no more, Wim would finally have avenged his blood mother's excruciating destruction.

* * * * *

On nights like these Alina could almost forget the danger that would always lurk as long as Louis Reynard drew vampire breath. She sipped daintily on a third flute of rare AB negative their host had found somewhere to serve at his daughter's wedding. He'd spared no expense, either at the beautiful ceremony in Chicago two days earlier or now, at the elegant reception in the courtyard of his New Orleans home. She was so happy for Stefan. And Julie too.

Still she couldn't quite stave off the crushing loneliness affairs like these made her feel. Most of the guests would probably laugh at the idea that the queen of the clan could feel this way when almost any male could be hers with as little as a look in his direction. But if she summoned them, they'd serve her, following her lead when what she really wanted was what most women of all species wanted. To be swept off her feet, compelled to set aside her life role and accept the pleasures her partner offered. Though vampires often enjoyed various forms of Domination/submission games in their romantic entanglements, the obvious expectation was that the vampire did the dominating when the games involved a mortal.

Alina often dreamed of submitting...

"You need to be dancing, *chérie*." She turned when she heard the deep, seductive voice of Julie's father, Sam Quill.

This was a mortal who'd intrigued her ever since they met, whose commanding height and take-charge manner had drawn her into his bed after the wedding...before he'd had to go to catch a plane and come back here to prepare for the reception. She loved his deep, Southern drawl, the incredibly sexy way he sometimes dropped a Cajun French endearment into their sex talk.

He hadn't asked then, and he didn't ask now before relieving her of her glass, setting it on a nearby table and sweeping her into his arms. "What a beautiful night...a beautiful party," she said, laying her head on Sam's broad shoulder.

"Had to send off my little girl right. You know, if it hadn't been for you, I'd have been feeling mighty old tonight." When he pressed his hand lower on her waist and drew her closer, she felt him growing hard against her belly.

She tilted her head enough so she could look up into his beautiful gray eyes, see how the pupils had dilated with his arousal. "You don't feel old at all. Besides, it's not safe to remind a female vampire she's outlived her partner by a few hundred years." His salt-and-pepper curls, cut no-nonsense short as though he was too busy to bother with trying to tame them, felt crisp against her forefinger when she circled the sensitive spot just above the hairline on his neck. His sigh and the nudge of his growing erection told her she'd found one of his erogenous zones.

When she parted her lips and pressed her body closer, he didn't draw back with embarrassment as a younger man might have done. Instead he welcomed her sign of invitation, drew her closer so not even the sultry breeze might have found its way between them. He slid his hand lower on her back, his smallest finger curved discreetly over the curve of her buttock. "I'd like to take you over in the shadow of that grandfather oak and fuck you..."

"Please don't tease me. I'm already wet for you." Alina looked longingly at the ancient tree with its wide canopy of darkness. But when she sensed an evil presence lurking there she tensed.

"What's wrong?" Sam's arm tightened around her and he swung them around, presenting his broad back to whatever danger she sensed beneath the tree. For a moment she was too astonished to reply. He thought—a human thought—to stand between her and danger, not questioning his deficit of strength or quickness against a male of her species. From the hard set of his mouth, which seconds earlier had been curved in a smile, she wondered if Sam might be far more dangerous than a vampire would expect. He certainly challenged her more than she'd expected, on several different levels. Despite the absurdity of it, she found his instinctive desire to shield her made her want him even more.

She cupped his cheek with one hand and looked over his shoulder, concentrating on identifying and reading the unseen foe. "It's all right. A Reynard lackey sent to keep an eye on us while their leader nurses his wounds. He's seething because his leader has ordered him to observe, not attack." *A good call,* she thought, considering the number and quality of defenders who would rush to the defense if he attacked. She found herself including Sam in her mental tally of strong male protectors, another foolish thought since not even the most powerful mortal was a match for the puniest of male vampires.

Sam curled his hand around her wrist, turned his head to put a kiss there and—she gasped at the audacity of the move—a graze of his teeth. His gaze held hers. "Your cousins may be otherwise occupied tonight. To keep you safe, I think I'd better keep you in my bed."

He wasn't sure where that came from. Yes, Sam was confident and assertive with women. And on the few occasions he wanted a woman—and he wanted Alina the way he hadn't wanted a particular female in years—he went after her. He didn't think she was using vampire allure on him, one of those vampire abilities Julie had told him about. Every time he looked into Alina's eyes, he sensed something he'd discerned before in women who had the sexual preference of submission. That called out the Dominant in him.

He'd think he was crazy, knowing what she was, except that when he told her he was taking her to his bed her eyes got hotter. Her nipples peaked, their hardness obvious through the material of the thin green dress she had on. "I will look forward to it," she whispered, punctuating her words with a soft nip on his earlobe. "Meanwhile you need to pay attention to your guests."

"I need to pay attention to shooing them out—politely, of course." As the music faded away, Sam turned them once more and came to a halt before the table where Julie and Stefan sat holding hands. The way lovers should. The way Sam held Alina's fingers laced firmly with his own, his knuckles brushing the firm flesh of her thigh through the thin veil of her skirt. When he looked at Stefan, he saw urgency that nearly matched his own. "It's getting about time to wind this party down," he said, and nobody voiced a word of protest.

When he nodded at the bandleader, the man held up his baton. A moment later the courtyard filled with a jazz rendition of "Good Night, Ladies".

Chapter One

ೲ

She was the most beautiful woman he'd ever seen. The most exciting lover he'd known in fifty-plus years on Earth. Lithe yet curvy in all the right places, she had satiny pale skin that reminded him of the finest China silks his importing company stocked for its most discriminating customers. She was his daughter's cousin-by-marriage. And she was a vampire, queen of her centuries-old clan.

Sam Quill rose early, as was his habit each morning, ready to greet a bright new day. Today, though, he hurried to the French doors that overlooked a courtyard garden and drew the drapes before stepping outside and plucking a creamy gardenia from a nearby bush. He moved to one of the wrought iron tables and picked up a champagne flute the caterers had apparently missed last night while cleaning up.

Despite the fact much of New Orleans still bore the decimation of last year's killer hurricane, the reception had gone well. Better than he'd hoped it would when his daughter had told him last month that half the guests would be vampires like her new husband…and herself, now that she'd opted to join Stefan for an eternity in a shadow world Sam still couldn't quite understand.

Saying goodbye to Julie when the party had wound down had been hard, but Sam couldn't have asked for a more loving bridegroom for his only child. By this time tomorrow the newlyweds should be settling in at Stefan's castle on the Normandy coast.

For a minute Sam wondered how Julie's mother would have felt about Julie giving up mortality to be with her lover. He honestly didn't know. Though he'd loved Madeleine with all his heart, remembering her now after so many years brought no more than a twinge of regret that she'd died much too young, before they'd had the chance to know each other as well as they knew themselves.

It had been just him and Julie for a quarter century, and if it weren't for Stefan's cousin Alina, Sam imagined he'd feel quite alone. The fact she was staying for a few more days, seemingly eager to explore this thing between them, made him feel young again. Eager to form the sort of emotional connection he'd avoided for so long. And to explore this sexual compulsion that had captured them both from the moment they met.

His cock rose at the prospect of more nights like the one they'd just shared, and he looked forward to showing Alina his world, at least the portion of it that had been left untouched by Hurricane Katrina the previous year. Drawing the gardenia close to his face, he inhaled the rich, sweet fragrance as he crossed his bedroom and laid it on the pillow next to her outstretched hand. As he did, a glint of sunlight off the dagger on the nightstand caught his eye.

Oh, no. Hadn't he heard somewhere that silver repelled vampires? No. It was silver bullets that supposedly would destroy a vampire while ordinary bullets had no effect at all. Folklore, he told himself. Still he put away the ceremonial silver dagger he kept on the table beside his bed and occasionally used to open mail. The dagger hadn't seemed to bother Alina when they'd come to bed last night, but he'd take no chances. No way did he want to repel his beautiful vampire lover.

"Good morning, love." Like a lazy cat, she stretched. "Tell me you're not rising at this ridiculous hour of the day." Her voice sounded husky, sexy as hell — almost like a big cat's purr. "Come to me."

"My pleasure." He picked up the flower from the pillow and laid it in her outstretched hand. God but she made him feel good. As if his life were just beginning instead of marching toward its inevitable end. He got as horny as a teenager every time she smiled at him with those gorgeous emerald eyes. After handing her the flower whose fragrance filled the room, Sam slid into bed and drew her into his arms. Sightseeing could wait. He wanted to hold her, feel the satiny smoothness of her cool, pale skin, crush the silken fall of her blonde hair in his fist while they made hot, sweet love.

Alina stroked the length of Sam's long, hard body, tangling her fingers into the nest of salt-and-pepper curls that cushioned his impressive sex. The scent of the gardenia surrounded them, reminding her that this was sultry New Orleans and they were in the master suite of Sam's beautiful home in a lush Garden District neighborhood not far from Audubon Park. She loved the heat that emanated from him…a sexual glow she hadn't experienced for centuries. When he shifted onto his knees and straddled her face, she took his big, rigid cock in her mouth and sucked while he buried his face between her thighs.

"Oh, yes, sweetheart. Like that," he growled, his warm, damp, very mortal breath tickling her clit and making it swell and harden with greedy anticipation.

He tasted so good, so alive, she wanted to consume him. No. What her body yearned for was for him to take over control, make her submit to his desires. She'd had to be in charge for much too long, for her vampire lovers deferred to her in bed as they followed her in life, never forgetting they'd been having sex with their queen—their mistress.

None of them would have dared bury their hands in her hair, force her to take their cocks deeper, swallow them, taste their essence. But Sam did. And she loved it.

She loved the heat of him, the warmth he brought to her cool flesh. The velvety moisture of his tongue on her clit felt so good when he lapped her there. She wanted more, wanted him to take that nub between his teeth and suck her the way she was sucking his cock. She wanted to feel his tongue in her cunt, tasting her honey, his cock sinking into her every orifice, him taking his pleasure of her in any way he chose.

She sensed he'd provide all that in his own time, at his own pace. The waiting was torture—delicious, tantalizing torture that fed her arousal toward the final goal of her surrender.

Alina closed her eyes. Darkness cloaked her, leaving her dependent on the sounds of Sam's breathing, the sweet smell of the flower petals crushed beneath her head. The contrasting textures of fine Egyptian cotton sheets against her back and Sam's hard, lightly furred body above her made her feel pampered, deliciously helpless.

Protected. Oh, yes. Sparks of sensation ignited in her cunt and radiated, heating each nerve as they traveled through. Building...and exploding, over and over. Sensations overwhelmed her. She clamped down on his cock and sucked him harder, surrendering to the ecstasy that came in undulating waves, carrying her to a place she hadn't been for much too long. He growled against her smooth labia then pulled away.

"Gotta get inside you," he muttered, whirling around, claiming in one smooth, hard thrust that fed her own orgasm, enhanced it.

Sam gave the best oral sex she'd ever had. He also knew how to wield his big, hard cock. He stretched her, filled her, suffused her body with his mortal heat. Alina twined her legs with his, moved with him toward nirvana, toward the sort of mutual satisfaction she hadn't found for centuries.

Until last night. Until Sam.

* * * * *

Until Alina he'd lived two lives, the mostly celibate widower, workaholic, father and—on those occasions when the needs of the flesh overwhelmed him—the masked Dom who imposed his sexual will on any number of anonymous

153

sexual submissives. As he and Alina walked through the French Quarter late that afternoon, Sam glanced at the unimposing brass nameplate that marked the *Club de la soumission*. He hadn't often visited there since having returned. He'd broken the pattern, he supposed, when he'd left New Orleans to stay with Julie in Chicago until electric and telephone services had finally been restored in the Quarter and his Garden District home.

Yes, Hurricane Katrina had changed his life, caused him to modify habits honed over the years. The big storm had done a number on his city and everyone who'd lived to remember it—more than he'd thought about until now.

The mental picture of Alina in the club's dungeon, laid out on a St. Andrew's cross with her alabaster skin in glowing contrast with the padded black leather restraints securing her for his pleasure, had him incredibly hard. Impossibly eager, for a fifty-some-odd-year-old who'd come three times in the past twenty-four hours. He ached, though. His balls drew up against his body. Sam willed himself to relax. After all, he had promised to play host, show her what remained of the attractions of the Big Easy. That's what he would do.

"There's the *Café du Monde*. If you were mortal, I'd suggest we stop and enjoy a beignet and *café au lait*."

Alina slid her dark glasses back to perch atop her silky blonde mane. "I'm perfectly willing to sit in the shade and watch you enjoy a New Orleans treat. Yes, I know the sun has practically set, but your late afternoon sun still has enough light to make me a little uncomfortable."

"I'm sorry, sweetheart, I didn't think. I wouldn't damage your soft, soft skin for anything."

"It's all right. But I'd enjoy sitting under that awning and feeling this sultry breeze."

When she gave him her hand, he led her to a corner table beneath the awning and held out her chair. "You don't need to feed?"

"After last night? Hardly. I must have taken enough nourishment to hold me for a week, as many times as I raised my glass in toasts to Stefan and Julie." When she smiled at him, her eyes sparkled like emeralds. "You need not fret that I'll suddenly become ravenous and decide to dine on you."

"I know." In the past few weeks Sam had learned a lot about Stefan's family. It had sunk in quickly that vampires, at least the d'Argents, were far from the creatures of old B-movies that flooded the TV airwaves every Halloween. Though he worried because Julie had chosen to join Stefan for eternity and had given up her mortality to be his mate, Sam had no doubt his new son-in-law would love and protect his daughter with all his considerable powers. Or that Stefan's family would stand firm behind him if need be, in defense of Julie.

Sam's earlier impression of vampires as bloodsucking creatures not to be trusted had taken a hundred eighty degree turn. For the most part. Julie's story of how one ancient, evil vampire had singled her out for death because of her resemblance to Alina weighed heavily on Sam's mind. Even though both Stefan and Alina had assured him that Louis Reynard now lay near death — if that was how one referred to vampire demise — in a hideaway in the Carpathian Mountains, Sam still suffered lingering doubts. Alina had assured him members of the d'Argent clan watched the would-be killer constantly, looking for signs he might be recovering. Still, if Louis Reynard had survived the attack of three healthy young d'Argent vampires as Julie had said he did, Sam reasoned that he might easily elude those who watched him convalesce.

Something here, in this place where he'd taken breakfast almost every day for more than twenty years, gave Sam an uneasy feeling. A sense of being watched by malevolent eyes. Alina felt it too, he guessed from the way she clasped her hands together and was giving each person who strolled by the once-over. "What's wrong?" he asked.

"I sense another vampire presence. Not one of the two from my clan that *Maman* insisted hover out of sight but in shouting distance, just in case I should need them. An evil vampire. Look. He's standing in the shadows across the street." She nodded her head in the intruder's direction. "There."

Sam turned to glance in the direction she indicated, only to see a tall, skinny man standing in the shadow of a canvas awning that shaded the display window of an antique shop. "Looks as though he doesn't want us to notice him," he commented, schooling himself to remain calm when he looked back at his companion.

"He's one of the Reynards." Alina closed her eyes. The tip of her tongue came out, moistening her upper lip. Julie's voice, filled with wonder when she'd spoken the other day about Alina's powers, flooded Sam's mind.

She's using her powers of telepathy, Daddy. It's amazing, how she can share thoughts with someone far away, without picking up a phone. I'm learning to do it too.

Fascinated, Sam watched Alina's expression change, reflecting myriad emotions though she never said a word. Emotions including, if not fear, at least a good bit of unease. Sam clenched his fists, started to rise.

Alina stopped him. "Wait. It's not Louis. I think—no, I'm certain it's one of the Reynard youngsters. I wager he's here to keep an eye on Louis' prey while Louis recovers."

"But Julie and Stefan have gone."

"It's not Julie that Louis truly wants. It's me. That's another reason I stayed here, so my protectors might have some respite from the fight." She looked into his eyes, smiled as she laid her hand on top of his. "That, and because I want to spend this time with you."

* * * * *

Wim let out a disgusted snort. It positively sickened him the way Alina simpered over the mortal. Even from his vantage point across the street from *Café du Monde* he had no trouble recognizing the sexual tension that sizzled between the two. No trouble at all. Resentment simmered for a moment then built to a full boil, overflowing his mind. Wim turned on his heel. He had seen more than enough. Damn it, he was no lackey fit only to baby-sit his leader's intended victim while Louis recovered from his wounds. For a moment Wim considered taking on Louis now, but he quickly reconsidered. Now was not the time. Besides, Wim wasn't at all certain he had the strength to defeat Louis one-on-one even now, while the ancient vampire lay nearly helpless in his lair.

After all, Louis had fought off three of the d'Argents' best fighters and survived, battered but determined to heal and take them on again. "Obsessed" was the word another of the Reynard elders had used to describe their leader's unwavering ambition to destroy the d'Argent queen.

When he had been back at the Reynard's main community, he'd noticed the elders were annoyed. Very annoyed. Wim understood and agreed. Business in the clan had largely ground to a halt for more than a year now while Louis pursued his bloody quest. When Wim had thought about it, he'd decided the clan was ripe for a takeover.

A takeover not by one of the other elders who had foolishly acceded to Louis' demands for personal vengeance, but by young blood—someone like himself. He wouldn't stay here any longer, blindly obeying Louis' orders. He'd head back, not to the clan leader's Carpathian mountain hideout but to the Reynard clan's main gathering place in southern France. Somehow he'd manage to persuade his fellow Reynards that the time was ripe for a *coup d'état*.

* * * * *

Sam sized up the deathly pale, skinny young vampire who stared at them from across Decatur Street. He could undoubtedly take the man in a fair fight, but...

"Vampires don't fight fair, Sam. Especially the Reynards. And even the puniest specimens of vampire males have strengths and powers that make them virtually invincible against even the strongest of mortals." Alina laid a hand over his, lacing their fingers together. "Especially Reynards. Leave it alone. See, he's going now."

Damn it, she knew what he was thinking. Sam found that particular vampire skill unnerving. "I see. Still, I wouldn't let anything—anyone—hurt you." *If I could help it.* He had a feeling he couldn't, and that rankled.

"I know. Come on, I want to visit that *fabricant de parfum* that Julie told me so much about. Perhaps the shop owner will choose a fragrance for me. I want one that will drive you wild."

When she leaned over and nibbled his ear, Sam's cock came to full attention. No woman had affected him so strongly for years. Perhaps none ever had. "Trust me, you don't need perfume to entice me. Behave. Now we'll have to sit here a while longer."

"But why, *mon cher*?" The sparkle in her eyes told him she knew damn well why, and it amused her.

"You like the power you've got over me, don't you? Wait until I get you home!" Or to his club. The more he thought about it, the more he leaned toward showing her the dominant side of his sexual makeup now, before she wound her way too tightly around his heart.

"I anticipate my punishment with the greatest of pleasure."

Her husky purr did nothing to relieve his arousal—nothing at all. "Be careful, my darling, or I'll show you what real punishment is." He slipped a hand under her skirt and stroked her cool, satiny thigh, not caring much whether the table provided an adequate shield.

"Is that a promise, *mon cher*?"

"Oh, yes. A promise I'll enjoy fulfilling." Sam moved his hand higher and traced the lacy tops of her stockings, then leaned closer and whispered in her ear. "I want to take you to play at my club. My dungeon."

Her eyes widened. "The *Club de la soumission* we passed on the way here?"

She'd noticed the words on the brass doorplate most passersby ignored. Noticed and remembered. Surely she wouldn't have unless... "Yes. Would you like to go there, play at being my devoted slave?"

"Play?"

"I certainly wouldn't expect you to embrace the lifestyle permanently. It would hardly befit a vampire queen."

Sam noted a shadow crossing Alina's face, almost as if his disclaimer disappointed her. When she laid a hand on his thigh, the electricity between them practically crackled. "Even vampire queens must have their times to be only women, submissive to their lovers. It has been so long..."

How long? Sam couldn't believe what he was hearing, even as unreasoning jealousy rose in his throat, for some unknown lover two weeks or two centuries ago who had apparently introduced Alina to the pleasure of being under a man's control. The thought that she liked being under a man's control made him want to take her, test how far she liked to go in the game of Domination and submission. Testing them both, he reached out and caressed her throat, watched her pupils dilate and her tongue dart out to moisten her full, pink lips. Having her look at him like that sent blood surging out of his brain, pounding in his sex. "You need wait no longer. Come. My dungeon awaits you."

But as soon as he'd said it, he realized it did not. His club was where he went to exert control over nameless, faceless subs. Alina was much more than that to him. She'd engaged his emotions along with his libido, the way no woman had done since he'd lost Julie's mother years ago. "On second thought, I believe we'll play our bondage games at my home."

Chapter Two

೫

Excitement—and a bit of trepidation, Alina admitted—bubbled up in her when Sam escorted her up a sweeping staircase to the beautifully appointed room where she'd spent the night before in his arms. Her own personal fragrance, created just an hour ago by a wizened Creole woman in a crowded shop on Royal Street, surrounded her, mingling with the scent of Sam's cologne and the sex they'd shared earlier.

"Tell me what you like." His breath bathed her neck in warmth and dampness, reminding her he was mortal and she was not. "The responsibility of a master is to please his slave."

"Take me. Tell me what to do to give you pleasure. Give me no choices. Let me be not a clan leader but a woman, at least for a little while. That is all I ask."

He traced the plane of her belly, the calluses on his long fingers grating lightly against the lightweight silk of her shirtwaist dress. "Take this off, then. Let me feel you with nothing between us." He sat on the bed, looking only at her, watching as though his only desire was that she display herself to him.

"Like this?" Slowly, in a dance of seduction older even than she, Alina shrugged out of the dress and watched him follow the soft material with his gaze as it slithered over her hips and floated to the floor. The longing look on his face told her, better than words could have said, that he desired her. That he found her beautiful. Emboldened, she raised her hands to the front clasp of her bra and opened it, freeing her breasts for his pleasure.

"Beautiful. Touch yourself. Roll your nipples between your fingers. Tell me what having me look at you does to your body...your mind." Sam's deep voice aroused her, sending waves of desire flowing over her, making her wet even though he hadn't touched her.

His gaze seared her as surely as the noonday sun would scorch her cool skin. She wanted to mesmerize him, make him take her as no one had for centuries. She longed for him not only to take her body but to capture her will and make it his own.

In slow motion she brought her hands to her breasts as he'd ordered. She stroked them and pinched the nipples until they stood in rigid peaks. Her flesh heated, and she longed to beg for the warm wetness of his mouth, the bite of mortal teeth.

"Talk to me, Alina. Tell me what you want. Remember, sweetheart, I can't read *your* mind."

"I want you. Only you. I'm wet for you...so wet." She slid her hands down her body, deliberately enticing him, enjoying the power of her own surrender when she hooked her fingers into lace bikini panties, lowering them slowly, baring herself completely to his appreciative gaze. "Take me, please."

"I'll take you, don't doubt that. In my own time, though." Sam grinned, a feral expression on his handsome face. "Sit on the edge of the bed and spread yourself for me."

As used as she was to being the one giving orders, Alina didn't think twice about complying with his request. His power was as potent as his cock, his command as sure as that of the most venerable vampire of her acquaintance. "Look at me." She couldn't stop trembling, but she managed to meet her lover's fiery gaze. "I like seeing how your cunt weeps for me. How its lips glisten with invitation." He bent, his hot breath scorching her mound when he tongued her swollen clit.

For as long as she could she stayed still, savoring the sensation of him licking her, nibbling her there. But she wanted more. Her centuries-old history of ruling males overcame her need to submit, and she threaded her fingers through his crisp salt-and-pepper curls to draw him closer, urge him to tongue her harder, give her the release her body craved.

He pulled away, his fingers surrounding her wrists in a steely grip and drawing her arms above her head, his action as clear an indication as anything he might have said to command her obedience. "Though you rule your people, I rule your body. It appears you need reminding. Don't move." Standing, his muscles rippling, he strode to a Louis XIV-style chest and snatched open a drawer.

Her cunt clenched. Her skin tingled. She clamped down on her lips to hold back the plea that threatened to pour from her, a plea for him to fuck her now, take over her body the way he'd conquered her mind and soul.

Neckties. A fistful of them dangled from his hand, their jewel tones a brilliant beacon to her gaze as he crossed the room, his sensual lips glistening with her own juices. Almost as though he'd just fed...

But no. His body heat and the ragged sound of his breathing as he secured her wrists in silk and bound them to opposite bedposts reminded Alina of his mortality. Of the temporary nature of their liaison.

It might have been temporary, but it felt so very real. The almost painful roughness of his fingers against her tender skin, the soft bonds that secured her for his pleasure brought her back to the here and now — and the anticipation of surrender...and fulfillment.

Alina. Her name echoed softly in the corners of Sam's mind. Otherworldly beauty, ageless and timeless, lay before him in a pose of total submission. Surrender. Her eyes, cool and regal to the world, flashed emerald fire — for him. Fire that fueled his own raging lust and more.

Oh, yeah. His lover might rule over a vampire country, but tonight he'd rule over her. He grasped her hips, brought her closer to the edge of the bed until her arms lay at perfect ninety degree angles to her lush body. Then he lifted her legs, bent them at the knees and secured her ankles to her wrists with more of the ties.

Seeing her there on his bed, hands bound to the bedposts, her slender legs spread wide, had him primed to take her. Her hairless labia glistened, the rigid button of her clit beckoned him...and her tight pink anus reminded him he wanted to sample that hole too. Soon. He bent, unable to resist tasting her dewy cunt, ringing her anus with his tongue.

God but he loved that nakedness. The satiny smoothness he was certain didn't come from shaving. No razor could have left her entire body so soft and kissable.

He stood, holding her gaze as he stripped off the rest of his clothes, revealing a body that wasn't perfect but thankfully hadn't been unduly ravaged by the inevitable ticking off of time. His balls tightened when her tongue darted out and she moistened her soft pink lips, the dainty flash of her fangs no longer alarming him.

"I command you not to feast on me," he said before taking those lips and running his tongue along the front of her teeth.

She laughed, but when he slid his lips along her satiny skin, nibbling his way to one tight pink nipple, that tinkling sound morphed into a soft moan. It was the neediest sound he'd ever heard. He flailed the rigid nub with his tongue before moving lower, across the flat expanse of her belly to her satin-smooth mound. The impudent nub of her clit protruded, seeming to beg silently for the rasp of his teeth, the stimulation of his tongue.

Knowing that with her vampire powers she could break the loose bonds that held her any time, but that she chose to lie here enslaved at his command, got Sam even harder, hotter. More determined to take her higher, show her more than the faceless vampires and mortals in her ageless past. He stroked along the curves of her body, warming her cool flesh.

"Beautiful." He bent his head, rubbed his beard-roughened cheek against her mound, inhaled her musk. The lift of her hips brought him closer to her prize. Hell, he was only a man. Resistance wasn't an option.

When he sucked her clit between his teeth it swelled and hardened more. So did his cock. He spread her outer lips, found her warm and wet and waiting when he slid a finger within the silken folds. God but he wanted to plunge inside her now, feel all that slick, tight warmth around his aching cock. He sucked her harder, eliciting little moans of pleasure that spurred him on.

"Yes, oh yes, please don't stop." The plaintive tone in her voice had Sam getting even hotter, knowing she was begging him to give her pleasure. In her passion she sounded not like the vampire queen but more like a woman loving his mastery, her own submission. He wet a finger with her cunt juices and used it to tease and circle the entryway to her rear passage. "Oh."

That single breathlessly uttered word held a world of surprise. He gave her clit one last nibble. Then he blew on it, watching her pale flesh tremble when he drew away. "We will do that too, love—later." Why hadn't he trimmed his nails this morning? He wasn't about to hurt her sensitive anal tissue by probing her now, when he didn't have a glove or a condom handy. "Right now I have to fuck you."

"Oh, yesss."

Sam knelt between Alina's legs and rubbed his cock head along her slit before plunging up to his balls into her warm, wet sheath. "Squeeze me," he rasped, nearly overcome when she did by her quick, unquestioning cooperation as well as by the pressure of tightening flesh around his cock. She lifted her hips, wanting…

Wanting him. The knowledge enflamed him. He wasn't going to last long. Bending over her, he took one of her nipples in his mouth and suckled. Slow. He had to go slow, make her come as she'd never come before. Give her what she so obviously needed. His muscles tensed with the need to pound into her, fuck her, claim her. Still, he withdrew almost completely and sank back into her slowly, deliberately. Had to fuel her flames.

She raised her hips to meet his thrusts, each time with more force, more demand. She grew hotter, wetter. He was so hard now he was about to burst. Stretching out above her, he took her lips, fucked her mouth with his tongue. He felt the rasp of her fangs when they grazed his lip. Her tongue darted out to taste the salty drop of blood that flowed.

For a moment he pulled back, stilled his hips. "I told you I don't want to provide your next meal. Don't make me stop and get out my belt." He made the admonishment as stern as he could, because admitting the streak of fear that had momentarily paralyzed him wasn't an option.

Nor was letting her know his first reaction, not when he didn't understand it himself. He understood the fear, that was easy. No mortal could fail to worry a little that his vampire lover might unleash the predatory side of her nature, feeding on his body. His blood. Oddly, the thought of feeding her, providing her sustenance, called to the Dominant in him. His balls tightened and his cock throbbed against her cunt when he imagined holding her head to his throat as he pounded into her. Had he lost his mind?

She misread his hesitation. "Do not fear, love. I can control my need for sustenance, but not my carnal need for you."

He gripped her face, his thumbs brushing her fangs. He watched her eyes darken in response. "Maybe it's you who needs to fear me, vampire."

"Oh, yesss," she hissed when he slammed into her again—hard this time. He fucked her harder. Faster. The slapping sound of flesh on wet flesh when he went in, of her flesh sucking his when he withdrew had him crazy. He had to come.

"Come now. Come for me." If she didn't, it would be too late.

Her cunt tightened around his cock. Her mouth went slack. He stared into her striking green eyes and saw fire there. Her scream of pleasure stole the last of his control, and he let go, his cock jerking as each hot spurt shot out into her convulsing sheath.

* * * * *

"Thank you, my love." Alina stretched when Sam loosened her bonds and pulled her to her feet. The rough feel of his big hands on her, the knowledge that he'd claimed her surged through her body, made her want to throw her arms around him as though she were a young girl with no worries other than how best to please her master. If only the specter of Reynard weren't hanging over her...reminding her she commanded the clansmen she had dispatched to destroy him, that if it weren't for her none of them would have been at risk. The men of her clan had made it clear such feelings were nonsense. Stefan had bluntly told her that she wasn't responsible for the evil of Reynard—that only Reynard could answer for that. But when she thought of the possibility of losing more of her clansmen...Stefan, Alex...Claude...those who'd already been lost...

"My pleasure. Come, I want to see you in moonlight, feast on every inch of your beauty." Sam hesitated, as if he sensed her concern. "No mortal would dare bother us in the courtyard."

"I know. And Philippe and Jacques are never far away." Not that the eight-foot, jasmine-draped brick walls would stop a determined killer vampire, but... When she saw his jaw flex, she put her hand up, not needing her ability to read minds in order to understand his reaction. "Just think. Having them out there means you can focus entirely on commanding your slave to serve your pleasure."

"Do they…watch?"

She lifted a shoulder, her expression deliberately teasing. "I'm sure they do, sometimes. Does that bother you?"

"Of course not. Does it please you to imagine your kinsmen watching a mortal pleasuring their queen?"

Sam answered quickly. Too quickly. Like most mortals she'd met, Alina imagined he might balk at joining one of the vampire orgies her clansmen enjoyed from time to time. "Do you not take part in group scenes at your club, my darling?"

"I have." He had a shamefaced look when she gazed up at him. "But I prefer my ménages not to be quite as spontaneous as just dropping in and watching me taking my lover."

"All right. Philippe and Jacques are more interested in each other than in taking voyeurs' pleasure from our love play." The two would certainly enjoy watching Sam, fantasizing about him joining them, but somehow Alina didn't think knowing that would reassure her gorgeous, very masculine lover. "Besides, I would feel another vampire's presence. And my clansmen would tell me immediately if Louis Reynard should venture from his lair. Please. For now, I am your loving slave." Alina squeezed Sam's hand and forced back more serious concerns.

"That's what I wanted to hear." Firmly yet gently, Sam led her through the French doors. Warm moist air kept her from shivering, and feeling his body heat behind her lent a sense of safety. A crescent moon hung in the deep-blue night sky dappled with ageless stars.

Alina dug her toes into the moss growing between stones of a pathway made smooth by time and the elements. Sighing, she leaned against Sam's broad chest, inhaled the fragrance of gardenias and the jasmine that climbed the walls, its tendrils tumbling over the top as if overburdened by an abundance of sweet white flowers. "You have a beautiful home, Sam."

"It's more house than I need, but I'm glad I've resisted selling it. Julie would have been heartbroken if we couldn't have celebrated her wedding here." He sat on a wrought iron bench and pulled her onto his lap. "And I wouldn't have had the chance to be with you like this."

"Surely you entertain customers here from time to time." It would be a shame if he didn't make use of a home that seemed to epitomize the charm of New Orleans.

"I haven't, not since Katrina hit. My importing company's warehouses were over in the Ninth Ward. After the levees broke, they were twenty feet underwater. Insurance covered most of my losses—I'm not complaining, I got off much better than the poor people who lived down there—but I haven't rebuilt them. Probably won't. Hindsight tells me it was lousy judgment that made me buy land that by all rights should have been underwater. Besides, I've made enough to keep me going the rest of my life. Starting the business over from scratch doesn't seem like all that great an idea. At least not here."

"I don't understand. Your warehouses flooded during the storm, but this house did not?" Alina glanced about, saw no evidence of damage.

"No. This part of New Orleans is several feet above sea level. We were without power for a while, and we lost a few trees and a roof here and there. But there was no significant damage from the storm, and more important, no flooding. The problem that made me seriously consider selling was looting. Can't say I blame the looters all that much, particularly the ones who were only looking for food and shelter."

Her first impression had been correct. This was a good man. Alina laid her head on his shoulder while she ran her fingers through the soft hair on his chest, finding a nipple and circling it with the tip of one fingernail. "As you told Julie at the wedding, you could do your business anywhere. But yes, I know. You love it here, just as I love Paris."

"I can't deny that. I was born and raised in New Orleans. Got married, had Julie, made a success of my business." His breathing slowed, and he tunneled a hand into her hair, holding her closer. "You know, love, no woman's attracted me the way you do, not since Julie's mother died." *It's been twenty-five years now. Over half my life.*

Twenty-five years. Forever for a mortal, yet a mere drop in time for a vampire. For her. Still his words rang with sincerity, made Alina wish for more than this short interlude with Sam. "I am glad." His heart beat strongly beneath her ear, its rhythmic pattern underscoring the differences between them. He stroked her arm, his work-hardened fingers abrading her skin, heating her passion and raising her curiosity. "How is it that a man who works with his mind has calluses on his hands?"

"I work out with weights to keep in shape. Have for years. I don't usually bother with putting on gloves before I start lifting."

"I like the roughness. It stirs my senses." Everything about him stirred her, made her want to keep him. But no. Sam loved his life, his business, the many friends who had come to help him celebrate his daughter's marriage. She had no business even fantasizing over a life together—a life of eternal surrender for her, eternal life in her world for him.

Chapter Three

ಞ

"Have you spoken with Louis, obtained his approval for your scheme?"

Wim smiled at the clan elder, a timid soul to his way of thinking. "I do not need his approval, only yours." Gesturing toward all the elders in the room, he included not only the man who'd spoken but all the members of the Council. "You do realize, of course, the losses our clan has suffered because of our leader's obsession with destroying the d'Argent queen. Of him playing a cat-and-mouse game with her by seeking out and killing her mortal look-alikes as a lead-in to her own destruction."

Another old vampire spoke, his voice heavy with the accent of an eastern European. A crony of Louis, Wim imagined. "We could hardly have missed noticing the economic impact. Still, Louis has been the leader of Clan Reynard since long before you were turned...before you were born, young one. I believe your ambition overreaches reason."

"Ambition? I merely want our clan to prosper. I wish for Louis to recover, once again to be the leader he was before he became fixated with the idea of tormenting and ultimately destroying Alina d'Argent. I propose we see to her destruction now, while Louis recovers from his wounds." Wim paused, gauging the expressions on the elders' faces. "That way, we will have accomplished what he sought, and he will have no reason to continue ignoring clan business by further pursuing his vendetta against mortal women—or the remaining ones of the d'Argent clan."

The timid elder who had wanted assurance that Wim had Louis' approval cleared his throat. Then he looked Wim in the eye and spoke. "What makes you think you can succeed where Louis has failed?"

Yes! At least Wim had planted the seed of possibility in one elder's mind. Now was not the time to remind him Louis had never targeted Alina directly. "Timing. As we speak, the d'Argent queen is enjoying a holiday in New Orleans with the father of Stefan d'Argent's bride. A mortal. Her usual contingent of bodyguards has dwindled to two, and they must watch her surreptitiously as she has ordered them to keep their distance. The mortal who is fucking her can be no match for even the weakest among us."

"What about Stefan d'Argent? And the other two who came very close to destroying our leader?" The Reynard elder with the eastern European accent rubbed his chin, as though considering the feasibility of what Wim had just proposed. "Are they not always within shouting distance of their queen?"

Wim stood and strode over to the flattened globe where Louis had marked each of his kills. He pointed toward a point on the Normandy coast. "Stefan and his bride are honeymooning here, in his ancestral castle. Alexandre is sampling Paris nightlife, as is his habit when not on assignment. According to my spies, Claude is honeymooning with his own bride in Paris while he recovers from his wounds.

"My friends, the time is ripe. I have seen with my own eyes how Alina's attentions are focused on the mortal, Sam Quill. She must believe herself safe for the moment, since Louis is temporarily incapacitated. If she had doubts, she would not have ordered her bodyguards to give her space. Give me your leave, and I will rid the earth of the d'Argent queen. Handed her destruction as *fait accompli*, Louis will have no choice but to cease this blood feud and get back to the business of making Clan Reynard profitable once more."

Wim sat back and watched the elders counsel among themselves. The longer they discussed his plan, the more confident he felt that they'd approve it. After all, they were all businessmen of sorts, and Louis had been neglecting clan business for too long while pursuing his senseless quest. When the eldest of the elders cleared his throat, Wim straightened and listened.

"We will not stop you from destroying the d'Argent queen. However, we will not give permission, either. This deed will be on your shoulders."

So cowards that they were, they would not stop him — but they would not stand behind him, either. Wim didn't care. Clan Reynard was long overdue for new leadership. Not only Louis but the elders as well. "Have it as you will. There is no need for us to discuss this further. I will apprise you all when the job is done." Wim stood, nodded to the elders around the table, and left the room. He'd do what needed doing, but first...

A wave of nostalgia came over him, compelled him to walk down the rutted roadway, toward the small community the Reynard clan called home. For a moment Wim paused before the thatched-roof hut where his blood mother had lived and died. How would she have dealt with the d'Argents? His throat suddenly became itchy when he thought of how the old vampire had cared for him, a mortal child turned vampire...and of the torture Louis had put her through after she'd tried and failed to conjure up a way for Louis to seduce Alina. Torture Wim had tried and failed to prevent.

The last time he'd been here, she'd been carried, bones broken, flesh tortured, to the clearing in front of the elders' council, where her fellow vampires had given her the merciful ending Louis had denied her. Staked in the sun, heart carved away, she had turned to ash before Wim's eyes.

Poised to escape that hideous, most recent memory yet compelled to go inside and meet it head-on, Wim stepped into the room where he'd grown up at the vampire healer's knee. His gaze settled on her supply of potions, specifically on a dusty amber vial. Her voice rang in his ears, as though he were still a child and she were still alive. *You must never touch that, child, for it contains a sleeping potion. A mere drop will kill a mortal instantly, and it can make a vampire sleep for days or weeks.* Hesitating for only a moment, Wim lifted the vial, checked the lid, and tucked it into his shirt pocket.

That evening Wim fed on an unsuspecting farm girl he found milking cows in a barn near the Flemish headquarters of Clan Reynard. Once he had drained her, he left her dead body where it had fallen. Satiated for the moment, he took to the air, propelling himself halfway around the world. After an uneventful journey, he landed atop a recently rebuilt levee overlooking New Orleans just as the sun was beginning to rise over the Mississippi River delta.

Blinking at the bright light that was his constant enemy, he set out to find a lair in which to pass the day. Tonight he would take on the d'Argent queen and destroy her.

* * * * *

Alina rolled over in bed, ducking under a pillow when Sam pulled back the curtain and let sunlight into the room. Why couldn't this man—the perfect Dom who wouldn't quit until he'd wrung the last bit of sexual pleasure from her—have been more considerate about her aversion to the morning light?

Because he's mortal, idiot. Unlike you, he thrives on sunshine. Which was why she shouldn't let herself fall in love, why the relationship between them had to be strictly temporary. Unless…

Unless she used her vampire seduction, made him beg her to change him, take him into her world. Her fangs itched and began to elongate. Suddenly she was ravenous. Starving for mortal blood. His blood. He'd be a made vampire, yes, but the d'Argents possessed the ancient knowledge of how to preserve his virility—his ability to pleasure her.

She tried to block the pangs of hunger. Hunger she'd assuaged for centuries from delicate crystal stemware…never directly from the source. Once more she reminded herself her lover wouldn't want to move into the shadows. He thrived on heat and light from the sultry New Orleans sun. More to the point, her powerful Dom wouldn't tolerate living in a woman's shadow—even if that woman were queen of a powerful vampire clan.

Sam was a born leader. Never a consort. If Alina took him as a mate, a consort would be what he would have to be, and she couldn't imagine him filling that role of his own accord. She tamped down this hunger…this compulsion she had never experienced before to use her seductive power for the purpose of luring a mortal into her vampire world. She dared not do it now.

Their liaison was a thing of the moment, a beautiful thing to revel in while it lasted, but not to extend into the future. Not even in her fantasies. Alina blinked back tears. Over the centuries she'd learned not to agonize over situations she couldn't—or wouldn't—change. She pasted on a smile and held out her arms to Sam. "Would my master care to take me to his club today?"

He bent and took her lips, obviously unaware how close he'd come to becoming something she knew he would hate to be. The taste of him was bittersweet, yet it fed her need. Her need to be taken, swept away from her world where the madness of Louis Reynard had to dictate her every action. "I wish to bring more pleasure here to you, *chérie*."

What did he mean? Alina pulled back enough to look into Sam's slate-gray eyes. *A ménage. Here, in my bed. Two mortals bringing you pleasure…* His thoughts came through crystal clear, made her nipples tingle and her pussy swell with anticipation. Oh, yes. If only they could both be Sam. "Tonight?"

"Tonight. Meanwhile, sleep well. I have things I must arrange, and I want at least some of what I'm planning to be a surprise, which I know won't happen as long as I'm here and you're reading my mind."

She smiled. No need to let him know she could divine his thoughts whether or not she could see him. No need to do anything now but close her eyes…sleep…dream.

* * * * *

Of home. Of a time long ago before her grandfather's destruction when she'd been just five hundred years old and free, when she'd joined her cousins in celebration of their uncle's birth. Tragedy hadn't touched their clan for years…and it had been much too joyful a night to fret about the tyrant Hitler and the storm he had begun to foment in neighboring Germany. Restless and growing aroused at the memory, Alina shifted against the covers, remembering the last time she and her cousins had performed the ritual celebration of birth to lend an infant vampire strength and power.

Recalling past rituals couldn't fail to rouse her body, already maintaining a low thrum of erotic heat just from remembering last night's sex with Sam, inhaling the smell of his body still on the sheets surrounding her. They performed a similar ritual more frequently to free a newly made vampire male to mate again as he had when he was mortal. When she thought of those rituals, though, the newly made vampire looked disturbingly like Sam, so she focused instead on the vampire ceremony that accompanied an infant vampire's birth.

"Come, cousin, let us celebrate the birth of our new uncle, Claude," Alexandre coaxed, his green eyes glittering with promise of vampire passion, his massive fist wrapped around a slim glass double dildo. "Stefan, join us."

Stefan hesitated just for a moment, before shedding the air of melancholy that had surrounded him since he'd accidentally destroyed the mortal he'd planned to wed. The grief in his expression faded, replaced by a look of carnal anticipation.

Instinctively Alina bared her throat for her cousins, welcomed the tickle of a chilly wind blowing through the arrow slits of the d'Argent's ancestral castle, damp and dreary on its perch above the English Channel despite a roaring fire that crackled in a massive fireplace. Candles flickered in elaborate wall sconces, casting golden shadows across her cousins' dark hair. Flames caught flecks of precious minerals buried in age-darkened stone of the massive hearth. A perfect setting, one that tied the present to their shared past. The way their passions flowed together in celebration of the infant Claude's birth heightened Alina's anticipation. In unison, like dancers at the cabaret, they shed their clothes and with them the cloak of humanity that let them walk freely with mortals. Alina welcomed the wet heat that was building between her legs, the tingling sensations playing along her nipples.

They moved together, so close she felt two accelerating heartbeats, the strength of two massive erections. Alex's sharp fangs pierced her throat first, the sensation mesmerizing, arousing. When Stefan duplicated the action on her other side, she experienced all his passion — and all the grief he wore with such determination.

A feeling of euphoria came over her. Senses heightened, she closed her eyes and saw...two beautiful males, naked in their perfection. Four hands, one holding the cool glass dildo, their motions smooth and sure, stroked her skin, heated it despite the darkness and chill of the night. Reaching down, she stroked both their cocks, rolled both sets of testicles against her palms. Anticipating them piercing her body. Claiming her aching orifices, stretching them and filling the emptiness there.

Two perfect male organs indistinguishable in the dark but for the guiche-piercing jewelry Alex wore in commemoration of a night of tantric sex magic he'd enjoyed not long ago in Paris. The egotistical youngster had told her about it, made her seethe with envy because she'd been away the evening the d'Argents had hosted a friendly vampire clan and engaged in a ritualistic orgy. "Must you continually remind us, Alex, of your prowess?" She caught the gold ring on a fingertip and gave it a small tug.

Alex's cock swelled more, grew harder against her thigh at the stimulation. Stefan's did as well when he completed the tantric circle by clasping her and Alex, drawing them closer until their two cocks touched as they probed her belly. As her two young cousins sipped her blood, she felt her fangs extend, brush against her lower lip. Apparently satiated, the two males raised their heads, bared their own throats as her blood dripped from their extended fangs. "Sheath us," Alex ordered, his dominant tone belying the fact he was barely three hundred years old. A mere child in vampire years.

When she'd done his bidding and rolled the thin latex condoms Stefan handed her over their erections, he bared his throat. "Take us now."

Alina drank first from Stefan, for he was the older by more than two hundred years. Then she sank her fangs into Alex's delectable young throat while Stefan guided them all to the fur rug before the hearth. She withdrew her fangs from Alex's throat when she felt the thick fur tickling her knees, beckoning her to lie down and let her vampire lovers pleasure her.

Not an inch of her skin escaped the stimulation of Stefan's hands or Alex's eager mouth. She guided Stefan's pulsating cock to her lips as soon as her fangs retracted fully, sampled the drop of lubrication at its rounded tip while Alex flailed her clit with his agile tongue and dipped into her swollen cunt with two fingers. He spread her juices along her slit, the sensitive opening to her anus. Her heart, usually so still she didn't notice its slow beat, pounded against her chest.

She skimmed her fingers along Stefan's hard-muscled chest, enjoying the feel of satin-smooth skin over bone and sinew, the slow pounding of his heart from within him. They rolled, taking her to her side, forming a sensual triangle. Mouth to cock, cock to mouth, mouth to cunt, they lay on their sides, legs raised, their sexes open for the heat of each other's lips and tongues. Pressure built in Alina's cunt, and she grew wetter and more swollen. Ready to take both massive cocks whenever they chose to claim her. Stefan's cock swelled even more as she took him deep down her throat. From the way Alex redoubled his licking and sucking and stabbing his tongue up her cunt in imitation of the act that was to come, she imagined Stefan was swallowing Alex's cock, toying with his guiche ring as he ringed the other man's anus and stroked his velvet-soft scrotum.

Pleasure exploded through Alina's body. It was time. Stefan lay on the fur, legs spread. Alina knelt and inserted one end of the double dildo in his ass. Alex slid into place, legs beneath his cousin's. Alina fed the other end of the dildo into Alex's anus as he slid in until his ass lay flush with Stefan's. Not an inch of the dildo was visible now. Two perfect cocks, jutting forward only inches apart, made Alina's mouth water, her pussy cream. She bent, wet first one cock then the other, then straddled them and took both cocks, one up her cunt, the other up her own rear entrance. The circle of possession was complete. Three d'Argent vampires possessing, being possessed, burning with the fire of sexual arousal, striving for the ultimate pleasure. She rose and fell like the waves against the shore, milking them with strong inner muscles, coaxing out their cries of pleasure, their hot seed. Her climax hovered just out of reach, waiting...

Then it came along with theirs, a perfect vampire ritual. Unanimous pleasure. Commitment to each other and the clan, though not the kind of sexual commitment that would last forever. Alina knew that, knew that in time they'd all take their lovers, mortal or immortal. But the vampire bond they'd forged would last and strengthen in many ways.

The picture in her mind faded, replaced with the face and body of the man who had left her in his bed to sleep. Sam. Her mortal lover who had brought back sensual memories when he contemplated a ménage. Who had made her dream of the sensual ritual of her clan, performed whenever a new d'Argent child was born...and within hours after a d'Argent female had changed a mortal to be her mate, if her desire was for that mate to retain his sexual abilities. Alina blinked once when she opened her eyes and saw the sun sinking, a great ball of orange on the western horizon. Not bothering to dress, she wrapped the top sheet around her naked body and waited. Anticipated...

* * * * *

Sam strode through the entryway to the BDSM club he'd rarely visited since the storm. Though everything inside looked as it had before Katrina, he sensed a subtle difference.

An aura of desertion, of gloom. Good thing he'd decided not to bring Alina here. She projected a sense of *joie de vivre* he'd have considered incongruous for a vampire before meeting his new son-in-law and the others of the d'Argent clan. He loved her smile, the incredible softness of her voice and the pale beauty of her alabaster skin. The emerald fire in her eyes when he'd aroused her.

Yeah, he'd do anything to see Alina smile. To hear her shout out her pleasure under his touch. He scanned the main playroom, considering then discarding possible partners to invite to the very private *ménage a trois* he'd hinted about to his beautiful, submissive vampire.

Beau Forte wouldn't do. The young club Dom with an angel face and a pedigree that went back to when Louisiana belonged to France possessed a streak of sadism. Sam had no intention of letting Beau practice on the woman he loved.

Loved? What the hell? He'd loved Madeleine, no one else except their daughter, and what he felt for Julie was a father's affection. Not this overwhelming feeling that encompassed not just sex but affection. This...this sense Alina was the other half of his being.

He didn't understand why, but Sam guessed he'd fallen head over heels in love, for what good that might do him. Alina belonged in Paris, in the vampire world she ruled. Despite the fact his business was in shambles and much of the city still lay in ruins, his home was here. Nodding a greeting to Beau, Sam spotted another of the club Doms, Chad Lalanne. At the moment the buff Cajun was occupied with one of the club submissives, licking her pussy while she lay spread-eagled across a padded sawhorse.

"It's been too long, Sam. Shall I book you with Tricia? She's running a little late today, but she should be on the floor in a few minutes." Andre, the hulking black manager who kept the club members in line, nodded toward the naked sub as she came through the swinging door from the women's dressing room. "There she is now."

"I don't think so, thanks. I'm waiting to talk with Chad." Sam's cock rose—apparently it was only his brain that had no desire for sex with anybody but Alina—as Tricia came his way, eyes downcast as a proper sub's should be. Her golden skin suddenly seemed too dark, her black hair too harsh. Contrasting the sub he'd enjoyed in past BDSM scenes with the woman who waited for him in his bed, he quickly lost whatever interest his hormones had aroused.

"Setting up a ménage?" Andre shot a knowing glance toward Chad. "Good choice if you're more interested in giving your sub more pleasure than pain."

"I am." Suddenly the sight of Beau using a metal-tipped flogger on his partner turned Sam's stomach. He only wished Alina were his, in truth. To love, pleasure and protect for the rest of his life—a period of a few decades at best, while her own future on earth was endless. God, but he'd flat out gone insane.

He didn't want to watch another man pleasuring her, a scenario he'd enjoyed many times here at the club with women who'd caught his passion but never his emotions. He wanted Alina all to himself. "No. I was, but I think I'll pass."

Andre laughed then sobered when he looked Sam in the eye. "Wedding bells, Sam? Sounds to me like you've been bit by the old love bug."

Bitten? Andre couldn't have known how aptly he described Sam's feelings. "Not likely, my friend." Though he kept his tone light, he couldn't help wondering if Alina would want to change him…and how he'd answer her if she brought the subject up. "I think I'll pay a visit to the toy store. See what I can find to liven up our sex games."

A few minutes later, Sam left the club with a bag full of toys. Thinking of the ways he'd soon make Alina scream with pleasure had him distracted—but not so much so that he missed noticing the young Reynard vampire, the same one Alina had pointed out the day before when he'd been lurking across Decatur Street from the *Café du Monde*.

How could he have missed the creep? Sam's skin crawled under the man's intent scrutiny. He turned, looked Reynard in the eye, his fingers curled into his palms so hard the short nails bit into his calloused flesh. He took a step closer then stopped.

Vampires don't fight fair, Sam. Leave it alone. Alina's voice rang in Sam's ears, made him stop, look around. There. He saw Philippe and Jacques, the two burly looking d'Argent vampires who'd stayed on in New Orleans after Julie's wedding. Both had Reynard in their respective sights, though they made no move to take him out.

One of them—they looked so much alike that Sam couldn't tell which was which—trotted over to Sam and stuck out his hand. "We won't let the bastard get near Alina. You go on, do whatever it is you're doing."

"All right." Damn it, Alina shouldn't have needed bodyguards. Not while she was under his roof. Sam should have been able to protect her from all comers. He had no doubt he could best most mortals, but against Alina's kind he apparently was impotent.

He'd never questioned his ability to protect the woman he was with, keep her safe and watch over her. In some ways, it was part of what he could offer, something instinctual as much as the ability to deliver pleasure. Knowing he couldn't offer Alina his protection, part of the package of his Dominance, made him uncomfortable. Almost as uncomfortable as knowing she didn't expect him to. Damn it, he might not be as strong as a vampire. He couldn't fucking fly or look into his enemy's head and know what he was thinking.

But he could fight. He had resources. Fighting was more than brawn, just as sex was more than shoving a cock into a willing pussy. Her enemies wouldn't find him defenseless if they came after her. He thought of the ceremonial dagger—the one he'd tucked away in case the silver bothered her—and recalled the old voodoo priestess who'd given it to him after he'd saved her from two street thugs in the Quarter.

Yeah, he wasn't completely impotent when it came to protecting her. That made him feel better. At least impotency wasn't a problem when she was in his bed. His cock twitched when he pictured Alina, her cunt glistening with lubrication, her green eyes dark with passion.

Chapter Four

෨

A crescent moon hung low in the sky as though it were dropping toward Earth this sultry late spring evening. The smell of gardenias filled Alina's nostrils when she threw open the French doors in Sam's bedroom. Moisture saturated the air, bathing her skin in evening dew. Strange how everything about this place—about Sam—heightened her senses, made her feel young. Hang the fact she could personally recall events Sam knew about only from his history lessons.

I want you now. Naked. I want to see you in the courtyard, your beautiful body lit by a Creole moon. She smiled. Her lover was testing out her telepathic powers, seeing if she could hear him. His command rang clearly in her head with an intensity so strong she could have heard him a world away, but her usually slow heartbeat quickened with the knowledge that he wasn't far away. And he was coming quickly, so quickly she didn't hesitate to do his bidding.

She dropped the sheet she'd wrapped around her like a toga, laughing aloud at her comparison of the fine bed linen with a garment from one of the few civilizations older than herself. Slowly, as Sam had commanded, she stepped out into the courtyard, her keen night vision allowing her to admire the graceful wrought iron-topped walls and arches draped with nature's own cloak of jasmine. She plucked one of the rich red hibiscus blossoms from a bush still ragged-looking now, almost a year after the storm that had laid waste to much of New Orleans. *A bit of beauty growing from the decimation*, she thought as she tucked the flower behind her ear.

Sam made her feel like a woman. He seduced her by the strength of his own volition, not by the mirage of desire conjured by her own vampiric seduction. *How will I ever be able to let him go?*

She sensed his presence, spied a table set for two, its brilliant white lace tablecloth a beacon in the moonlight. Fat candles flickered in a breeze so slight it caressed her naked breasts like a very careful lover. The romantic setting, an occasional caress of the wind against her cheek, the brush of her hair against her own bare shoulders seduced her, not with one bold stroke but with a subtle harmony of small stimulants blended into a powerful aphrodisiac.

As she approached the table, the spicy smell of crawfish jambalaya, a spicy Louisiana specialty she dared not sample, tickled her nostrils. A steaming plate of the fragrant dish sat at one place setting. At the other was a single blown-glass wineglass. Only two? She'd been so sure he'd been planning a ménage.

It didn't matter, so long as Sam was there.

Still dressed in the khaki slacks and blue striped shirt he'd worn this morning, he emerged from the shadows, a dark green cushion in his hand. His gaze locked on hers, he laid it on the chair in front of the wineglass. "Sit here, my angel."

Angel? Seldom if ever had Alina been compared before with one of the celestial beings. She wouldn't challenge her mortal lover, though. Not now, when every fiber of her being longed to have him take her, claim her. In slow motion she moved to obey his softly spoken order.

The crushed velvet cushion brushed her thighs, her ass cheeks. So soft, it pampered her skin, reminded her Sam cherished her, would protect her as if she were his own...his beloved slave. She knew he wouldn't stand a chance against an attacking vampire, but for reasons she didn't understand, Sam made her feel safe and protected, her heart guarded from worry, surrounded by his love. She knew he'd give his life to protect her, which made her feel safe in a way she'd never before experienced. Perhaps that was what it meant to be truly loved.

He traced a path along first one of her forearms then the other, catching her wrists and shackling them to the wrought iron chair arms with padded manacles. "Spread your legs for me," he ordered once he had her hands secured.

His gray gaze scorched her flesh when she did his bidding. Her juices began to flow, the female musk tickling her nostrils as it dampened her slit. The touch of his fingertips in the slick lubrication had her muscles clenching...releasing...her cunt contracting with sheer animal lust. When he inserted a finger then withdrew it, her usually slow heartbeat pounded against her chest. Her skin warmed, a flush of heat that fed her already raging arousal.

He raised his head, met her gaze. "I saw your bodyguards this afternoon. They have the Reynard bastard in their sights, so I command you not to concern yourself with him. Concentrate instead on the pleasure a mere mortal can give you. Meanwhile, allow me to feed you."

Alina caught the undertone of resentment in Sam's voice and understood his frustration at his own impotence against her enemy, but not her own compulsion to put him at ease. "I feel safe with you, Sam, in ways I've never felt safe before."

"Don't patronize me. Just do as I command." He held a finger up to her lips, as though to take away the sting of his words.

She smiled up at him. "All right, *mon cher*. Your slightest wish is my command...tonight."

"Then drink." Sam brought a fine crystal wineglass to her lips, its contents a dark, rich red. Strong. Sweet with just a tinge of metallic bite that told her it had been freshly drawn.

His deep, melodic drawl mesmerized her as she did his bidding, savored the sustenance and her lover's attention. Then she noticed the stark white bandage on his left wrist. Alina froze a moment then reached out an unsteady hand to lay it over the bandage. "You..." *offered your blood for me.* "You didn't have to—"

"I wanted to give you part of me, just as I want to give you all the pleasure at my command."

She looked up at him. "Is there any wonder I feel safe with you, Sam Quill? You make me feel you'd lay the world at my feet if you could."

As he reached out and touched her face, she heard his thoughts. I *wish I could keep you forever, love you. I wish you were mortal*…

Alina quickly slammed the door shut on Sam's thoughts. Some things, it was better not to know. Especially when those emotions echoed loudly in her own mind. Just as it was better not to long for things beyond one's reach. She took another sip from her glass then smiled up at him. "Thank you, *mon cher*."

"And I thank you, for bringing me the sort of joy I've been missing for so long." He knelt at her feet, his head tilted back so he met her gaze. "*Mais oui*, but you are beautiful."

His oddly melodic Cajun dialect sounded beautiful yet strange coming from a man so boldly Anglo. "*Merci*."

"See how you make my cock salute you." Standing, he shed his shirt, tossing it carelessly on the brick-paved floor of the courtyard beside his shoes. Never taking his eyes off Alina, he unfastened his pants and shoved them down and off, along with the silk boxer shorts she thought looked sexier than the briefs favored by so many men.

"Oh yes." His cock rose against his belly, long and thick. She wished she weren't restrained because she wanted to sample the drop of lubrication in the eye at its plumlike head. She longed to massage his testicles that drew up high and tight in their sac as she watched. His male beauty, as yet seemingly unravaged by time, made her want to take him, change him, make him hers for all eternity so they'd grow old together…but not for many years, the fates willing.

"Yes." He reached for the wineglass, held it to her lips once more. "Drink up. Pretend you're taking it from here," he gestured toward a prominent vein in his muscular neck, "taking your sustenance from the man who loves you more than life."

Did he? Love her more than his own life? Alina silently took his offering, savored each taste in her mouth before letting the warm, rich fluid trickle down her throat. His blood. Warm, vibrant, like the man himself.

For a moment she imagined them in Paris, him at her side as she meted out justice to the other vampires of her clan. A tear that rolled down her cheek tickled her skin, as though it were trying to tell her this could never be. Illogical as it might have been because she'd wanted him to render her helpless to his emotional and sexual assault, she wished her hands were free so she could wrap them around the wineglass, feel as well as taste the essence of the man. ·

His touch as gentle as she imagined it had been when he'd handled Julie as an infant, he caught her tears on his fingertips. Absorbing her doubts, her regrets, her sadness that their love was destined to play out and die. "I command you, get rid of your tears. Focus for now on your lover. Your master."

An involuntary smile curled the corners of her lips when he withdrew the empty glass, set it on the table and came back to her, his own eyes glistening. This strong man would never allow his tears to fall...yet she sensed a depth of emotion there that eclipsed that of a virile lover's affection for the woman currently sharing his bed. "I thank you for my dinner," she said, every cell in her body tingling with anticipation for his touch.

"My pleasure."

"Are you not going to eat that luscious-looking jambalaya?" Savory-smelling steam still rose from the plate set before his chair. "You might need your strength for the night ahead."

He laughed. "I ate in the kitchen. Up until I saw you coming toward me, I'd toyed with the idea of asking a friend to join us, so I set a place for him. But I found I wanted you to myself this evening." *I've never minded sharing my lover before, but I won't share you.*

His words echoed in her head, making her dizzy. *I won't share you.* A purely mortal sentiment, but one Alina welcomed even as she feared where it might lead. "I don't wish you to share if doing so doesn't please you."

Sam moved behind her chair, laid his big hands on her shoulders, his touch light, caressing. Suffusing her body with heat and something else. The kind of love she'd sought for centuries but never found, more potent now that she sensed Sam shared those feelings…

"Everything about you pleases me. You've cast your vampire spell over me, but I can't object. I haven't felt this young, this alive, since…" *Since Madeleine died and left me when Julie was only four years old.*

Twenty-five years. A third of a human lifetime, yet a blip in time for those of her kind. Alina leaned her head back, resting it against the hard-muscled expanse of his abdomen. "I've cast no spell, Sam. It may be that some power greater than mine has destined this."

Julie stepped over to the other side. There's not any good reason I couldn't do the same. Sam slid his hands down the silken length of her arms, laid them over her manacled wrists. *Except control. I need to be in control of my lover…and there's no denying she's the power behind her clan.* "What power might that be?"

She wished she could tell him she'd relinquish her position in return for his love. But she couldn't. Not now. Soon, maybe, once Louis Reynard was returned to the Transylvanian dust from whence he'd come. Once Claude matured enough to take his rightful place as his late father's successor. Until then, Alina had to live up to her responsibilities. "The power of your God? He's mine too, you know, even though most priests would run in horror if they realized some vampires prayed to the same God they do."

"What would it be like if I—"

"You'd sleep by day and move about by night. Sustain your life with blood. Engage in the sort of vampire sex orgies you decided not to indulge in on a smaller scale tonight with me and another mortal partner. You could run your business successfully—yet have many of your mortal customers keep arm's length away for fear you might suddenly become ravenous and select them as your next meal. And Sam, if I changed you, you'd be more under my power than I am now under yours."

He toyed with the bonds that held her, as if he was imagining himself bound and helpless for her pleasure. "Even in bed?"

"Sometimes." Turning her head, she nipped the lightly furred skin of his belly. "You'd become as smooth as I am, except for your face and throat."

Sam laughed, a deep rumble she felt vibrating against her cheek. "I could deal with that. I'm not so sure about becoming the filling in a *ménage* sandwich, though." She sensed his mind churning, though, projecting silent pictures of orgies where everybody claimed all the others' orifices and vice versa—the part that seemed to make Sam shudder.

"It's our way, *mon cher*. Not so much different from your own, except we gain sexual pleasure with each other rather than with strangers at a club or dungeon. Only those of us who are incredibly fortunate find a life partner...a mate." She paused, turned her face to his, saw both intrigue and fear in eyes already dark with passion. "Like Stefan. And Claude."

"I don't know. I'm no youngster." The doubt rang out in Sam's voice as he bent and loosened her bonds. "I imagine there's no way you'd stay with me in my mortal world until..."

Until he grew old and died? "I couldn't. Before my grandfather died, he named me head of the d'Argent clan. It's a responsibility I can't shirk, and I can't pass it on to Claude until he is mature enough to rule." Alina reached up, laid a hand on Sam's broad chest as she looked into his eyes. "I couldn't bear to watch you age and die, helpless to do anything to ease your pain."

The look he gave her was one of sadness, resignation. "Then we'd best enjoy what little time we have together. Come here and let me hold you."

In slow motion she rose, stepped into his arms. She laid her head on his shoulder, felt the play of muscles there when he moved to encircle her. His heart beat strongly against her breasts, reminding her of his mortality. As though he'd willed it, soft music began to play, the distinctive sounds escaping through an open window, surrounding them in a melancholy melody. A New Orleans instrumental rendition of an old Gershwin song. "Summertime." Haunting, melodious, the song reminded Alina of other times, times when her clan hadn't lived under the constant threat that in his mad quest to destroy her, Louis Reynard would bring down mortal vengeance on the d'Argents and all vampires. "Dance with me, please."

"Relax. Let the music carry us away, just the two of us." His left hand splayed out across her lower back, his right clutched her left when she laid her right hand on his shoulder. They swayed, naked flesh to naked flesh, his hard cock searing her belly, his chest hair stimulating her nipples. As though the courtyard were an island far from civilization, she let go the tension, the fear that they were being watched, stalked.

A crescent moon winked down from a starry sky. Cicadas chirped all around them, and lightning bugs gave off bursts of golden light that illuminated fragrant gardenias and jasmine vines. Sam nuzzled her ear where she'd put the scarlet hibiscus blossom. "I hope you don't mind that I picked it," she said, her voice husky as though touched by the warmth and humidity of a New Orleans night.

"It's like you." He sounded so wistful she had to ask why.

"Both of you will stay in my life just a few days. Yet you're so vibrantly beautiful, I can't imagine never having known you." He held her tighter as the music waned. "I do mind that you can't stay, but I'll take all the time with you that I can get." His cock nudged her belly. When it did, it sent waves of need coursing through her body, making her go wet with anticipation. "I want to fuck you here, underneath the stars. Make memories that will have to last a lifetime." Sliding his hand down her arm, he clasped her backside, lifted her. "I'm going to fuck you now."

"Yesss." The imprint of his fingers on her flesh fed her arousal as he lifted her, impaled her, filled her cunt with mortal heat as he lowered her slowly, smoothly until his balls pressed against her wet slit. "Don't stop."

"Wrap your legs around me. Oh, yeah. Like that." *Feel us, baby, and tell me loving you isn't right. I dare you.*

She couldn't. Having Sam inside her felt perfect, like two halves suddenly made whole. "Fuck me, Sam." She didn't dare say what she was thinking, pour out her heart when they both knew it couldn't last. "I want to carry some memories too," she said, trying as she did to still the tears that came pouring from her eyes.

He sank onto a bench, taking her with him. For a long time he didn't move except to stroke her flesh, claim her mouth with his voracious tongue, seemingly unafraid that she might puncture him with her fangs. She clenched her inner muscles, squeezed his cock, offering herself. When he freed her lips she whispered, "Are you certain you won't come with me when I must go?"

Though she tried not to intrude on his private thoughts, they came to her almost as if he'd willed it...almost as though he shared some of her ability at thought telepathy. *I want to...can't. God, why did you send her to me?* She took in his pain, absorbed emotions as jumbled as her own.

"No." With power approaching violence, he lifted her then slammed her back down on him. Almost as if he wanted to hurt her and himself. "I don't have the mindset to become consort to a vampire queen, no matter how much I want her."

"All right. I won't ask again." Taking over and holding his rhythm, Alina fucked him hard, didn't try to hold back. When he shouted out in triumph and filled her cunt with burst after burst of hot semen, she shuddered and came. She'd never felt so full, or so empty, as she did when she slumped against Sam's chest, listening to the hard pounding of his mortal heart against her ear.

If only she could stay…but no. She'd given her promise to Alain d'Argent as he lay dying. Claude wasn't ready to take over the clan yet, but a voice inside Alina's head kept saying he would be—soon.

Not soon enough for her to follow Sam. Follow her heart. Two more days and she would leave this place where hope mingled with sadness, beauty with the lingering horror of Nature's destruction. Where she'd found love with this strong, dominant mortal. Their paths might cross again when he came to visit his daughter. It wouldn't be the same, though, for they'd fallen in love yet he wouldn't change for her…and she couldn't abandon responsibility to her clan to stay with him.

* * * * *

Darting in and out of narrow streets in the French Quarter, Wim thought he'd lost his shadows several times the last hour, only to find one or both of the d'Argent clansmen waiting for him at every turn. *Patience.* Although this cat-and-mouse game was becoming old very quickly, Wim schooled himself not to make any foolish moves.

It was fucking almost as if he were the prey, they the stalkers. A bell rang out twelve times, its sound muffled by air heavy with moisture and the mingled sweat of hordes of mortal bodies. The eerie shadows cast by street lamps should have scared the hell out of the tourists, but the idiots seemed determined to party, oblivious to the evil that might befall them under the curtain of darkness.

If he had time, he'd sip life from the throat of one of the foolish women who stared at him with horror…and apparent fascination. He didn't, though. Not seeing his nemeses, he darted through the swinging doors of a bar, determined to escape them.

The sounds of jazz music, mellow saxophones and blaring trumpets assaulted his ears. He glanced around, found a corner table. It took him only a moment to realize this was no ordinary bar — but one of the upscale vampire establishments where those of his own kind who were too timid to take nourishment direct from mortals went to get their nourishment. His d'Argent shadows appeared seconds later, taking seats at the carved antique bar and shooting him matched stares after ordering whatever it was they intended to drink.

He watched them, wished he dared try to take down both burly specimens while they quenched their thirst. Discarding that idea as foolhardy, Wim tried to relax, prepare himself for the moment he could ambush them from behind. They had to sleep sometime, though Wim had never been out when at least one of them hadn't been lurking, watching him.

"What can I get you?" A waiter, dark-haired with prominent fangs, shot Wim an expectant look.

"O Positive." Though he'd never considered the blood type of his victims, he'd overheard another customer ordering A Negative in a haughty sounding voice. He figured his taste was more plebeian, as was his wallet.

In a moment the waiter set a draft before him then disappeared with the ten-dollar bill Wim had laid down. He lifted the glass, took a sip of the vapid stuff. Damn, but he'd rather take his sustenance from the source, where he had no need to pay. He studied the menu, scoffed silently. Reynards had no need for the fancy vintages or additives this place charged dearly for — niceties that catered to d'Argents and their like. And, he added, to the local offshoots of evil African sorcerers. The Owengas of the world seemed to have congregated in New Orleans and made this bar their own. A large party of them gyrated to the beat of the music, a sensual dance as sultry as the Louisiana climate.

Wim hated to admit it, but he was no physical match for both burly vampires. Possibly not for either one of them. He wasn't certain they possessed all the usual vampire skills, but he dared not take chances. Reaching in his pocket, he clutched the vial. What did it contain? His blood mother had never said. Not that it mattered so long as the potion worked. It had to work. He couldn't get rid of his shadows any other way. He stared at the dark red fluid in his beer stein and wondered...

Would the powder dissolve in blood? He opened the vial and shook a small amount of it into his own drink. Watched it disappear into the drink. He held up the glass, found it looked the same—like the blood it was. Yes, this could work. If he could get close enough to the two vampires, he could drug their drinks. The potion might not be strong enough to destroy them, more was the pity, but it should put them out of commission long enough for him to get away and destroy their queen.

To do it, though, he would have to get close to them without arousing suspicion, but that was impossible in the crush of bodies. Mellow sounds of jazz filled the small room, and a clutch of Owenga swayed to its rhythm on the dance floor that separated him from his nemeses. Wim sighed. He'd have to do something quickly, before he used up the paltry store of money he'd taken from the pockets of his last meal down on the levee.

"You look like a man who needs a woman, *monsieur*." The whore—apparently a vampire herself, as she was sipping from a champagne flute filled with dark-red fluid—perched on the corner of Wim's table and hiked her skirt up to where he could see her pale cunt lips, smell her musk. Her blood-red talons caught his eye when she ran the tip of one nail along the inside of his forearm. Obviously she wasn't aware he had no use for her services.

Yet— Wim hesitated, glanced over toward the bar. "How much for a dance, *chérie*?"

"Twenty dollars."

That would leave him with only thirty more to pay the woman to drug the d'Argents' drinks. But he had no choice. Reaching in his pocket he fingered the vial before pulling it out with a dingy twenty. "Here." Wim took the whore's hand and dragged her onto the dance floor, pushing his way through the crowd of Owengas until they stood at the corner of the bar. "I'll give you thirty more if you spill some of this into the drinks of those two."

She snatched up the money, slid it down between her two generous breasts. "This will not destroy them, will it?"

Fuck. He'd picked a whore with some semblance of conscience. "No, *chérie*, it will only make them sleep. Now do it, or give me back my money."

"Don't be quarrelsome, now. You can't expect me to destroy macho males like them for thirty dollars. Give me the vial and I will help them to sleep."

She popped the cap off the vial and shot Wim a disgusted look. "Most of my customers prefer a more personal kind of service." Her smile bordered on a sneer as she stepped up to the bar and began to hustle the d'Argent vampires he'd pointed out to her.

Wim dared not breathe. Pure torture, it was, watching and waiting to see if the woman did his bidding. She laughed then turned to her second target. *Do it now, bitch.* He clenched his fists, felt his fangs elongating.

In slow motion, she leaned across one broad chest and dropped some of the powder from the vial into one drink. Then she turned back to the other vampire and stroked between his muscular thighs. *Finish it. I'll fucking destroy you if you fail.* Why had he picked a whore who obviously enjoyed plying her trade?

Just as he was about to go, fling the woman out of the way and drug his other enemy, himself, Wim saw her empty the vial into the second bodyguard's drink. Fuck, it was taking too long. As he was about to slip away, hoping the whore had his shadows' full attention, he saw first one and then the other hit the floor.

The whore swirled around his way, obviously distressed that she'd put both of her potential johns out of commission. The bartender looked surprised when he delivered two more drafts to the empty places where the d'Argent guards had been sitting. "Hey, what's going on there?" he asked.

The whore knelt beside one bodyguard. "Better get a healer. I think this one's close to dead."

Wim couldn't have cared less. But he had no desire to be caught up in the investigation the stupid bitch's comments had surely triggered. Not when the guard who'd gotten the smaller dose of poison would likely be up and after him before too long. Making his way through the crowd of Owenga, Wim stepped out into the warm, humid night and made his way out of the Quarter. Taking to the air, he headed toward the house where he'd first begun his assignment of watching over Alina d'Argent. He'd watch over her, all right, destroy her and any mortal foolish enough to challenge him.

Chapter Five

🕉

Alina woke suddenly. She sensed…but no, this uneasy feeling had to have come because she'd been sleeping at a time when she generally was wide awake. She looked over, warmed at the sight of Sam, his face younger-looking as he slept. Laying her hand on his muscular chest, she enjoyed the reassuring beat of his heart, the feeling that he cherished her.

His eyelids fluttered then opened. "What's wrong, sweetheart?"

"Nothing. I guess I'm not accustomed to sleeping at night." But there was something. Some danger she couldn't quite define but which permeated the heavy air like the slowly rotating blades of the ceiling fan at the center of Sam's bedroom. She focused her gaze on the lightly swaying curtains — pale ghosts, formless yet giving a silent warning. She couldn't will herself to stop trembling. "Sam, I'm afraid."

"Come here and let me hold you."

She couldn't move other than to shake so hard the bed vibrated beneath her. This wasn't… *Philippe, where are you. Jacques?*

Sorry. Shouldn't have trusted that Owenga wench… We let him get away.

That had to be Philippe, but why did he sound so sleepy? *What is wrong? Where is Jacques?*

Drugged. Both of us. Jacques got most of it. He's…destroyed. Alina heard the catch in Philippe's voice, imagined him checking Jacques for some sign of life. *Watch out. Reynard bastard is coming after you… I'm coming, my lady… Hang on.*

Philippe's voice trailed off. Nothing more came from his mind. Alina turned to Sam. "Reynard has drugged the bodyguards who were tailing him. Quickly. Hide. I will try to dissuade the bastard from destroying me." Helplessness ate at her gut like a forbidden serving of mortals' *crème brûlée*. Why couldn't female d'Argents fight as well as their male counterparts? "Go. Go now. I feel his presence."

"I'm staying." Sam stood, gloriously naked, his fists clenched. He'd barely had time to grab a silver dagger from the nightstand drawer when Wim Reynard burst through the French doors, his eyes red with bloodlust, his yellowed fangs extended for the kill. "Come on, vampire, I'm not afraid of you."

Oh, no. Alina tried to step between them but Sam flung her aside. Damn it, she couldn't even stop Sam—a mortal— even if it might have saved his life. She recalled Stefan telling her where she might have lacked fighting skill, she had the strongest mind of them all. Heartened, she summoned all her strength, sent an urgent mental call for help to the men of her clan.

She watched Wim Reynard survey his surroundings, size up his opponent. Bloodlust glowed in his eyes as he took one step toward Sam, then another. His fangs elongated. "I am going to destroy you, mortal. Suck out your blood."

"Sam, run. He's going to kill you." Alina couldn't bear the thought of losing another one of her own. And she definitely considered Sam hers.

"Not if I destroy him first." Sam charged Reynard, got in a punch that set the vampire reeling against the wall. A picture fell, glass shattering all over the floor and hindering Sam's motion. Alina tossed a blanket over the shards of glass to protect Sam's bare feet. Breathing hard, he lifted the dagger, lunged at his enemy. "Take a look. It's silver. That's right, duck away. I'll get you anyhow."

Male bravado. Alina moved in again, hoping to distract Reynard and give Sam a clear shot at putting the vampire out of commission. She looked with horror as Sam stabbed Reynard—and Reynard's clawlike hands closed around Sam's thick neck, their hold vicious...killing...

"Stop. I order you, stop." Alina dug her nails into Reynard's skinny arms until his blood flowed over his pale fingers...over Sam's cooling flesh. Tears obscured her vision as she pounded on the bastard's back while he kept on choking Sam. *Why couldn't I have been a man...or at least been given a man's strength?*

"Because the fates willed that you be a woman. Strong in mind so as to lead us well." When Alina turned to the voice she saw Philippe. "Get out of my way. I'll take special pleasure in finishing the bastard off. He destroyed Jacques."

Alina moved, her attention now not on Wim Reynard but on Sam, whose face had turned to a mottled mass of blue and red—listening for a heartbeat, a noise, anything to give her hope that he still lived. She barely noticed when Philippe pried Reynard's hands from around Sam's thick neck and tossed the evil vampire onto his back. From the corner of her eye she saw Philippe pull Sam's silver dagger from Reynard's chest and plunge it once again into his black heart. The fetid odor of toxic vampire blood filled her nostrils, and the sucking sound of death rang out in the darkness.

"He is finished." Philippe sounded tired, his bloodlust apparently tempered by the knowledge his friend and lover lay dead at Reynard's evil hand. Alina, too, had mixed feelings. For her clan's sake she rejoiced in this Reynard henchman's death. For her own sake she mourned for the man she loved. The man whose existence could only be spared by doing what he'd specifically told her he didn't want. Turning him into one of them—a vampire destined never to have the power of one born, ineligible for a position of authority in her clan. "Sam, I don't have any choice now," she whispered. Yet she hesitated. Did she have the right to make him into something he'd already refused to become?

"This Reynard lackey will not be harming anyone again." Philippe's voice, still slow and deep as though the drug still held him in its evil clutches, made her turn and look as the bodyguard jerked the bloody dagger from Reynard's chest. "Not after I do this." Raising the dead vampire's head by his hair, Philippe made a vicious chop with the dagger, burying it deep into his throat.

"Be very certain Reynard does not rise again," Though bloodlust generally sickened her, Alina relished the thought of this enemy being staked out in the fierce New Orleans sunlight until his remains turned into a cloud of dust...or beheaded. She let out a small shudder. "I don't care how you accomplish this."

"Yes, ma'am. I will do it. With pleasure." *Only wish I were not so sleepy. Got to avenge my lover...my queen...for what you did this night.*

She felt for Philippe, shared his pain for the loss of Jacques. But right now her concern was for Sam. Frantically, she felt for a pulse that wasn't there, found his heart deadly still when she placed her hand over his chest. She looked up at Philippe. "The Reynard upstart has destroyed the man I love too."

Philippe laid his bloody hands on her shoulders, pulled her away. "Perhaps not, my queen. Perhaps Sam Quill is but ready to come over to our side."

"He didn't want to be one of us," Alina said, her voice so low she could barely hear herself. "I asked him."

"You know, I wasn't too keen on changing, either, but I've got no regrets now for having had a lot of good years with Jacques." Philippe's eyes clouded then cleared as he looked down at Sam. "Well, now, this one has a choice between becoming a vampire and being dead. And it looks as though you're going to have to make that choice for him." Philippe's fangs elongated as he spoke. "I can turn him if you wish." He sounded drawn, tired. Some of the drug that had killed Jacques must still have been coursing through his veins.

Alina bent and placed a kiss on Sam's cooling cheek. Then she looked up at Philippe. "No. I will do it, even though he may very well hate me afterward. You finish off Reynard, until you are very certain he is destroyed, never to attack anyone again. Then find yourself a bed and rest. I cannot lose you too." With infinite care she lifted Sam's head and rested it on her lap. As Philippe dragged Reynard's carcass out into the courtyard, Alina steeled herself to do what she knew Sam wouldn't have wanted. And summoned Stefan, Claude and Alex to her side to take part in the ritual that must follow the change.

Then she smoothed her hair back and lowered her head. "I'm sorry, my love. I'd never go against your wishes again. Wouldn't do it now but I can't bear to lose you this way." Moving quickly before she could lose her courage, she sank her fangs into his jugular vein, now still where before it had pulsated invitingly when they made love. And drank her fill. And sat there, holding the newly made vampire in her arms, watching the transformation from mortal to vampire take place. When he woke, he'd be ravenous for his first meal. And furious.

* * * * *

"This one looks to be destroyed beyond recovery, even for a Reynard." Stefan d'Argent looked at the decapitated vampire on the whitewashed brick floor of the courtyard beyond the door. Then he stepped inside and saw Alina sitting on the floor, cradling his wife's father on her lap. "Julie, wait outside." He snatched the coverlet off the bed and tossed it over Sam's naked body.

"I will not. That's my father's room. What is it you're not telling me?" Ignoring her new husband, Julie bounded into the room, her pale blonde hair tangled from what Alina imagined must have been a frantic flight from Stefan's castle. "Sam! Oh God. Tell me he's not dead."

"He is not dead…" Should she tell Julie now, or wait until Sam awakened, when his change would become evident. Alina hesitated a moment, then met Julie's gaze. "But he is now one of us."

"Oh, no." Julie's eyes widened with apparent dismay. She tightened her hold on Noodles, the sleek red Dachshund that was hers and Stefan's constant companion.

"No? I remember you begging me to turn you, my darling." Stefan looked up from the floor where he'd knelt to examine the remains of Wim Reynard, his look one of gentle amusement. "Have you not been happy?"

"Oh, yes. But I *wanted* to be with you. Daddy wouldn't have wanted—"

"He wouldn't have wanted to die now, either, but that's what he did, while he was saving me from *him*." Alina gestured toward the open French door where the villain's headless body lay just outside. "I hope you can help me persuade your father that becoming a vampire is not a fate worse than death."

Julie sighed when Stefan stood and gathered her in his arms. "He looks so pale. So…uncomfortable. Stefan, please put him on the bed."

"Alina?" Stefan's voice registered concern, reminded her she was behaving more like a lovestruck child than the queen of their clan.

She gathered her jumbled feelings, managed a small smile when Stefan squatted beside her and tucked the coverlet around Sam before lifting Sam and laying him on the bed. "I'd have put him there before I changed him, but he was too heavy for me…" *Strong enough to lead a clan yet too weak to lift your lover a distance of only three or four feet. Some queen you are.* Acutely aware of her nakedness now, she snatched up the top sheet and wrapped it around her like a toga. Its softness enveloped her, somehow gave her hope that Sam would embrace his new life…embrace her…when he awakened.

As if he weighed twenty pounds instead of two hundred, Stefan lifted Sam and placed him gently on the bed. "Lie beside him, as I lay with Julie while she transformed. You look as though you've been through hell."

"I have. Where are the others?" If the message she'd projected to Stefan had reached his ears despite the presence of his new bride, then they should have also made their way to Alexandre and Claude. "Jacques is destroyed, and Philippe is in one of the other bedrooms, sleeping off the effects of the poison Reynard used to get rid of them both."

Stefan sat beside her on the bed, drawing his trembling bride down beside him. "They are going to meet us at the castle. Claude is bringing Marisa to join in the ritual since we've not had time before to welcome her to the family."

Of course Julie wouldn't feel comfortable taking part in a vampire orgy with her own father, and Alina felt sure Sam would be even more reticent. "Thank you. I hadn't considered…"

"It's all right. I thought Julie might remind Sam that living as one of us can be tolerable—even pleasurable," Stefan said, giving Julie a hug. "Remember the night Claude was born?"

"I thought about it yesterday, when Sam hinted about a ménage. It was almost as though…" Alina suddenly realized she was about to talk about an event she doubted Stefan had shared with Julie, as well as confirming to Sam's daughter that they'd been lovers. "You two—and you too, Noodles—may as well go home and enjoy your honeymoon now that the immediate danger is over. We will want to hold the ritual in our ancestral castle."

If Sam is willing. Alina hoped he'd enjoy the freedom of taking to the air, floating over land and ocean without the noise of jet engines reverberating in his ears. She doubted he'd relish losing out on a lot of mortal pleasures, and she shuddered to think he might refuse the ritual and exist for centuries in limbo, a virtual eunuch in a world very different from his own. "Stefan?"

He reached over and patted her arm. "We will stay in New Orleans a few more days, but in the suite where we started our married life at the Monteleone. That way we will be close by in case you need us." Stefan bent and brushed his lips across Alina's cheek then rose. "Come, Julie, leave Alina to take care of your father. You need your rest." Alina watched as Stefan met his wife's gaze, shut down her scan of his thoughts as he drew Julie to her feet and hurried her from the room. Some things should be kept private, even from one's clan elders, she thought, adjusting her body to fit the curves and angles of the man—no, now the vampire—of her heart.

She said a prayer to every deity she knew and some she didn't, that Sam would accept his new lease on life...and that he'd want her now as much as he had when he had been mortal.

* * * * *

He was dead, wasn't he? Sam's eyelids felt as though they'd already been weighted down with coins in preparation for the funeral. No, they didn't do that anymore, did they? Besides, if he were dead he wouldn't feel anything at all.

He felt strangely cool, but for the warmth of an angel whose hips cradled his cock and balls. She felt familiar. Almost like the marble perfection of his woman...his Alina. Not a woman. A vampire. Cousin by marriage to Julie.

"Alina?" Her name rattled off his dry lips, the sound coming out raw from a throat that felt it had been constricted.

"I'm right here." Her low, slightly accented voice gave him temporary comfort until he realized the sheets felt different. Softer against his back and the arm that rested beneath her silky hair, as though...

He moved his other hand over his body. His? Yes, he was running his palm over himself, but it was different somehow.

Cold. His skin was smooth as a baby's ass. The muscles beneath it seemed harder now than they'd been when he was a young man. Could she? No. He'd forbidden her. But a voice in his head reminded him she could. She was his submissive lover, but she also was a vampire. A vampire queen.

Tentatively, he rubbed his tongue over his top teeth, then the bottom ones. Awareness came suddenly, like the hurricane that changed his life last year. "Goddammit, Alina. I told you I wanted to stay mortal."

She turned, caught his head between her hands. "Wim Reynard killed you when you were defending me. I couldn't bear..." Her voice trailed off. As it did his memory started to come back. The vampire he'd seen this afternoon. And again tonight, after Alina had wakened and ordered him to hide. He saw himself grabbing the dagger, going on the attack.

And he remembered feeling as though he was choking. Everything going black. "He got in here. In this room. How?"

"He drugged the guards. The poison destroyed Jacques, but Philippe apparently got a smaller portion. He staggered in here as the Reynard bastard was choking you. I tried so hard to stop him..." A sob came from deep in Alina's throat.

That sob made Sam feel guilty. He should have been able to protect her from the skinny bastard. Bits and pieces of the fight flashed through his head. The dagger. The satisfying feeling of silver slipping between ribs, finding purchase in the vampire's evil heart. And the imprint of ten skinny fingers digging into his neck with superhuman strength, cutting off his wind. "Where is he now?"

Alina rolled away, leaving him suddenly cold. "You destroyed him. Philippe arrived in time to deliver the *coup de grâce*. And to save you." She reached out and stroked Sam's neck, her touch gentle as she traced the imprint where Reynard's fingers had been. "If he had not come, I couldn't have stopped Reynard and turned you quickly enough, before life had completely left your body. No, don't open your eyes. They will become less sensitive in time, but for now the morning light will harm them." She slid off the bed and drew the drapes. "There. That's better."

Better? Sam doubted it. Crazy as it was to mourn something as simple as a morning walk down Decatur Street, he couldn't help thinking about the things he'd lost with one long bite by his vampire lover. He looked at her, saw the fear—and the love—in her beautiful green eyes. "You did what you thought you had to do," he said, surprised that he managed a civil, almost friendly tone. "Come back here and tell me what all this means. Don't leave me with any surprises."

She sat beside him, legs folded under her ass. "It means you'll still age, but slowly. You'll drink blood instead of eating and prefer night to daytime. Your mind will stay the same as ever. You'll find some perks, I'm sure, such as being able to move through time and space without the need for planes and such. And in time you may develop the ability to communicate telepathically. Some made vampires do. Others don't." She smiled at him, as though hoping to wipe away his anger. "It's a mixed blessing, reading others' thoughts."

"How'd you do it?"

Taking his hand, she rubbed his fingers along one side of his throat. "Feel the two marks?"

The two small marks along his jugular vein felt insignificant, yet they'd apparently changed his life forever. Once more he traced his tongue over his upper teeth. As impossible as it seemed, he was now a vampire. Like Julie. Like Alina. Tentatively he opened one eye and then the other, found the dim light uncomfortable but bearable. A chilling thought ran through his mind. Was he now her slave? He had to know. "Does this mean you are now my mistress?"

Alina bared her throat. "I am your creator, in a way. But I am also your sex slave, as much now as when you were a mortal. Go ahead. Take me now. Drink from me as I drank from you last night."

He couldn't help recoiling at the thought of drinking blood. "I can't."

She lay on her back, drew him down beside her, baring her throat, offering herself to him in a way that gave him back some control, some sense of who he was that he'd felt quickly slipping away. He stroked along the curve of her hip, expected the usual stirring of arousal as he looked at her perfect body, imagined plunging his cock into her tight cunt...her lush mouth...the tight little asshole he'd yet to claim.

Nothing.

"It's easy. Arousing. Come on. Bite me." Her voice was husky, different. Was she using vampiric compulsion to bend him to her will?

Sam didn't care, because he was feeling his first attack of bloodlust. It began as an itchy feeling, a longing for the salty, metallic taste of his mate's blood. A throbbing in his balls that quickly had his cock as hard as he'd ever been. An ache that began deep in his belly and spread until he could do nothing but take her. Taste her. Take life from her as she'd taken it from him. "I still am not happy you did this," he said, laying his hands on her shoulders and drawing her onto his lap.

Driven not by reason but by compulsion, he aligned his fangs so they'd pierce the inviting vein she'd bared as he flexed his hips and buried his hard cock deep inside her. He felt nothing there. Not the wetness or the warmth of her tight little cunt, only a building ache in his testicles that demanded release. "Do it now," she whispered, "give me a vampire bite while you are deep inside me."

"I am a master, not a slave." He hoped that still was true as he sank his fangs into her tender flesh, felt them pierce the vein she offered. Warm, slightly salty fluid filled his mouth when he bore down and sucked. He swallowed once, twice. On the third taste of his lover's blood, feeling started to return to his cock as it swelled against her damp cunt. She moved on him, coaxing...rubbing her clit against his now hairless groin, the hard nubs of her nipples against the newly smooth skin that covered his chest. When he drew on her blood, her cunt contracted. Her skin warmed. The moans he heard from her lips made him realize she was about to come. "Make me come, my darling. Now," Sam ordered.

"No, love, you can't come. Not now." Alina ground herself down hard on his cock, let out a feral scream as her inner muscles clasped him, as though trying to squeeze out an orgasm that wouldn't come. "Made vampires are impotent until they've been accepted into the clan."

He sure as hell didn't feel impotent. His balls were about to burst, and his cock had never grown so thick and long. His body had never before felt the delicious sensation of skin on skin, unimpeded by the body hair that had somehow disappeared when he made the change. He drew back his fangs, lifted his head so he could look into her eyes. "How long must I wait for this acceptance?"

"Until tonight when the elders of my clan join me to welcome you and take you to the d'Argent's ancestral castle. Until the ritual." Her words reminded Sam of the ritual at Julie's wedding to Stefan, the surreal fantasy mating of Julie not only with her lover but with a representative of the clan — his cousin Alexandre. Though the act had shocked him at the time even though he'd thought it an act of minds not bodies, it now seemed natural. A real part of their vampire world that now would be his too. A sense of acceptance flowed through his veins as he drank Alina's blood while his cock lay deep in her body, seeking yet not finding release. "Meanwhile you must learn how best to serve your queen."

Sam served no one. Nothing but his own desires...or did he? For the last few days of his mortality he'd dominated Alina, but he'd done it to pleasure her. Was that not a form of submission? "I serve my queen best as her lover. I command that you come."

Alina laughed as she lifted herself off his throbbing flesh and twisted around, straddling him so her wet, musky cunt made contact with his mouth. "Taste me while I tell you what must happen if you are to regain your potency. I forget you've just now crossed over."

Panic coursed through Sam, but he couldn't find the words to protest. Not while she was rubbing her female flesh against his lips. A voice in his head said he didn't even want to stop her sensual movements, especially when he felt her wrap one small, soft hand around the base of his cock. "Mmmm," he managed to say against her swollen clit as his arousal grew to an exasperating fever pitch with no relief in sight.

"Most made male vampires are sexually impotent. Over the centuries, though, the d'Argents have found themselves short of new blood — pun intended — and have therefore discovered a way to restore the potency of the mortals we have turned." Her tone mesmerized him, made him concentrate not on the delicious musky taste of her pussy or the hardness of her impudent little clit but on the breathless sound of her voice. "We've managed to keep our methods secret for hundreds of years, but I believe Louis Reynard came to me because rumors had spread. Even if I would have taken him, I couldn't have restored his ability to have sex, because the method only works on vampires when they've been newly made by a member of the d'Argent clan." She paused, let out a little moan when he took her clit between his teeth and nibbled none too gently.

Bitch. She deserved a little pain. Besides, Sam had learned the second time they fucked that pain aroused her. He lapped up the warm, slippery fluid that escaped her cunt when he'd bitten her. His cock became larger, harder — damn painful. His denuded skin registered every motion, each brush of her hand on his sex. Even the press of her knees against his shoulders heightened his need to take her, prove to her that vampire or not, he was boss in bed. *I won't be your sex toy.*

"Yes. You will. This is the first part of the ritual I discovered as a young vampire...the rest will take place at twilight."

Sam recalled her enthusiasm when he'd mentioned a ménage. Who'd take part? *Not Julie.*

"Not Julie. I wouldn't be so cruel as to ask her to take part in a sex ritual with her own father. Not Stefan, either, for participating with Julie's mate would be awkward for both of you. Alexandre and Claude will be the two d'Argent males taking part, along with Claude's bride, you and me." Alina paused then continued. "Philippe will come here just before nightfall to prepare you for the ritual. Like you, he is a made vampire. Go gently with him, for last night he lost the lover who changed him. He and Jacques were inseparable." Her cunt released its juices and she shuddered with the release he wanted so badly for himself.

Sam wasn't at all sure he liked the idea of males taking part in this vampire initiation. "Tell me more about this ritual," he demanded, drawing her hand to his aching balls. "I have a feeling I'm not going to enjoy it."

"Lie back." She paused, bending to lick the slit in his cock head before rubbing her cheek along the taut skin of his shaft and scrotum. "All made male vampires are pierced. Have you ever played with sounds?"

"No, but I once watched a Dominatrix use a set of them on her slave at the club." The idea of having a metal object threaded through his cock had never been a turn-on. It wasn't now, either. "I thought you mentioned piercings."

"The piercing is to place a ring that will hold the sound in place during the ritual. Philippe will explain more when he prepares you."

The more Sam heard, the less he liked the idea. The prospect of having a gay male vampire—a virtual stranger—handle his private parts made him want to stop this before it even began. "I don't think—"

"Do you want to stay impotent, unable to get release for the rest of your life?" Alina worked the tip of her forefinger into his anus and moved it in a slow circle. "Your very, very long life?"

Of course he didn't. But... "The whole thing sounds distasteful."

"It won't be. The purpose of the preparation is to purge the remnants of your mortal body and prepare you to be reborn, fully potent, as a d'Argent vampire. As my consort, if that's your wish. By the way, vampires heal almost instantly from any but the most serious of wounds."

"I'm not worried about the pain." He had to say it, but he wasn't sure that was true. Sliding her hand down the inside of his thigh, she cuffed his ankle and bound it to the nearest bedpost. "Hey, what are you doing?"

"Before you can become a vampire master, you must be reborn a vampire slave. Spread your arms and legs, and we'll get this done quickly." There was that low, compelling tone again—vampire compulsion that had him meekly positioning himself so she could bind him. "That's good, *mon cher.*"

He didn't think he could have stood it—the humiliation and discomfort his subs often begged for—if it weren't that he knew her soul ached to have to do it. "What now, my vampire queen?"

She bent and brushed her lips over his. "Take a nap, my darling. Philippe will be coming soon. I have things I must do to ready everything for the ritual."

The ritual that would make him whole...and hers for all eternity.

Chapter Six

∞

How many hours had gone by? If the light streaming through the open French doors didn't burn his eyes so much, he'd have been able to figure the answer by looking out into the courtyard. The clock on the nightstand was just outside his limited range of motion. Never in his life had Sam felt so helpless.

Or so alive. He pictured Alina taking him in some sensual vampire ritual and grew even hotter and harder. Fuck. His cock was about to burst. He went back in his mind to the fight...the sensation of claws choking the life from him...Alina's gentle touch. As if he were in real time he felt the first touch of her fangs, the sensation of floating outside himself as she sucked the lifeblood from him. Leaving his mind and body a void waiting to be refilled.

He had no feeling of urgency, no need to relieve himself. Those, he guessed, were feelings unique to mortals. And he was mortal no more, but a newly made vampire hovering in the shadow world between his old world and the one he would inhabit for a long eternity. Forever.

The door opened. Footsteps clattered on the hardwood floors then softened to muffled thuds when they moved over the antique Persian rug. Soft at first then louder as they approached Sam's bed. "I've been through this too. Our queen felt I could prepare you better than she could."

When he opened his eyes, Sam recognized Philippe at once. The vampire's pleasant smile and the look of sympathy in his eyes was obviously intended to put Sam at his ease, but Sam still didn't like the idea of having another man's hands handling his private flesh. He tensed when Philippe approached the bed but managed to look him in the eye and express his gratitude. "I understand I owe you for my life."

"Not me. Alina's the one who changed you. I suggested she send me to prepare you and explain the ritual that will make you whole once more."

"How would you know?"

"Because my master Jacques made me. Because I am the only made male vampire here today, the only one who has experienced the ritual as you will. Mostly because Jacques would never have allowed me to back away from a duty to our clan, no matter how painful it might be." Philippe's eyes glistened with unshed tears, and his lower lip quivered for a second before he schooled his features into an impersonal, professional mask.

"Does this involve pain?" When Sam glanced to his side and saw the array of tools and jewelry, he shuddered. Needles had always done that to him.

"No more than what you can bear. I am going to insert a sound, pierce your cock and thread a ring through the sound. Only your mate will be able to remove it."

Sam shuddered. "And if I say no?"

"Then you'll be impotent. Of no use to your mate. Is that what you want?"

"No!" Closing his eyes so tightly the lids hurt, he clenched his fists in anticipation of agony. "Do it."

"First, I'll do a thorough cleansing." Philippe lifted Sam's ass and placed a thick pad beneath his genitals. Then he donned latex gloves and picked up what looked like a baby wipe.

The feel of Philippe's hands on Sam's cock and balls made him even harder, which he wouldn't have thought possible. The initial embarrassment of lying helpless while another male manipulated his genitals eased with the other vampire's impersonal touch. Even the internal cleansing of his bladder and anus wasn't as bad as he'd feared. Philippe turned away for a moment then came back with a set of Rosebud sounds and a jar of lubricant that he placed beside Sam's hip. "What?"

"I will insert sounds until I find the largest one you can accept. At that point I will pierce your cock head and thread a captive bead ring through the eye of the sound."

Sam had never gone for sex play that involved putting toys into his own orifices. The very idea made his erection start to subside, but when the sound slid down his cock and into his bladder it felt surprisingly good. "Hey, how long is that thing?" he asked when he felt the tip move through his scrotum and rest against his prostate gland. "Hell. It feels good."

It felt better each time the other vampire replaced one sound with a larger one. "There. You took a thirteen-millimeter Rosebud, twelve inches long. Hang in there now. I'm drawing it out far enough that I can attach the eyelet and cap."

"Cap? How the hell can I—"

"You are a vampire. The only uses for your cock and ass now are for giving and receiving sexual pleasure. There. I got it." Philippe pushed the sound back inside Sam once again, and he felt himself harden once more at the stimulation to his insides. "Hold still. This is the part that's tricky."

"What are you doing?" Sam wished he could see what Philippe was taking out of a square white envelope.

"Providing some insurance to be sure the sound stays where it belongs. I'm going to thread this needle through your cock, just behind your cock head. You'll feel a little sting."

A little sting, hell. He'd never hurt so much, but Sam was determined not to scream out loud. He bit down on his lower lip instead, drawing blood. "Damn, these fangs are a pain."

Philippe looked up at Sam, his expression indulgent. "You'll learn how to keep them retracted except when you feed. Now I'm stretching the hole I made so it will take an eleven millimeter ring."

Sam could tell. His cock felt like it was on fire when Philippe threaded the ring through his cock, right behind the head. The icy metal sent sensations down the sound when the ring passed through the eyelet. When it emerged on the other side, Sam felt another sharp pain. "Are you finished?"

"Take a look," Philippe said. "The piercing is called an Ampellang. You may want to keep on wearing the ring after the ceremony. It looks delightful. Master Jacques liked to see me wear the sound. He even had a barbell made to secure it. My lady Alina may gift you with a similar piece." Sam gasped at the sight of the thick ring that passed through his cock horizontally, and the rounded metal cap of the sound that covered its tip.

His cock still hurt, but damn if he didn't like the look of the hardware. And the idea of Alina choosing some additional baubles for her greater pleasure." Are you finished?"

"Almost." Philippe picked up a large, well-lubricated anal plug and set it between Sam's splayed legs. "Relax and this won't be too uncomfortable."

Strangely enough, the plug didn't hurt at all once its thickest segment had passed through Sam's anal sphincter. Having the plug stimulating his prostate from one end while the sound worked from the other side felt damn good. The pain from the piercing had already subsided, faster than he'd have imagined possible considering the weight and thickness of the ring Philippe had just forced through it. "The pain is almost gone."

"It will be completely healed by the time the ritual begins. Vampires heal almost instantly from all but the most severe of injuries. One of the many benefits," Philippe said. "I will leave you now. Rest, for you will need your strength for the ceremony. You will be one of the clan's elite, so you may as well observe carefully so you'll know what to do next time. The d'Argents are more civilized than most, but we do enjoy performing some of the clan's ancient sex rituals. In a few hours we all will be winging our way to the d'Argent family castle."

* * * * *

"It's like floating through space, Daddy," Julie said after she'd closed up Sam's house. "We'll be at Stefan's castle in no time."

Sam didn't know about this, but his daughter had done it several times now, so he had no business being afraid. Of the trip, at least. He was glad Alina had taken pity on him and tossed his black evening cape over his shoulders. As long as he held it closed, the cape hid his permanent hard-on from Julie's eyes and kept the ring from swaying in the breeze and driving him to the brink of insanity. His new fangs scraped his lower lip as Alina rose into the air, taking him with her. Once they were airborne, his cape fanned out, helping him stay aloft but exposing his cock to the night air, making the ring sway and the sound reverberate constantly through his vampire sex.

"Are you all right?" Alina asked when he began to moan from the overstimulation to his new jewelry.

He glanced around, saw none of the others in the immediate vicinity. "I want to fuck you until you can't see straight. Until I come and relieve this—this monster hard-on."

"Patience, *mon cher*. We will be home soon now." Their small group moved through the night, eastward over America and the Atlantic to come to earth again on the other side. Waves crashed against the cliff below them.

"Welcome to the d'Argents' ancestral home," Stefan said, motioning toward a castle perched beside them on the cliff. "Come, let's get inside out of the cold."

* * * * *

Flickering candles lit the high table in the great hall, where Stefan's servants had set out wineglasses for eight. Alina murmured her approval to the housekeeper whose family had lived and worked here since the days of her grandfather and before. The distinctive smell of incense filled her nostrils. As she did every time she came to the great castle, Alina imagined she heard voices from those long gone, from d'Argents and from the warriors who had held off Hitler's army and preserved the so-called vampire castle. The sounds continued, their tones eerie, muted whispers coming as if from a great distance.

"Alex. Claude and Marisa. Thank you so much for coming," she said, crossing the drafty hall to the fireplace and embracing each of them in turn.

"Wouldn't miss a restorative ritual. Marisa's been pestering me to try doing one for her brother."

"Be sure to invite us if you do it. I've often wondered how long it's possible to wait and still achieve full restoration." Alex paused, grinned. "I remember the last time we met here to welcome a new life to our world. That was when you were born, e*nfant*."

Claude shook a fist Alex's way. "I'm no child now, nephew." The two were close, almost like brothers despite the difference in their ages.

Alina held up a hand. "There will be no quarreling amongst ourselves this night, for we have a newly made vampire among us. Stefan, take Julie and go to bed. It's not fitting for Sam's daughter and son-in-law to take part in the ritual."

"Come on, Noodles, you'll just be in the way," Stefan said, picking up the frisky pup and holding her in one arm while looping the other over Julie's shoulder. "We will be with you in spirit."

Alina wished they could have stayed. Particularly Stefan who, along with her, had guided the d'Argent clan since their grandfather's death. But it was time. Time for her to take Sam as her vampire mate. Time for Alexandre to lead the hunt for Louis Reynard. And time for Claude to be acknowledged as their equal, no longer a child to be cosseted. "Claude, you will lead the ritual." Soon he would lead their clan, and Alina would be free to enjoy her time as a woman, no longer burdened with the cloak of leadership.

In slow motion Claude began removing his clothes. As sure of himself as he would have been if he had done this many times before, he stood naked at the head of the table and surveyed the crowd. At his instruction they all stripped naked. "Marisa, love, disrobe the one most recently brought into our midst."

Flickering candlelight from the wall sconces and at the high table lent a gilded tone to pale vampire flesh, caught highlights in the men's dark hair. Marisa's too. Alina wished she could allay the confusion in Sam's eyes when Claude's bride caught him by the ring that pierced his cock, led him behind the table and shackled him to a heavy wooden "X" set up against an age-darkened stone wall.

Neck, wrists, thighs and ankles. The ominous sound of metal hitting metal sent a wave of excitement through Alina. Moisture dribbled down her thighs. Marisa's, also, unless Alina missed her guess. A glance at the men told her Claude and Alex were not unaffected, either. Their cocks rose up against their bellies, showing testicles drawn tightly to their groins, displaying Alex's guiche ring.

"Alina, do you wish to service this vampire before the ritual begins?" Claude's voice seemed darker, deeper than she recalled as he began the ritual.

"Yes." When Marisa knelt before Claude and serviced him, Alina didn't need to be told to kneel and taste Sam's cock, deliberately letting her fangs scrape the tender flesh, catch and tug at the ring behind his thick, rigid cock head.

His thoughts came through clearly. The desire to be whole, to dominate her once more. The anger at being confined, helpless to do anything but accept the will of each participant. The stoic determination to go through with this even though the thought of being penetrated by another male repelled him. Alina almost called a halt. She loved Sam, would still love him if his potency were not restored.

But Sam's virility was such a huge part of him. He wanted badly to restore it, or he wouldn't have let Philippe go through with the preparation that had to have been beyond painful.

Alina stepped back, holding Sam's gaze as Marisa moved beside her. Claude and Alex came forward and grasped Sam's rock-hard cock, at the same time leaning in to sip blood from the prominent veins in his thick neck. His puzzled look when the other two males touched him intimately reminded Alina once more that her love was an American heterosexual as well as a newly made vampire. He must have been taken aback by his fellow vampires' casual handling...and more so by the fact their touches aroused him.

From somewhere in the distance a bell chimed twelve times, its tone piercing the silence of the night. A cool breeze rattled through the ancient castle walls, its rhythm caught in the flickering of the candlelight, the shifting shadows of another time, a time before even Alina had been born. "The ritual will now begin," Claude declared, moving back from Marisa and helping Alex loosen Sam's bonds.

"In the year of our Lord 935, Alain was born a vampire, son of Rolfe d'Argent and the lady Elaine. I am his last surviving son, born seventy-five years ago, not even a year before he met an untimely end. The d'Argent clan has thrived, thanks to my older brothers and their children—Alina, Stefan and Alexandre. This night we gather to restore virility to Sam Quill so that, if the gods be with us, he may get a son on Alina to perpetuate our clan.

"Let the strength of all of us flow into him, make him whole and strong so he may serve his mistress well." When Claude paused, Alina stood and led Sam to the spot where the brightest firelight reflected off the hardware in his cock. "Sam Quill, are you ready to become one with Alina?"

"Yes." Though he sounded sure of his reply, Sam's flesh quivered beneath Alina's hand. She didn't blame him. Rather, she admired him for accepting his state and bravely meeting every challenge with courage. He'd been a man to adore. He would be the vampire to make her wildest fantasies come true.

Alexandre moved behind them, his cock large and ready for the lubricated condom Marisa supplied. Grasping Sam's hips, Marisa removed the anal plug and stepped aside. Alex filled the void as Claude stepped forward and fed his own cock into Sam's mouth.

Alexandre's cock moved in and out, burning Sam's ass as his flesh stretched to take the other man's sure, steady thrusts. Alex's testicles bounced against Sam's. He'd have protested because the ass fucking hurt like hell, but he couldn't talk while Claude was fucking his mouth, making him swallow cock until his throat felt as though it would explode. Marisa tugged at his nipples while Alina knelt between his widely spread legs and stroked his own jutting cock. The sound reverberated inside him, its humming increasing each time Alina rotated the ring through its eye.

God but he'd never felt so full in his life. So helpless yet so stimulated, as though his vampire family were pouring its collective sexuality into his own empty shell. For the first time he understood a woman's need to take a man as he experienced the incredible pleasure of feeling Alexandre's hot male flesh stretching his ass while he licked and sucked Claude the way he often ordered his mate to do to him. Tension built in him, like nothing he'd ever experienced. His balls drew up tight against his groin. His heart pounded in his chest the way it had when he was alive—but more so. The sound inside him thrummed wildly. It seemed to have grown, but he knew his cock had to be expanding, throbbing. Fuck, he had to come. But he couldn't.

Then Alina opened the captive bead and fed the Ampellang ring through his flesh, freeing the sound but sending waves of sensation along its embedded length. "Come, Sam. Come for me now," she whispered against his burning flesh.

"Can I?" He remembered her telling him she was his mistress now.

"You can and you may." Her soft breath on his cock sent him over the edge, and he came, great spurts of semen that shot the sound out of his cock and into his mistress's hand.

"Now you can come inside me," she told him after they retired alone to a guest chamber in the venerable castle. He blinked at the sight out the narrow window, as the dawn of a new day turned the eastern sky to pink and purple.

Sam was content…as content as a newly made vampire could be while the specter of Louis Reynard hung over his mate, his life…his love.

Epilogue

ℬ

Alina's luxurious townhouse in the Marais District of Paris, within easy reach of clubs and bistros that reminded him of the French Quarter back home, suited Sam much better than the clan's elegant but somewhat spooky castle that Stefan and Julie seemed to prefer. Alina was glad, because the life in Paris suited her, as well. Word had it her nemesis, Louis Reynard, was up and about now, after several months' hibernation in the Carpathian Mountains. And Philippe, whom Claude had put in charge of watching Louis' movements, had said Louis apparently decided to bypass Alina for the moment, moving instead to the warm climes around Miami to resume his killing spree by stalking young women on the vacation mecca known as South Beach.

"Who is Claude sending to destroy Reynard?" Sam looked up from the English-language paper he'd been reading and smiled at his mate. "Alexandre?"

"Alex...and Philippe. I doubt Philippe will leave the bastard's trail until he can avenge Jacques' untimely demise. You know, you took away the pleasure Philippe would have had by destroying Reynard's lackey."

Sam raised a gently arched brow. "You'd have wanted me to let him destroy you instead?"

"No, love, and I thank you. But if you had, you might still have been a mortal, going about your business in New Orleans." When he pulled her down on her knees, she loved the dominant side of him that he always showed when they were alone in their rooms.

"Suck my cock, love."

"With pleasure." When she freed him from his clothes she took him in her mouth, rolling her tongue around his corona, over the eye made more sensitive since they'd been experimenting with different ways of using the sounds. She rolled his heavy testicles between her palms, loving the silky feel of him. The drop of lubrication there tasted good. So good she hated to stop sucking him when he lifted her head and looked down into her eyes.

He rubbed his palm over Alina's cheek, his touch full of tenderness. Of love. "I've found I enjoy being a vampire, much more than I ever dreamed I would." He handed her the largest of the Rosebud sounds he'd come to enjoy wearing and held the ring he often wore in his Ampellang piercing in the crook of one finger. "Put these in for me before we dress and go downstairs. Your *maman* tells me she has planned another vampire orgy, and I'm anxious to watch the scene."

"Watch? My darling, you will be the star of tonight's vampire scene…" Alina threaded the full length of the sound through his flesh until he sighed with pleasure. When the rosebud tip hit his prostate, she worked the thick ring through his piercing then inserted the anal plug. She bent and licked off the salty essence that pooled around the sound's rounded cap then stood and pulled him to her side. He didn't need to know just yet that he'd be the Dominant to her submissive, or that tonight and forever she'd promise him her eternal surrender.

* * * * *

You'll be the star of tonight's vampire scene. Sam couldn't help wondering what Alina meant, but he wouldn't torture himself by imagining what she might have had in mind. No longer self-conscious as he'd been at first about partying stark naked with the others of the clan, he mingled easily with the others, stopping now and then to stroke a particularly tempting belly, a golden fall of female hair.

Like the submissive males of the clan, Sam wore the sound and retaining ring with pride. With love for Alina, gratitude that she'd snatched him from mortal death into her erotic, sensual world. He'd thought to shave his head as a further sign of his submission, but she'd said no, she didn't want him to look like the other submissive males because in private he was her Master. Besides, she liked the bristly feel of his closely cropped curls on her pussy, her nipples...every inch of skin he could reach.

Even though he'd often thought having a lover caress his bare scalp would have to feel incredibly erotic, Sam had settled for having her caress the smooth-shaven strip at the back of his neck, where he had the barber keep his hairline raised. His ring swayed when he moved, sending auditory waves that kept him as painfully aroused as the others who wore the accouterment of vampire slavery.

When he noticed the cut crystal bowls of condoms his mother-in-law had placed strategically around the room, he laughed out loud. The woman had ranted for weeks after the last orgy because several guests had dripped semen on her priceless Oriental rugs, and this generosity with the latex barriers had to have been her solution to potential housekeeping problems. After all, she must have realized her guests had no place to carry their own protection since nudity was the dress code for d'Argent orgies. As Sam crossed the room, he glanced down at his cock. No way would he be coming on Mother's rug, not as long as he had the sound locked firmly inside his genitals. Not that a condom would have fit over the ring, and there was no way he could remove it until Alina unlocked the captive bead.

Alina. He loved her more each day, gave secret thanks each night that she'd brought him into her life...her world. Like the queen she was, she sat on a raised dais, her female musk perfuming the room as one by one her subjects slid beneath her fucking chair and licked her wet, fragrant cunt. Marisa sat in a similar chair, her body incredibly alluring now that her pregnancy was showing, while Alex fucked her ass and Claude sucked her clit.

What would have seemed unheard of in New Orleans outside the observation rooms at *Club de la soumission* seemed perfectly acceptable in this world where there was no room for inhibitions or mortal social rules to stifle freedom of sexual expression. When a d'Argent vampire he'd met bent and presented Sam his ass, Sam didn't hesitate to fill it.

Who'd have ever thought Sam Quill would fuck another male? Enjoying the freedom and the sensation of tight anal rings gripping his flesh, Sam pumped into his partner's ass, steadying himself by grasping and spreading the young vampire's muscular buttocks. First slow then fast, Sam accelerated the pace, going deeper with each thrust until he was buried to the balls. His partner shuddered and spurted his semen into the condom Sam had noticed he donned before making his proposition. Focusing his gaze on Alex's sister taking one cock in her cunt, the other in her ass, he considered inviting himself to fill her only vacant hole.

Before he could get to the girl, Alex approached him. "Mind sharing my cousin with me just this once, before Claude sends me off on yet another hunt for Louis Reynard?"

Sam did. There was still the streak of mortal possessiveness in him that wanted to destroy any vampire who touched his mistress. But he'd arranged ménage scenes to please past lovers, lent out his submissive of the moment to other Doms. How was this loving, no-holds-barred sex that much different? "Come on. I think I've watched enough of her subjects pay homage." Like a good slave Sam prostrated himself before Alina then rolled over and slid beneath her well-licked pussy. He rubbed the top of his head over her wet slit, enjoyed feeling her squirm. Oh god. Alex had come up onto the dais behind him, grabbed Sam's cock, held it steady as he rotated the ring he wore.

As hard as he was, the motion inside his cock was pure torture. Sam changed the angle of his head, ringed Alina's tempting ass with his tongue. *Please. Please mistress, take it out. Let me come in your mouth…your cunt… Here.* With his fangs extended, he bit her puckered rosebud, not hard enough to hurt her but plenty hard enough to make her yelp.

I will. I gave Alex the tool to unfasten the ring. Finally he'd managed to communicate telepathically with her. Sam wanted...her. Only her. Not the dozens of other willing vampires ready to drain his pent-up semen.

It was always like this after she had him wear the jewelry. Desperation fueled by denial. Desire born of love for the beautiful vampire queen who'd given him back his life. Fear she wanted more than love, more than devotion...more than the Domination he craved to give her. She stood on the dais, her pale gold hair surrounding her like a cloud. Her nipples were red—probably some abrasion from his hair gotten when she'd rubbed them against his bristly scalp before the orgy. Sam fantasized about piercing her there, running a thin gold chain between her nipple rings and one he'd thread through her clit. Or one he'd thread through a thick gold collar around her neck.

One like the collar that caught the sun's waning light when Alex rolled the table it sat on to Alina. "Yours?" he asked Sam, a grin on his face.

Sam didn't know. It looked too small. But if she wanted him to wear it, he would. What was it but another public symbol of her Dominance. "If my mistress commands it," he said, kneeling before her and baring his throat.

"Stand up, my darling. I have an announcement...one I believe is past due. Claude d'Argent may be hardly beyond childhood, but none of you can doubt his power or maturity. I've held the clan together for three quarters of a century. Now it's time for Claude to take his rightful place."

The revelers all gathered around Claude, bestowing vampire kisses, offering cunts and cocks and asses for his pleasure. All except Alina and Sam. They stood on the dais, facing each other, their gazes locked on the collar between them. "I've been a queen far too long. Now all I want is to be your beloved slave. Forever."

Sam's heartbeat accelerated, something that hadn't happened often since the change. His cock reared up against his belly as he reached above her head. "Come here." He couldn't stand having that table between them for one more minute. "And hand me that collar."

He bent and lifted her hair, finding and sipping from her jugular vein then soothing the faint marks with his tongue. As he worked the key in the decorative padlock, he read the inscription she'd had engraved for all to see: *alina, loving and beloved slave of her vampire Master, Sam Quill.* The snap of the padlock broke a charged silence, and cheering broke out in the room.

"Take her!"

"Fuck her now!"

Alex grinned. "Better do as they say, my friend."

Alina dropped to her knees, worked the loosened ring from Sam's piercing. "May I please service you?" she asked as she worked the sound from his body.

"Oh, yeah." Incredibly, Sam's cock grew thicker and longer after she'd freed him, arched her neck and taken him down her throat. "Suck me. But not too long. Tonight I'm gonna claim every hole. Every inch of you. Then I'm gonna bite right here and take me a vampire feast." He crushed her hair in his fist, lifting it, freeing the nape of her neck for his attention. "Just me. Someday soon I may want to share you, but for now you're only mine."

When he lifted her mouth off his cock, he bent and licked the spots of his lubrication off her lips then drew her to her feet. "Bend over the table and spread your legs."

His hot cock seared her when he pressed it hard against her anal sphincter. "I—love—you," he ground out as he inched his way inside that tight opening. He curled his long fingers around her breasts, cupping them. Drawing out every sweet, erotic notion she'd ever entertained. Making her want to crawl inside him, learn all the things he wanted from the perfect slave she swore she'd be.

The collar she wore was like him. Hard, sometimes a little heavy, always reminding her of his dynamic presence. His groan distracted her, made her tense as he slid out of her ass and into her wet, needy cunt. Two hard thrusts and he came, filling her with his love and, the gods willing, his child.

Never again would she have to pretend to rule her master, nor would he need to call her mistress. For now and always, Alina pledged eternal surrender.

Why an electronic book?

We live in the Information Age—an exciting time in the history of human civilization, in which technology rules supreme and continues to progress in leaps and bounds every minute of every day. For a multitude of reasons, more and more avid literary fans are opting to purchase e-books instead of paper books. The question from those not yet initiated into the world of electronic reading is simply: *Why?*

1. *Price.* An electronic title at Ellora's Cave Publishing and Cerridwen Press runs anywhere from 40% to 75% less than the cover price of the exact same title in paperback format. Why? Basic mathematics and cost. It is less expensive to publish an e-book (no paper and printing, no warehousing and shipping) than it is to publish a paperback, so the savings are passed along to the consumer.

2. *Space.* Running out of room in your house for your books? That is one worry you will never have with electronic books. For a low one-time cost, you can purchase a handheld device specifically designed for e-reading. Many e-readers have large, convenient screens for viewing. Better yet, hundreds of titles can be stored within your new library—on a single microchip. There are a variety of e-readers from different manufacturers. You can also read e-books on your PC or laptop computer. (Please note that Ellora's Cave does not endorse any specific brands. You can check our websites at www.ellorascave.com

or www.cerridwenpress.com for information we make available to new consumers.)

3. *Mobility.* Because your new e-library consists of only a microchip within a small, easily transportable e-reader, your entire cache of books can be taken with you wherever you go.

4. ***Personal Viewing Preferences.*** Are the words you are currently reading too small? Too large? Too… ANNOYING? Paperback books cannot be modified according to personal preferences, but e-books can.

5. ***Instant Gratification.*** Is it the middle of the night and all the bookstores near you are closed? Are you tired of waiting days, sometimes weeks, for bookstores to ship the novels you bought? Ellora's Cave Publishing sells instantaneous downloads twenty-four hours a day, seven days a week, every day of the year. Our webstore is never closed. Our e-book delivery system is 100% automated, meaning your order is filled as soon as you pay for it.

Those are a few of the top reasons why electronic books are replacing paperbacks for many avid readers.

As always, Ellora's Cave and Cerridwen Press welcome your questions and comments. We invite you to email us at Comments@ellorascave.com or write to us directly at Ellora's Cave Publishing Inc., 1056 Home Avenue, Akron, OH 44310-3502.

COMING TO A BOOKSTORE NEAR YOU!

ELLORA'S CAVE

Bestselling Authors Tour

UPDATES AVAILABLE AT
WWW.ELLORASCAVE.COM

erridwen, the Celtic Goddess of wisdom, was the muse who brought inspiration to story-tellers and those in the creative arts. Cerridwen Press encompasses the best and most innovative stories in all genres of today's fiction. Visit our site and discover the newest titles by talented authors who still get inspired - much like the ancient storytellers did, once upon a time.

CERRIDWEN PRESS

www.cerridwenpress.com

Discover for yourself why readers can't get enough
of the multiple award-winning publisher

Ellora's Cave.

Whether you prefer e-books or paperbacks,

be sure to visit EC on the web at
www.ellorascave.com

for an erotic reading experience that will leave you
breathless.